For Chad, the only guy on my kiss list for eternity

PART 1: THE LIST

CHAPTER ONE

I needed a license plate frame that said, "I'd rather be kissing." Because, honestly, if I could be doing anything right now, it would be kissing.

Which was why I pressed my freshly glossed lips against my boyfriend's somewhat dry lips. They wouldn't be dry when I was done with him. Dylan didn't hesitate—he pulled me into his lean chest, and our lips moved in perfect harmony like Pentatonix. After being together for over a year, it all came naturally.

We were on the leather couch in the front room of my house, me in his lap, his firm arms wrapped tightly around me, holding my body close, and his warm hand cradling the back of my neck. His long fingers drummed like they wanted to move, but he knew better than to let his hands wander. He'd get a solid smack across the cheek, like every time he'd ever tried.

I drew the line at kissing. A dark, thick line that wouldn't be going away any time soon, no matter how big of an eraser Dylan tried to use.

"Break it up." At Dad's deep voice, Dylan picked me up off his lap and set me down next to him.

Dad had one of those voices that no matter what he said, he came across serious, and slightly life-threatening. Add in his short-cropped military hair and huge muscles, and a lot of people stayed clear of him.

Dad didn't really care that much about us kissing. As long as we weren't alone in my bedroom, he was okay with it. But, obviously, it wasn't his favorite thing to watch.

"Hey, Mr. Collins," Dylan said, showing his dazzling white teeth and using his charming tone that made every adult smile. Except my dad.

Dad was in his 'at ease' stance, feet shoulder width apart, arms folded, and chin tilted up. He had on his hardly worn button-down shirt and slacks. The blue paisley tie was tied like it had been an afterthought. Mom would fix it when she got the chance.

Dad exhaled loudly through his nose—his calming technique—then turned his attention to me. "Camille, your mom and I need you to watch Seth tonight."

As if on cue, my little brother bounded into the room and put his hands on his hips. "Dad, I'm ten. I can take care of myself." He had his blond hair in a short mohawk and wore his favorite Minecraft shirt that was developing a few holes since he wore it so often.

Dad broke out in a fit of laughter, the rumbly sound making Dylan and me laugh as well. With his habit of opening the door for anyone, Seth couldn't stay home by himself, but Dad loved how grown up he tried to be.

"You all suck." Seth glared, his blue eyes too adorable to take seriously.

Dad's laughter cut off, and he slapped Seth upside the head. "Language."

Seth rubbed the back of his head, the glare intensifying. "Camille says it all the time."

I leaned my arms on the back of the couch and kneeled on the cushion, my bare knees sliding on the leather so I could face them. "That's because I'm seventeen. I can get away with almost anything."

Mom rounded the corner of the hall, dressed in her typical form-fitting black dress, her blue eyes intently on her smart phone, her manicured thumb moving across it at lightning speed. She put my friends and me to shame when it came to how often she used her phone and how fast she could go. She was a teenage girl in an adult's body.

"Not true." Mom didn't take her eyes off the phone as she went into the kitchen and opened the fridge. She had a new case at her law firm that was occupying most of her time.

I held up a finger. "I said *almost*."

Dad snatched the phone from Mom's hand. She threw out her hands to retrieve it, but he just turned his back on her, a sly grin sliding onto his face. He loved to see Mom squirm.

"I was using that," Mom said with the same tone she used on Seth when he was misbehaving.

"I know," Dad said, dropping the phone into his jeans pocket. "But your clients will live until tomorrow. I promise."

Mom dropped her hands with a sigh. She opened her mouth, her eyes ready to challenge him, but instead, she grabbed a lime Diet Coke from the fridge, popped it open, and downed it.

"That's so impressive," Dylan whispered next to me.

I elbowed him, and he grunted, rubbing his stomach where I hit him. Mom didn't like anyone commenting on her "drinking problem," as Dad called it.

Dad pointed his thick finger at us. "Dylan can't be here."

I rolled my eyes. "Yeah, I know."

He told us that every time he and Mom left me in charge. He didn't like the thought of Dylan and me being alone in the house without them there. I once tried to argue that we weren't alone since Seth would be home. The intense glare that followed, with Dad's jaw pulled tight, and veins popping out basically everywhere, forced me to never bring that up again.

Dylan kissed my cheek, leaving behind some of my lip gloss I'd given him earlier. "I gotta get home anyway. Have fun tonight, Mr. and Mrs. Collins." He jogged over to Seth and held his hand high in the air. Seth jumped up, slapping his hand against Dylan's, smiling brightly the whole time.

Normally, I hated seeing him go, and I'd beg him to stay just a little while longer. But as I watched his backside as he left the house, nothing flitted inside me—good or bad. I shook the random thought from my head. I was probably just tired.

Dad took the opportunity to come up behind me and slap the back of my head—his favorite thing to do.

"Not in my house," he mumbled.

"What? Looking at my boyfriend?"

He rubbed the top of my hair until it became a tangled mess. "Lusting after him."

I threw my head back and laughed so hard, I snorted. It took me a few seconds to calm enough that I could talk. "*Lusting?* Seriously, Dad? Gah. Will you please not use that word around me?"

Dad folded his arms, emphasizing his muscles. "If you stop lusting, then I'll have no reason to use it."

Seth had his small fingers in his ears and his eyes closed as he hummed the Star Wars theme song.

"Maybe we could grab an early dinner as a family before Dad and I leave for the party," Mom said, tossing her empty can in the recycle bin. She brushed back the blonde curls blocking part of her eye.

"Who has a party on a Thursday night anyway?" I asked.

Dad pointed his thumb at Mom. "Her weird clients."

Mom slapped his arm, and he huffed, smiling the whole time. A smile finally broke out on her face as well. Until she noticed Dad's tie, huffed, and stepped in to fix it.

When she finished, she went to Seth—still humming and plugging his ears—wrapped her arms around him, squeezed him tight, and pressed her lips close to his ear. "Food."

Seth took his fingers out of his ears, but couldn't lower his arms since Mom still had him in her grasp. He smiled wide, showing off his crooked front teeth. "Can we go to McDonald's?"

Dad scrunched his face, disgust filling every wrinkle. "No."

"You never let us go there," Seth said, flapping his hands awkwardly. Mom wouldn't release him, but he wasn't trying to get away.

"Because I'm being a responsible parent," Dad said. "I love you kids and care about your wellbeing."

I hopped over the couch, landing on the tile, shuffling closer to them and swaying my hips like a little girl. "Is that why you're going to take us to Chick-fil-A?"

Dad wiggled his eyebrows, his smile splitting wide. "You know it."

"What's the difference?" Seth asked, holding his palms up. "They both have chicken nuggets that are delicious."

"Oh, Seth." I squeezed his cheeks since Mom held him in place and he couldn't do anything about it. "One day your taste buds will develop, and you'll know the difference between gross and delicious."

Mom kissed the side of Seth's head, avoiding his Mohawk. "I personally love McDonald's chicken nuggets. Maybe we could go there, and your father and sister can go to Chick-fil-a."

Dad held up a hand. "We eat as a family." When Seth pouted, Dad sighed. "They're right next to each other. You two can bring your food over and eat with us."

Seth tried to pump his fist, but couldn't move. He grunted. "Mom, you're making it hard for me to do anything."

"I know," she said, rocking him left and right.

Dad caught my eye, and I nodded. Seth saw our interaction and squealed, trying to wiggle away from Mom. "Stay away!"

With wicked grins, Dad and I swarmed in on Seth and tickled him while Mom held him in place. Seth squirmed and giggled, his eyes closing tight.

"Stop!"

We kept on tickling, getting his sides, armpits, and stomach. When I ventured down to his feet, he kicked out his legs, smacking his foot into my cheek. It hurt a little, but it was all too funny for me to care.

"Stop!" He laughed. "I'm going to pee my pants!"

Dad immediately stepped back and threw up his hands. "I don't want to clean that up."

Seth danced where he stood, so Mom let him go and pushed him toward the hall. He took off running, his socks sliding on the tile as he neared the bathroom. He already had his pants unzipped.

I leaned over laughing, clapping my hands. Tears pricked at the corner of my eyes. It didn't take long until Mom and Dad were laughing uncontrollably like me. Seth came out of the bathroom glaring, but couldn't help laughing when he got a good look at us.

He threw his arms wide. "Glad I can entertain you guys. Can we go now? I'm starving, and those chicken nuggets aren't going to eat themselves."

Dad patted Seth's shoulder and turned him toward the front door, but then spotted Mom on her phone, probably emailing a client. He glanced at his jeans pocket, looking both annoyed and impressed that Mom had somehow wrangled it free. He opened the door, and they were about to step outside before I spoke up.

"I'm thinking Seth should probably put some shoes on," I said, pointing at his socked feet. What would they do without me?

Dad looked down at them. "Huh." He rubbed Seth's shoulders. "Hurry before I beat you to the car."

Seth plopped down in the entryway and scrambled to get his shoes on. Dad kept jerking like he was going to take off toward the car, causing Seth to whine. When he finished with the laces, Seth flew to his feet, past Dad, and out the door. Dad had to sprint to keep up.

"Mom, can I go to a concert with Dylan next weekend?" I asked. The best time to ask her for things was when she was preoccupied. Which was actually most of the time.

"Uh huh," Mom said, her eyes glued to her phone. We walked out the front door, and I locked it since that would be another thing they'd forget to do.

I could tell her anything, and it wouldn't register. "It's one of those wild ones. Lots of drugs, clothes coming off and such."

"That sounds fun." Mom opened the passenger door of the car, her thumb moving across the screen of her phone.

"Also, I'm an assassin."

Mom pressed *send* on her phone and smiled up at me. "That's nice, dear." She got into the car and closed the door.

With a sigh, I joined my crazy family in the car and wished for once that Mom would pay attention to us during dinner. But I never liked to get my hopes up.

CHAPTER TWO

*W*e were at the end-of-the-school-year party down by the lake. It was a tradition for all of the juniors to get together before the last high school summer began, so it was our turn. I was wrapped up in Dylan's arms, enjoying the salty taste of his lips and our moment alone.

Dylan tickled my side until our lips peeled apart, and I busted out laughing. He kissed my nose. "I love your laugh."

Rolling my eyes, I played with the collar of his baby blue polo shirt. "You tell me that all the time."

"Because it's true." He buried his face into my neck and gently kissed my skin. I teetered a little on the uneven pebbled ground.

"You two are seriously so disgusting." The annoyed voice came from my right.

I turned to see Hayley, one of my best friends, gagging. She fiddled with the star pendant filled with blue stones hanging from the silver chain around her neck.

"How many times do we have to have the PDA convo?" Hayley asked. Her bright red hair made her green eyes pop.

No matter where we went, people stared at her. Never in a bad way, just in a captivating way.

Dylan left a trail of kisses along my neck.

"Apparently, often," I said, trying to push him away from me, but he held on tight, his arms wrapped around my back and holding me close. I finally gave in and just let him continue to kiss my neck, even though Hayley still gagged and rolled her eyes. For the briefest of moments, I felt like doing the same. Awkwardness strangled my stomach.

She'd never actually cared about PDA until her boyfriend dumped her and, suddenly, she hated every relationship within a five-mile radius of her.

"Camille! Hayley!" My other best friend, Kaitlyn, jogged up to us and smiled brightly. She had her thick, curly black hair hanging over her shoulder. "Guess who just asked me out?" Her eyes were on me, completely ignoring Dylan. While Hayley loved to harass us, Kaitlyn chose to shut out our affection altogether.

Hayley took the opportunity to pry me away from Dylan, yanking at his arm, and then shoving his chest repeatedly.

"You're no longer needed," she said, a forced smile on Dylan.

With a chuckle and a shake of his head, he left us alone, going to find one of his friends.

I turned my attention to Kaitlyn, rubbing my neck where Dylan's lips had just been. "Ethan?"

She shook her head, her brown eyes dancing in excitement. She had a couple inches on both of us, making us look up at her.

"That dude who stalks you on social media, whom you find 'endearing?'" Hayley used air quotes. We were huddled close, creating our 'gossip triangle' that told everyone to stay back.

Kaitlyn's smile grew—flashing her bright, white teeth—as

she shook her head. There were a lot of guys at our school who desperately wanted to date Kaitlyn. She was the captain of the girls' basketball team, downright gorgeous, unapologetically kind and friendly with everyone at our school, and, from the most recent rumor created by the captain of the boys' basketball team, an excellent kisser. She hadn't denied the rumor, because really, who would?

Hayley glanced over her shoulder, making sure no one was eavesdropping. I got a good look at her daith piercing, a hot pink star. She'd just got both sides pierced to help with her constant migraines, and so far, they had done the job. She turned back to us, folding her arms close to her chest. "You're just going to have to tell us before Dylan comes back over to maul Camille."

Kaitlyn placed her long, slender fingers on our arms and leaned in closer. "Garrett!"

Hayley's eyes bulged. "Wow. So, he finally caught on to what the rest of the universe already knows? And here I thought he had no balls."

Kaitlyn's crush on Garrett started all the way back in second grade when he'd helped her to the nurse's office after she fell during recess and scraped her knee. She'd always teased me about being a hopeless romantic, but I wasn't the one holding on to my hope of a second-grade prince charming.

"That's huge!" I said, trying to keep my voice low. "I thought he was dating Angie."

Kaitlyn clapped her hands together and jumped up and down, almost in a prance. "They broke up! Two weeks ago. They just hadn't told anyone, so they could work through it all without everyone knowing."

"Smart," Hayley grumbled. "I should have done that with *him*." We weren't allowed to say her ex's name, and I was fine with it. Kaitlyn and I were ecstatic when they broke up because he was a jerk to Hayley. She was too uncharacteristically smitten to see.

She did get a tattoo of some stars behind her right ear after they broke up. He wouldn't let her get one, but she'd had a special attachment to stars since she was a little girl. Her mom, who passed away from cancer when Hayley was seven, always told her to be a shining star, no matter where life took her.

Kaitlyn and I rubbed Hayley's arms, and while she tried to appear tough, her eyes said *thank you*. We'd been best friends since we were in diapers, and nothing would ever tear us apart. Even if we did have different interests. We had a bond, and in the end, that was all that mattered.

"So, where's he taking you?" Hayley asked, turning the attention back to Kaitlyn.

"Not sure. He just asked if I was free next Friday night." She took our hands and squealed. "I can't believe he finally asked me out. I seriously thought this day would never come."

"Me, too," I said, placing the back of my free hand against my forehead. "I thought I'd have to deal with all the pining for the rest of my life."

Kaitlyn let go of my hand so she could shove my arm. "Thanks for the support."

I wrapped my arms around her. "I'm so happy for you. I hope it all works out." Because if it didn't, I wasn't sure if we'd ever hear the end of it.

Angry shouts broke out near the fire pit. The three of us turned toward it, arms linked together.

"Seriously, man, leave her alone." Dylan's voice rang out over all the commotion.

Both Hayley and Kaitlyn glanced at me before we took off running. A crowd had gathered around to watch whatever was happening. We pushed through the bodies, making our way forward. We were almost to the front when stupid Liam Elliott stepped into view and held up a hand to stop me. His dark eyebrows were as thick as his brown hair, which was perfectly messy tonight—liked he'd tried for hours to get the I-woke-up-like-this look.

"Might not want to see what's going on, Cam-Bam," Liam said, his arms folded and his resident smirk on his full lips.

"Pretty sure I told you not to do that with my name." I tried to push past him, but it was like his tennis shoes were stuck in the pebbles, keeping him in place. I glared at him, thankful he wasn't much taller than me so he could see the intensity. "Like every day since we were five."

Liam chuckled, rubbing his hand across his smooth chin. "That's not possible. You pretty much stayed hidden all of middle school."

Yeah, because I didn't want to hear his endless teasing.

He wrapped his arm around my shoulders and turned me toward the fire, his hand firmly on my shoulder. "See, Cam-Cam, your dear boyfriend is fighting for another girl." He woe-is-me sighed. "Love is such a fickle thing."

I shoved him away from me to get a good look at what was happening. Dylan had Brady Tucker, the captain of the football team, in a headlock, holding on tight.

"I told you to leave her alone," Dylan said through gritted teeth.

Brady's as-of-last-week-ex, Raelynn, cried near the fire, tears and mascara streaming down her cheeks. All her friends surrounded her, trying—and failing—to console her. She wailed like she'd just lost a loved one or puppy or something. It was so over-the-top that it was almost hard to take her seriously. Almost.

"Get off me," Brady rasped under Dylan's hold.

"Not until you promise to leave her alone," Dylan growled.

Brady was actually much stronger than Dylan. I mean, he was in his home gym for hours on end each day. Dylan was just a tall twig. But for some reason, Brady didn't seem to be putting up much of a fight.

Liam leaned in close, his warm breath tickling my ear. "On a scale of one to ten, how awkward is this for you right now? You know, since Dylan's had a thing for her for years."

Dylan has a thing for Raelynn? What was Liam talking about? I'd never seen Dylan give her a second glance. But he was wrestling her ex at a party in front of practically all the juniors.

Shaking the thought from my head, I motioned to them. "Why aren't you doing anything to help to him? Brady's your friend."

Liam shrugged. "Brady can handle himself." There was more to his tone that I couldn't quite figure out, but I didn't push it.

After elbowing Liam out of the way, I rushed to Dylan and placed my hand on his arm until he finally looked up at me.

"What are you doing?" I asked.

His arms squeezed tight, the veins bulging out. He actually seemed more muscular than usual. How had I not noticed that earlier? "He was harassing Raelynn, and she was begging him to stop."

All of Brady's friends were trying to intervene, but Dylan's friends were doing a decent job of keeping them back.

With a strained smile, I glanced around at everyone before I stepped close, trying to keep my voice low. "Doesn't mean you need to kill the guy. I think he gets the point."

Brady slapped at Dylan's arms. His face turned a dangerous shade of red, getting close to purple. Why wasn't Brady stopping him? Or Liam?

"Seriously, Dylan," I hissed. "You're going to kill the guy. He can't breathe. Let him go."

Brady's legs buckled, and he fell to his knees. Dylan finally let go and threw up his hands like he was innocent. I took him by the arm and yanked him away from the crowd. When we finally cleared the last spectator, I shoved Dylan in the chest.

"What was that?" I asked.

Dylan rubbed his arms. "You should have heard the things he was saying about Raelynn. Someone needed to defend her."

I folded my arms. "And that required almost killing the guy?"

He rolled his eyes. "He just would've passed out. Don't go all dramatic on me."

"There are other ways to defend her without resorting to a choke-hold."

He tucked some of my hair behind my ear and stroked my cheek. "My adrenaline was pumping, okay?" He leaned in to kiss me, but I so wasn't in the mood now. I'd never seen that violent side to him, and I really didn't like it.

I stepped away from him. "I'm going to catch a ride home with Kaitlyn tonight."

He frowned. "Fine." After a quick kiss on the cheek, he headed back near the fire and all his friends.

I suddenly felt cold standing there all alone. Shivering, I went in search of my friends. I needed to get the image of Dylan all worked up over another girl out of my mind.

CHAPTER THREE

I didn't talk with Dylan at all until the next night when we were on our way to a party at none other than Brady Tucker's house. I really didn't want to go, seeing as Dylan had him in a headlock the night before, but somehow Dylan's pouting lip talked me into it. That bottom lip had talked me into a lot of things.

Plus, my only other option was to stay home and help Seth with his swing, and I hadn't wanted to do anything soft-ball related in over a year, no matter how persistent the kid was.

The whole ride in Dylan's tiny Chevy car had me rehashing the whole fight, my skin itching like when I wore that oversized cashmere sweater Mom had gotten me for Christmas. She'd somehow forgotten I was allergic, and I didn't have the heart to upset her. She'd been so proud that her law firm had been doing so well that she could afford to get me something that nice.

Dylan was singing along to The Weeknd, completely oblivious to my uncomfortable mood. Things had shifted between us—and not just because of the altercation at the lake. We'd been slowly dying out over the past few weeks, but I hadn't wanted to admit it.

I glanced over at Dylan, taking him in. His long fingers beat along the steering wheel, trying to keep rhythm with the song, but doing a terrible job. I used to think his off-key singing was adorable, but now I wanted some earplugs. He must have sensed me looking, because he glanced over and winked at me. I forced a smile before he turned his attention back to the road, his pitch cracking worse than a boy going through puberty.

I turned up the volume, hoping to drown out his singing, and stared out the dirty window until we got to the party.

Brady Tucker had an amazing home, the kind pictured on the front of all the home magazines, and every mom across America envied. Curved driveway. Spacious house. A mix of gray rock and stucco, but mostly rock. Lights lined underneath the roof, casting a glow over the entire home. The windows were ridiculously large and spotless.

We went up the steps to the wraparound porch. Dylan opened the door and motioned for me to join him. I eyed the white wooden swing hanging to the right of the door. It was looking awfully tempting. I needed a moment to collect myself and get into party mode.

"I just need a minute," I said.

Dylan kissed the top of my hair. "I'll be inside." His hand lowered from around me, brushing against my back before he swept into the house. That used to cause a chill to run through me—the good kind. But now there was nothing.

I really needed to talk to Kaitlyn and Hayley, but I knew exactly what they'd say: dump him and move on. I wasn't sure if I was ready for that. I'd been Dylan's girlfriend for so long, I had no idea who I was without him.

Brushing off what looked to be bread crumbs, I sunk into the floral cushion and swung back. It only took seconds to find the perfect speed to calm my soul. I closed my eyes, trying to drown out everyone pounding up the porch steps and into the loud house.

Parties were fun, but there were times when I loved the quiet of life and wanted to bask in it for as long as I could. It gave me a moment to clear out my mind and focus.

What would happen if I let Dylan go? I'd have no one to hold my hand or hug at school. No one to sneak off with into a corner and steal some kisses. I'd become Camille—the girl who dumped Dylan. Because, let's face it. I'd become the villain, and he'd be the war hero.

There were so many things about him I'd miss. His smile. His laugh. His kisses. Using him as an excuse to get out of the house, away from the reminders that my mom wasn't around, and Seth constantly begging me to pick up softball again. His nagging had grown beyond annoying.

The swing suddenly jolted. I almost fell to my side, but put my hand out in time to stop myself. I swayed side to side in a jerky fashion, like I was on a ride at Universal Studios. I wrapped my hand around the arm of the swing to steady myself.

"Nice night." Liam was sitting next to me on the swing, arm rested behind me, and an annoying smile on his face. He winked when we made eye contact.

My eyebrows bunched together of their own accord. "What are you doing?"

He swept out an arm. "Enjoying a nice evening."

I had to bite back a yell. He'd completely messed up my peaceful vibe. "Have you ever sat on a porch swing before? It goes front to back, not side to side."

"What?" With the force of his hips, he got the swing moving side to side, the choppiness messing with my innards, which I foolishly said to him.

"Did you just say 'innards'?" His eyebrow quirked up, and

a smile tugged at his lips. They didn't look as dry as Dylan's normally were. I shook the thought from my head, not sure where it had come from.

I folded my arms, pretending like the jerky swaying didn't bother me. "Yes, Liam, I said innards, because that's what they are. And my *innards* aren't liking you using this peaceful swing as a bumpy rollercoaster."

With a sigh, he settled the swing and moved it in the correct fashion. My innards truly appreciated it. I couldn't help but notice his blue sweater brought out the color of his eyes. If he wasn't so annoying, the guy could have potential.

"There you go, Cam-Tam." He flicked my shoulder. "Saved you. There was a vicious ladybug about to move in for the kill."

I stared at my shoulder in horror. "You flicked a ladybug?"

He rested his left ankle on his right knee, bumping our knees together. His checkered Vans were spotless. "Hey, I'm an equal opportunity bug flicker. Lord or lady, I'll flick if necessary."

"How is flicking a ladybug off my shoulder necessary? It wasn't anything creepy or dangerous." Why was I arguing this with him? It was stupid. "You're missing the party."

He pinched my cheek. "Why go inside when I have your charming personality to keep me occupied?"

I slapped his hand away. I hated that he always treated me like I was still a kid. He was the one who obviously hadn't grown up.

A bubbly sophomore bounded up to us, her brown eyes melting for Liam.

"Lee-uhmmm! There you are!" The girl, Sadie, worked her way onto Liam's lap, which was awkward considering he had one leg resting on the other. She draped her arm around his neck, giggling the whole time. Her long, brown hair fell over her shoulder. She wore a summer dress that didn't leave much to the imagination.

I was impressed that Liam was able to keep his eyes on hers and not on her boobs that were on the verge of popping out. I almost leaned over and smashed them back in her dress. I'd be doing her a public service.

"Sadie." Liam poked her nose, and her giggle intensified to the point my innards flipped. "If I had known you were here, I would have been in there forever ago."

I was about two seconds away from losing my dinner. With more force than necessary, I stood, sending the swing back and Sadie's boobs into Liam's face.

"Oops!" Sadie bit her lip like she was embarrassed, but with the way her eyes sparkled, I'd just made her night. By Liam's sparkle, I'd made his as well.

"Well, you two cutesy-wootsy lovebirds have fun." I poked Liam on the nose, and then gave his cheek a solid smack. "Have fun at the party. I hope I don't see you again!" With a smile, I went into the house.

CHAPTER FOUR

The loud pop music vibrated my sandals as I weaved through the large front room to the kitchen. The place was packed with almost every junior, plus a few seniors and sophomores that had crashed the party. From one look around, it seemed most girls had taken the opportunity to bust out the barely there summer wardrobes, even though the heat hadn't quite settled in.

I adjusted my blue cotton skirt that hung just past my knees. I had my thin, pink blouse tucked in the front, the light material soft on my skin. Dylan had picked out the outfit because it minimized my curves. Ever since I ditched softball, my muscles had lessened, but it hadn't completely wiped out my thick build, no matter my diet.

Two arms wrapped around my neck from behind. Dylan tucked me close to him, my back pressed up against his torso.

"Find your peace?" His warm lips pressed against my ear.

I placed my hands on his arms, giving his forearm a soft kiss. "For a moment."

We swayed with the music, and I breathed him all in.

Everything felt off, like there was a light taint to our normal harmony. I wondered if he felt it, too.

Dylan turned me around, his clammy hands landing on my cheeks. They shook against my skin, so out of the ordinary for him. He swallowed, his large Adam's apple moving up and down. "We need to talk."

I blew out a long breath. "Yes, we do."

Taking my hand, he steered me away from the crowd and into a semi-quiet corner of the kitchen. He leaned against the wall, folding his arms. "Things have changed between us, haven't they?"

I slowly nodded. "Yeah."

His eyes held the smallest amount of hope, like he hadn't been sure if I'd agree with him or not. "I've been doing some thinking."

"Me, too."

Unfolding his arms, his fingers ran along my hair, gently tucking it behind my ear before resting his hand on my neck. "Camille Collins, you've been the best first girlfriend a guy could ask for."

I took a shaky breath. "But it's over."

Dylan bent down, his lips brushing against mine. "I'm going to miss you."

"I'll miss you, too," I whispered against his lips.

He kissed me, short and sweet. "But it needs to be done."

"Uh huh." I held in a sigh. He was right, and I hated it. We were hanging on to the past and what we felt at the beginning. A little spark ignited in me, but it was more about remembering our first weeks together than the moment we were currently in. My first boyfriend. Gone.

I held my clasped hands behind his back. Tears pricked at the corners of my eyes, but I wouldn't let them escape. I wasn't going to cry over Dylan, and I definitely wasn't going to cry at Brady Tucker's party.

We'd had a good run, but it was over. I had to accept it.

"You've been the perfect first boyfriend." A sincere smile landed on my lips. He really had been great. Aside from all the pressuring to move things further, he'd never once crossed the line.

He stared into my eyes, deep and sure. When his lips found mine for the last time, I didn't hold back. My glossed lips slowly wet his, making them smooth. Without me, where would he get his moisture?

A throat cleared next to us, trying to break us up, but we pulled each other closer, our lips moving with a heated eagerness. It wasn't until a firm hand landed on my shoulder that I released Dylan from our embrace.

Both Hayley and Kaitlyn were standing there, both looking beautiful in their own way. Hayley had a black headband in her red hair, pulling it away from her gorgeous eyes. Her red corset and black skirt were the perfect blend.

Kaitlyn's shiny, curly hair basically looked like it should be on the cover of a magazine. Add in her button-down pastel dress with a thick brown belt, her long, silky brown legs, and she was stunning.

Kaitlyn wrapped her arm around my shoulder and steered me away from Dylan. "Okay, seriously, what was that?"

"What was what?" I asked.

Hayley rolled her eyes. "You two were seconds from undressing each other right here in Brady Tucker's kitchen." She stared at the marble counter. "At least we can assume their maids do a decent job of keeping it clean. But still. Gross."

I glanced around and noticed that a lot of intrigued eyes were staring at me. I folded my arms close to me. "Just saying goodbye."

Kaitlyn frowned, highlighting her thick lips. "What do you mean, goodbye?"

Taking their hands in mine, I escorted them outside and off to a quiet spot around the side of the house. There were tons of people playing around in the humungous rock pool, making it not much quieter than the music in the house.

"Dylan and I broke up." I stared at my two friends, wondering what their reactions would be.

Hayley threw her arms up toward the heavens. "I'm so happy and completely sad. Happy you finally got rid of that sack of . . . garbage. Sad that I'll have to come through on my promise to never swear again since God finally answered my prayers."

Kaitlyn scrunched her face in confusion, yet she still looked adorable. "That kiss didn't look like a break-up kiss." She put a hand on her hip and fanned herself with her hand. "I've never seen you with that much passion about anything before. Well, aside from softball." She sucked in a sharp breath. That was one topic we hadn't broached in a while, and I chose to ignore it for the moment.

I lowered my arms, unsure of what to do with them. It was uncomfortable for me to talk about. While I was a deep romantic, I also was a 'what happens behind closed doors stays behind closed doors' kind of girl. I finally stuffed my hands in the pockets of my skirt. "I'm just sad to lose my first boyfriend."

"Do you mean in general?" Hayley asked. "Or Dylan specifically?"

I shrugged, my hands moving up in my pockets. "I hate that this chapter of my life is over. I mean, I'll miss Dylan, but I'll miss having a boyfriend even more. Does that make sense?"

Kaitlyn put her hand on my arm, her smooth skin soft on mine. Since her favorite things—basketball and doing people's hair—required frequent use of her hands, she always made sure to moisturize like crazy. "Yeah, we get it. But you don't need a boyfriend."

"Seriously," Hayley said with an edge to her tone. "You have us. Boys suck."

I stared up at the sky. The sun was almost down, and the stars were waking up. "I just don't know who I am without Dylan." I leaned back against the side of the house, the stucco clinging to my shirt.

Hayley leaned next to me, her body turned toward me. "You're Camille Collins. One of the toughest, smartest girls I've ever known."

Kaitlyn saddled up on the other side of me. "Driven. Smoking hot. A good person. Loyal."

They paused. My eyebrows slid up. "You didn't have to stop."

They both shoved me on the arm, squishing my body.

"You're not defined by Dylan," Kaitlyn said, linking her arm with mine.

Hayley fingered one of her daith piercings, something she often did but probably didn't realize. "In fact, I think you're better without him."

I turned to her. "Really?"

She nodded, a fierceness in her eyes that gave me courage. "You kind of got lost as Dylan's girlfriend. This will give you a chance to focus on you."

"I agree." Kaitlyn rested her long arm on my shoulder. "I know I'm going on a date with Garrett, but it's just one date. Let's focus on some girl time for a while."

"Yes!" Hayley squeezed my arm. "That's what I'm talking about." She snapped her fingers. "Oh, there's a new band playing at The Shack next Saturday. I've been dying to hear them play. Let's go. No boys allowed."

"Perfect," Kaitlyn said.

The two of them wrapped their arms around me, and we stood there on the side of the house, hugging like I hadn't just lost my first boyfriend. I was so lucky to have them.

CHAPTER 5

*A*fter ten more minutes, we wandered back into the house. There was a weird buzz below my skin that I didn't know what to do with. I had my two best friends at my side, but I wasn't sure I was in the mood to party. I'd rather be at home, curled up under a blanket, and watching Easy A for the billionth time. Add in a bowl of caramel popcorn, and I'd be the happiest girl in the world.

But, instead, I was pretending like I was having a fun time. Which, really, after a few dances with my friends, I was enjoying myself. There was something freeing about being with my two gal pals, completely unattached to a guy, and just letting loose. Maybe I could survive. Maybe I didn't need Dylan.

Bruno Mars came on, and Hayley, Kaitlyn, and I all held hands, swaying and singing along at the top of our lungs. Nothing could ever come between us.

Until a slow song came on, and Garrett batted his pretty brown eyes at Kaitlyn, and she all but swooned. They somehow melded together in the middle of the living room, and I wasn't sure if we'd be able to pry them apart. He was tall and strong like her and played volleyball. Kaitlyn used to play, but she was having a hard time juggling between it and basketball, so she finally settled on basketball since she loved it more. I wouldn't be too surprised if she found her love of volleyball again, though.

"So much for girl time," Hayley whispered in my ear. She squeezed my arm. "I'm going to go get some water. Want anything?"

"No, thanks."

She left me standing there all alone in a sea of couples dancing. My momentary high vanished into the overly-perfume-and-cologne air, swirling among the sweaty bodies grinding on each other.

I squeezed my eyes shut tight, wishing I could transport myself to my bedroom.

Someone bumped into me. The giggle that followed made me dig my fingernails into my skin so I wouldn't say anything mean. Sadie. I spun around to find her and Liam all cuddled up in a disgusting display. Liam winked at me when he saw me gawking at them.

I snapped my mouth shut and whipped around, only to fall right into the arms of Brady Tucker. He thought it meant I wanted to dance, so his hands landed on my waist. I almost pushed him away, but thought, "why not?" It was just a dance. And Brady was hot. Plus, it was his house. It would be rude to deny the host a simple dance.

Brady wore a dark blue button-down shirt, the long sleeves rolled up to the elbows, and the top two buttons undone, showing some of his smooth chest. His shirt was tucked into his jeans, showing off his thick brown leather belt. The guy certainly knew how to dress.

"Your boyfriend is a loser," Brady said. His sharp jaw was clenched tight, highlighting the muscles.

"Then why did you let him win that fight?" I asked. "We both know you could have won if you wanted."

His muscles loosened. "Because I deserved it for saying those things about her." He arched an eyebrow. "I was surprised it was your boyfriend that intervened."

I patted his shoulders. "He's no longer my boyfriend."

Brady's gorgeous brown eyes swept to mine, and his smolder took over. "Oh, really?"

I intertwined my fingers behind his neck. "Yep. Totally over. He and Raelynn can hook it up all they want now." The thought made my stomach roll, but I shoved the unease away.

"So could we." Brady wiggled his eyebrows. He probably had meant it to be seductive, but for some reason, I found it hilarious. I busted out laughing until his glare cut me off.

"Yeah, I'm so not dating anyone for a while," I said.

"Who said anything about dating?"

Sighing, I patted his cheeks. "Brady, it's not going to happen. Deal with it."

He doubled my sigh, his whole body sagging. "I think she really likes him."

"Raelynn?" I didn't want to picture her and Dylan together. No way he'd move on that fast. I mean, we'd only been broken up for less than an hour. Considering we'd been together over a year, no one moved on *that* fast.

Brady held me close, like I was a stuffed teddy bear that would wipe away his worries. "I've seen them making eyes at each other at school."

What was he talking about? Had they? I'd never noticed. But then again, I'd never been looking. I didn't think I *had* to look.

"How could she move on so fast?" His eyes glistened. I had to lean in to see better. Was Brady Tucker crying?

"That's life for you," I said. "One minute everything is fine, the next, someone breaks your heart."

He used a palm to massage his eye. "Sorry, there's something in my eye." He sniffed, wiping his nose on his shirt sleeve. I had to lean back so I wouldn't get elbowed in the face. "Stupid allergies."

I had a feeling it wasn't allergies, but I wasn't about to say anything. "Looks like you could use some water." I dropped my arms and stepped away from him. "Want me to get you one?"

His chin fell to his chest. "No."

Moping Brady was not attractive. It gave me all the more reason why I wouldn't cry over Dylan in public. He looked like a sad puppy. I kinda wanted to hold him in my arms and rock his worries away. Honestly, I think he would have let me, even though we were in the middle of his living room surrounded by all the other juniors.

Liam's hand landed on my shoulder. "Always making the boys cry, aren't you, Cam-Sam?" He scrunched his nose. "I don't like that nickname. I'll take it off the list of options."

I shrugged away from him. "There shouldn't be a list."

"I'm not crying. There was something in my eye." Brady took in all the guests dancing around us. "I shouldn't have had this party. I thought it would be a good distraction."

Liam's smirk dropped, and he stepped in close to his friend. "Say the word, and I'll get everyone out of here."

With a slow nod of his head, Brady patted Liam's arm. "I'm gonna go watch a movie in my room."

Liam leaned in close to Brady, keeping his voice low, but I still heard. "Please tell me you aren't going to watch *The Notebook* again."

"Of course not!" Brady's eyes flickered over to me, and I did my best to pretend like I hadn't heard, which was hard because I kind of wanted to laugh. "Why would you even ask that?" He huffed and pushed Liam away from him before he disappeared up the stairs.

Liam turned to me. "I feel bad for the guy. Raelynn really did a number on him." He glanced around the room. "I'll go outside and shut it down out there. Want to do the inside?"

"On it."

With a soft smile, Liam headed out the back door with his hands in his pockets. When he wasn't teasing me, he was a pretty good person and a real good friend to Brady.

I stared around the room. There were so many bodies moving to the rhythm. There was only one way to end the party. Muttering apologies, I shuffled my way to where DJ Ice, aka Isaac Lee, was set up. He had his headphones pressed up against one ear, his whole body moving along to the beat. He didn't like to wear his headphones over his head like a normal person because that would ruin his perfectly gelled black hair. He currently had question marks shaved into the sides of his hair, wrapping from ear to ear behind his head.

I waved my arms in front of him, trying to get his attention. He answered with a head nod, like I was some buddy of his. I pushed my way around to Isaac and stood on my tiptoes.

"Turn off the music," I shouted.

Isaac narrowed his brown eyes. "What?"

With the speakers blasting just feet away from us, he couldn't hear me. Even if he had, Isaac wasn't one to just turn off the music and send his partiers packing.

I followed the extension cord running along the wall until I found the outlet. With a mighty yank, I removed the cord, and the whole sound system shut down. Immediately, shouts rose up, demanding that the music be turned back on. On the down side, I was finally able to hear Isaac's voice, the profanity stringing from him so unattractive.

Ignoring him, I stood on the coffee table in the middle of the room and cupped my hands over my mouth. "The party is over. Go home."

"Why?" Garrett yelled. He was right below me, so he flinched when he realized how loud he'd been. He rubbed a hand over his slick, close-cropped hair.

"Uh, because." No way I was telling our junior class that Brady was having a sulk fest with Rachel McAdams and Ryan Gosling and needed some privacy. Especially since I needed to do the same thing. Just with Emma Stone. "The cops are coming."

"There's no alcohol," some guy said.

"Sure." I winked at the crowd. "Of course not. But seriously, leave."

Kaitlyn tugged on the bottom of my skirt to get my attention. "What's going on?"

I yanked her up on the table with me. The juniors might not listen to me, but they'd listen to Kaitlyn Hawkins. I whispered in her ear. "Brady needs everyone to leave. I'll explain later. Just get them out of here."

With a firm nod, Kaitlyn clapped her hands. "Alright, everyone, the party is officially over."

A bunch of moans echoed through the house. They all sagged out like she'd just announced she was taking away their prized pony.

"Wow." I put my hands on my hips. "They ignore me, but one word from you, and bam, they're gone."

She flipped her hair back. "Technically, it was six words, but you know, who's counting?"

"You."

She stuck her tongue out at me. Garrett helped her down from the table, even though he didn't need to. It was a coffee table. It wasn't like we were high off the ground. Which was why I jumped, landing on both feet at the same time.

"You're adorable when you leap." Liam grinned. "Almost everyone is out of the pool. I'll go check for stragglers in any of the bedrooms."

I blanched. "Have fun with that."

He groaned. "Yeah, I'm pretty afraid of what I'm going to find."

I put my hands on his shoulders and turned him toward the stairs. "You got this, champ."

"Thanks, sport."

There were still some voices coming from the kitchen, so I rounded the corner, ready to tell them to jet when I saw it was Dylan, his friends, and none other than the reason the party ended: Raelynn.

My feet thought on their own and scooted back until I was out of sight. I had this itching urge to hear what they were talking about.

"So, it's over?" one of Dylan's friends said. Pete. I so wouldn't miss him.

"Yep." Dylan almost sounded relieved.

Pete hollered. "So glad. She drove me crazy."

What? Pretty sure he was the one who drove me crazy. He was always hovering around like an annoying helicopter mom.

"What are we doing?" Hayley whispered behind me. I turned to see her and Kaitlyn staring at me. I held my fingers to my lips, pointed at the kitchen, and mouthed *Dylan*. Both their mouths went into the shape of an O, and then they stepped forward, pushing into me so they could hear better.

"She's such a prude," Pete said. That didn't bother me. I had no qualms with being a virgin.

"What do you mean?" Raelynn asked. Her tone was sweet, bordering on high-pitched annoying.

"She wouldn't do anything other than kiss," Pete said.

All their other friends snickered. Raelynn gasped. "Seriously? That was it? You only kissed for what, over a year?"

Hayley pushed forward like she wanted to run into the kitchen, but I held her back. I really didn't care what Raelynn thought of me.

"Crazy, right?" Dylan said. "I'm ready for a *real* relationship."

My hands balled into fists.

"Not to mention," Dylan continued, "she wasn't that great of a kisser."

I gasped. I hadn't realized I was moving forward until both Kaitlyn and Hayley wrapped their arms around me and pulled me away from the kitchen. I dug my feet into the ground and tried to push forward. That good-for-nothing tone-deaf prick. I wasn't a good kisser? Please. He enjoyed it. He always did. I could tell.

"Leave it," Kaitlyn warned.

"He's not worth it," Hayley added.

"You were just about to take down Raelynn!" I cried.

Hayley jerked her head back like I'd said something stupid. "Yeah, because she *is* worth it."

They shoved me back, keeping me from raining down destruction on Dylan and his stupid friends. Oh, Pete. I swear, if I ever got my hands on that guy, he'd never be able to walk straight again.

They fought against me until they pushed me into the wall. Only, it wasn't a wall. It was Liam.

"What's going on?" he asked.

I swatted at my friends. "They won't let me go kick Dylan's butt."

Liam chuckled. "Since you used the word *butt*, you shouldn't be allowed to kick him anywhere."

"Not helping," I said through gritted teeth. "I can't believe he said that. I'm a bad kisser? Really? That's just insane."

Kaitlyn's eyes were soft. "He didn't mean it. He's probably just trying to make himself feel better about the break-up."

Liam whistled, rocking back on his heels. "He said you were a bad kisser?" He tapped Kaitlyn on the arm. "From what I hear, you're amazing. Maybe you could teach her a thing or two."

I rounded on him, ready to throw a punch, but Kaitlyn and Hayley ruined all my fun.

"Not tonight, Camille," Hayley grunted as she pushed me toward the front door. "We are getting you home, into something incredibly comfy, and watching movies until we fall asleep."

Kaitlyn helped her get me outside of the house and onto the porch. "We'll stop and get candy and Dr Pepper on the way home."

I finally stopped fighting against them and dropped my arms. "I can't believe he said that. In front of all his friends."

They shared a look. The pity look I so hated.

"He's an egotistical jerk," Hayley said. "I've always said you were too good for him. Now you can see I'm right."

I sulked down the porch steps. "I'm getting like ten different kinds of chocolate and the biggest Dr Pepper they have."

Kaitlyn and Hayley's hands landed on my shoulders as we walked to Kaitlyn's car.

"We should get some shakes, too," Hayley said.

"I like where your head's at," I mumbled. I really did, I was just too sad to act enthusiastic.

I'd just been told that I was bad at the one thing I loved to do more than anything: kissing. This day officially sucked.

CHAPTER 6

The next morning, I woke with a bad sugar hangover. The three of us were sprawled on my queen bed. Hayley's hand was smashed against my cheek, and Kaitlyn's long legs were draped over mine. Typical sleepover for us.

I moved Hayley's hand off to the side and stared at the ceiling fan. I could live without Dylan. I *would* live without him. It just . . . sucked. Big time.

And really. "I am not a bad kisser." I folded my arms across my chest. "Am I?"

Kaitlyn moaned. "I wouldn't know."

"He had to have been making it up." I wiped some sweat from my forehead. When had it become so hot in the room? I shook out the top of my Maroon 5 T-shirt. "No way he would have stayed with me *that* long, kissed me *that* much, if he hated it."

Hayley threw her hand over my mouth. "Please stop talking."

I lowered her hand, but kept my hands wrapped around hers, holding it on my chin. "He was just trying to impress

Raelynn," I huffed. "But, why would saying I'm a bad kisser impress her?" I didn't realize how hard I was squeezing Hayley's hand until she shrieked and yanked it from my grasp.

She propped herself up on her elbows. "Okay, seriously, stop talking about him. He's a loser. We hate him. He could fall into a dark pit filled with rats and never come out for all I care." She wiped some sleep from the corner of her eye. "Actually, I'd probably push him in there."

I turned onto my side, leaning on my arm. "What if I am?"

"Are what?" Kaitlyn yawned and sat up. When she saw Hayley and me next to each other, she wiggled up on her stomach, her body between us, until her head was near ours. "Why are we up so early?"

I waved my hand in front of my face. We all had horrible morning breath. Couples kissing when they got up in the morning was the biggest lie they showed on movies and TV. So gross.

"It's almost eleven," Hayley said.

Kaitlyn rubbed her eyes. "Anytime before noon on a weekend is early."

I stared at the wrinkled sheets. "What if he's right?"

Hayley threw her head down on my pillow and stared up at me, her bold eyes serious. "He's wrong."

"How would you know?" I asked.

Kaitlyn lay her head down on Hayley's hip, so I shuffled so I could lay my head on hers. Always in our little triangle.

"You can't let this get to you," Kaitlyn said. "I'm sure you're a fabulous kisser."

"Or maybe you could use some work," Hayley said. When I glared at her, she laughed. "Practice makes perfect."

I thought back over my year with Dylan. "I've had plenty of practice. I have to face the facts. I, Camille Collins, am a terrible kisser."

Hayley swore under her breath, then looked at the ceiling and mumbled an apology before she slapped my butt, which I'd conveniently placed near her. "There are no facts. You have one guy claiming that to impress another girl."

Kaitlyn cracked a smile. "You could prove him wrong."

My eyebrows shot up. "How? I'm not kissing him again. Not after what he said."

"But there are so many other guys you could kiss." Kaitlyn wiggled her sculpted eyebrows. "How fun would that be? All in the name of science."

Hayley snorted. "What, you want her to just start asking guys to kiss her, and then rank her? Like a taste test, but in this case, a kiss test?"

I stuck out my tongue. "No way I'm doing that." I may like to kiss, but not just any random guy. Kisses were supposed to mean something.

Kaitlyn patted the covers. "I gotta pee." She shimmied out of bed and jogged to the bathroom attached to my room.

My phone vibrated on the nightstand. With a grunt, I rolled over and snatched it. My blinking eyes tried to focus on the screen. I smacked my lips together. I definitely needed to apply some lip gloss and brush my teeth. And gargle.

Tons of notifications from every social media outlet, plus text messages, filled my screen.

"Uh, oh." Hayley bit her lip and flew forward, trying to grab my phone from my hand.

"What are you doing?" I asked, swatting her away.

She stretched for my phone, which I held away from her. I pushed my hand into her face. Her lips moved along my palm. "Let's have a technology-free day. It'll be therapeutic, or some crap like that."

Kaitlyn trotted back to the bed, pausing and tilting her head to the side when she saw me and Hayley tangled together. "What did I miss?"

"Hayley being weird," I replied.

Kaitlyn grinned, flashing her teeth. "So, what's new?"

Hayley glared at her. "We need to get Camille's phone from her. It's important. Like 9-1-1 important."

Kaitlyn's eyes went wide at the same time she dove for me. Hayley had let me go when she saw Kaitlyn coming, so I took the opportunity to roll off my bed, barely going under Kaitlyn, and sprinted to the bathroom, slamming the door behind me.

Hayley and Kaitlyn were pounding on the door seconds later.

"Don't do it," Hayley said, her tone like that of a scolding mother. "I'm warning you, Camille. You need to listen to me."

If she'd just casually suggested a tech-free day, I probably would have been on board. But with her freaking out, I knew something was going on.

I scrolled through my notifications, instantly regretting it. The news about me being a bad kisser had spread like wildfire. Everyone was talking about it online, tagging me in posts, making gifs and memes, and I suddenly hated life and everyone in it.

The things people were saying about me were horrendous. They blamed it on the fact that I wouldn't do more than kiss, so my experience was limited. Some guy said it was because I was "thick," like being a little bigger boned and having muscles immediately qualified a person to suck at kissing.

I hated people.

I slammed the back of my head against the door.

"You know they're idiots, right?" Hayley said through the door. "I'll beat them all up, I swear."

For some stupid reason, I couldn't stop myself from reading everything. People who I thought were my friends were getting in on the jokes, saying how they just knew I'd be bad at it. A 'friend' of mine said it was because I was blonde.

Seriously? They were just grasping at straws, and I knew it, but it still pissed me off.

Liam had responded to that comment. *But I thought blondes had more fun. I think there should be an investigation into the matter. There's only been one accuser.*

Pete responded: *That's because there was only one guy willing to kiss her. But Dylan wised up.*

Liam: *It took him over a year to wise up? Maybe he's the one with the problem.*

Pete: *Why are you siding with Camille? Everyone knows what a selfish brat she is.* Only, he hadn't used the word *brat*.

Liam: *I'm siding with the truth, which is yet to be found out.*

My fist wrapped around my phone like it wanted to break it in half. I was *not* a bad kisser. I needed to prove it. I was a summer away from my senior year, and I wasn't going to enter it with everyone in the school thinking I couldn't kiss.

But there was no way I was opening a kissing booth. If Liam had taught me anything, it was that guys could easily lie. No matter if the guy liked it or not, he could say he didn't.

I needed a list of guys who were honest. Who would tell the truth, no matter what. It would also help if it were someone I wanted to kiss. No, it *had* to be someone I wanted to kiss. I wasn't dropping my standards over some stupid rumor Dylan started.

Standing, I straightened my back and opened the door. Kaitlyn and Hayley scrambled to their feet and searched me over in a panic, trying to read my mood.

"I'm making a kiss list."

They exchanged a wary glance.

Kaitlyn licked her voluptuous lips, reminding me of the rumor that she was an excellent kisser. "What do you mean?"

Pushing past them, I went back into my room and got some paper and a pen from my backpack. I sat down on my bed, using the cushioned headboard as a back support. I tucked my legs close to my chest and put the paper on my knee. On the top of the page, I wrote: *Kiss List*.

Then I numbered underneath that, stopping at four. I needed four guys to prove Dylan wrong. I could have done more, but I honestly didn't think I could find more than four guys I'd be willing to kiss for scientific purposes. Or any purposes.

Kaitlyn and Hayley sat in front of me, the wariness still hanging on their faces.

"I'm going to find four guys I want to kiss and who can prove Dylan wrong."

"That's the stupidest thing I've ever heard." Hayley's gaze flickered to Kaitlyn. "Back me up here."

I continued on like she hadn't said anything. "There are plenty of guys over the years that I've wondered what it would be like to kiss. I don't want a relationship with them, just a nice make-out session. But I can't just walk up to a guy and ask him to kiss me. He could get the wrong idea. I have to somehow make it natural."

Kaitlyn patted my knee. "Do you think maybe you're not thinking clearly? You're just worked up over . . ."

"Oh, I'm thinking clearly," I snapped.

Kaitlyn snatched her hand away, her eyes wide. "Yeah, okay. Totally clear." She cleared her throat. "Go on."

I held up a finger. "First one is easy: Brady Tucker."

"I've actually wondered what it would be like to kiss him," Kaitlyn said. She pointed at me. "Let me know how it goes and if I should cross him off my list."

Hayley didn't look as excited. Her nose twitched up. "Why Brady?"

He'd seemed open to the idea the night before when we danced. Yeah, he just wanted to make Raelynn mad, but Brady would do it. He'd be honest, too. He might side with me, even if I was a bad kisser, just to make Raelynn and

Dylan feel like crap. We both had stakes in it. "Because he's hot and he will."

I wrote his name on the list. I held up another finger. "Isaac Lee."

Kaitlyn gagged. "DJ Ice? Gross. He's so . . . short." Everyone was short compared to her, but I didn't point that out.

Hayley smirked. "Now, there's a guy I could sink my teeth into."

He'd been the DJ at Brady's party. He was the DJ at everyone's party. He also didn't give a crap what people thought of him. He'd tell me the truth, whether I wanted it or not. No way I'd ever date the guy, but he was good-looking. I couldn't deny that fact.

"Three?" Kaitlyn leaned back on her arms. She seemed to be loosening up to the idea.

Hayley slapped a pillow against her face. "For the record, I still think this is the stupidest thing you've done to date, which is saying something." She threw the pillow at my head. "But since there's no way to stop you, I'll give you some advice: you need someone with cred. Someone who everyone would believe and has kissed so many girls, he'd know what he was talking about."

At the same second, Kaitlyn and I declared: "Alejandro Ramirez." We both laughed. He'd been a fantasy of ours for a long time. Just one hot make-out session, and nothing more. He'd be the steamy kind who would make you fan yourself afterward. Kaitlyn didn't even mind that he was an inch shorter than her.

Hayley smiled slyly. "Even I'd get on that train."

I added his name to the list. Just one more.

"Who next?" Kaitlyn asked, rubbing her hands together.

I twisted my lips to the side. "Okay, there's been one guy I've been *dying* to kiss since middle school."

"Who?" Kaitlyn asked.

"And why haven't you mentioned it before?" Hayley asked. "I could have been mocking you about it all this time."

I shrugged, drawing circles on the top of my list. "He's not well known at school. He's kinda shy and quiet. But I've wanted to get my hands in his hair and kiss him good for a long time." My hand hovered over the number four spot on my list. "He's someone I could see having a relationship with."

Hayley narrowed her eyes, her finger flicking a daith earring. "Oh, *brilliant* idea. Let's throw you into another relationship with a stupid guy who's bound to break your heart and annoy the crap out of me."

I shook my head a little too fast. "Oh, I definitely don't want a relationship right now. Maybe I'll save him for last." Maybe by then, I would have sorted through all my feelings about Dylan.

Kaitlyn shook my arm. "Who? You're killing me!"

I leaned forward, a sultry smile tugging at my lips.

Hayley held up her hand. "Please don't say Liam Elliott." She motioned to the trashcan in the corner of the room. "If you are, I might need that to throw up in."

I pulled back, not hiding the disgust on my face. "Liam? Ew. Why would you think that?"

Kaitlyn took a hairband from her wrist and pulled back her curly hair. "Pretty sure the guy has had a crush on you since elementary school."

"What?" A weird, uncomfortable feeling crept over me, and I wanted it gone. "No way."

"Guys tease the girls they like," Hayley said. "Which is lacking in the creative department, if you ask me."

"Yeah, in elementary school," I said. "Not high school. If he's still using that tactic, then I definitely don't want anything to do with him."

Kaitlyn shook her fists in the air. "Enough about Liam! Who, Camille?"

My smile came back. "Mason Payne."

They both sat there in stunned silence. Hayley folded her arms across her knees, which she had tucked into her chest. She opened her mouth, and then snapped it shut. She finally leaned over to Kaitlyn, her lips twisted to the side. "Are we supposed to know who that is?"

Kaitlyn scrunched her nose. "The guy who ate paste in first grade?"

I threw up my hands. "Why is that the one thing people remember about him?"

Hayley clapped her hands together. "Oh, *him!*"

"Because it was gross," Kaitlyn said.

Ignoring their stares, I added his name to the list. "Pretty sure his paste-eating days are over."

"Look on the bright side," Hayley said, shoving my arm. "If he likes the taste of paste, maybe he'll like the taste of your lips."

I shoved her so hard that she fell onto her side. Both Hayley and Kaitlyn laughed, but I read over my list. A kiss list. A perfect, beautiful, luscious kiss list.

By the end of the summer, I intended to have every name crossed off the list.

CHAPTER 7

There were only two days left of junior year. The boring days where the teachers don't know what to do because all the finals have been turned in, and none of the students want to be there. They really should cancel those days since they're pointless.

I had this small hope in the back of my mind that when I showed up at school, everyone would be so excited about the year being over that they wouldn't be talking about me.

I hated when I was wrong. Because I was. So wrong.

Pete draped his puny arm around my shoulder the second I walked through the doors like he'd been waiting to ambush me.

"She's here, everyone!" Pete shouted, surprisingly loud for such a scrawny guy. "The worst kisser in the school."

I tried to shove him away, but he kept a tight hold, making it hard to proceed with my original leg-demolishing plan I'd concocted the night of the party. So, I punched him in the stomach, not holding back. He grunted and released me. I narrowed my eyes at him. "How would you know? It's not like I, or any other girl for that matter, would be desperate enough to kiss *you*."

He laughed loudly, but anger brewed in his hazel eyes. "Deflecting won't work, Cami."

"I'm surprised you even know what that word means," I said, my glare not going away. This day was officially going to suck.

All morning, people whispered as I past them in the hall. Some were brave enough to shout vulgar things at me, but only when I was alone. If I had Hayley or Kaitlyn next to me, no one said a thing. But I couldn't lug them everywhere I went, no matter how much I wanted to.

On the way to fourth period, a freshman approached me, a smug smile on his lips. "Hey, sugar. If you need someone to practice kissing with, I'm willing to offer up my services."

Taking him by the scruff of the shirt, I lifted his tiny body off the ground. One of the perks of having muscles. Or being 'thick.' Gah, I hated that word.

"Listen to me, boy," I growled. "If you ever talk to me again, or talk about me to anyone, I will snap you in half."

His wide eyes blinked fast. All the color had drained from his face. His feet dangled, searching in vain for the floor.

"Alright, Cam-Jam." Liam pried the boy from my grip. The second his feet hit the floor, the freshman took off running.

"She's crazy!" he yelled, waving his arms in the air. "The bad kisser is crazy!"

Liam sighed and rubbed the back of his neck. "I think that backfired."

I huffed, folding my arms close to me. "You think?"

He motioned to the door of our fourth period class. "I hear we're watching a movie." He leaned in close and patted his backpack. "I snuck in some popcorn. If you're a good little girl, maybe I'll give you some."

"What movie?" I could leave. Really, I had no reason to be at school.

His light blue shirt made his eyes light up. "It's Mr. Palm. It's probably something alien related."

I threw my head back. "Just my luck. Why can't we watch something fun? Like Easy A."

Liam held up his palm for a high five. "Love that movie."

I slapped his hand and went into the classroom. All the chatter came to a screeching halt, and every head whipped in my direction. I turned to leave, but Liam put his hands on my shoulders to stop me.

Liam clucked his tongue at the class. "Have you guys been talking about me again behind my back? That's just rude." He pushed me toward my desk and forced me into my seat. Then he patted my head. "That's a good girl."

With a groan, I slapped him away from me. He laughed as he went to his seat near the front of the class.

Val, the stringy brunette next to me, leaned toward me. "Bad weekend?" She wore baggy clothes, probably trying to conceal the fact that she was basically just skin and bone, but her gaunt face gave it away.

"Oh, it was just great," I said with a forced smile. "Thanks for asking."

"It's okay," she said. "Not everyone can be good at kissing. You should just focus on your better qualities. Like . . ." She tilted her head to the side. "You know, I can't think of one right now."

Everyone around her laughed.

Mr. Palm started the movie, a homemade alien documentary, and I wanted to kill myself. Any time I made eye contact with someone, they'd make a kissy face at me. I slunk lower and lower into my seat, wishing I could disappear.

Liam turned around and pulled at the side of his lips, telling me to smile. I bared my teeth, snarling, which made him laugh. I wasn't trying to be funny. How could he make light of my horrifying situation?

Val threw a rolled-up piece of paper at my face, smacking my nose. It bounced onto my desk. I knew I should've ignored it, but I couldn't help myself. I opened it only to find a drawing of me puckering my lips to kiss someone, and the guy next to me bent over and vomiting all over his pants and shoes. So clever.

Reaching into my backpack, I found a blank piece of paper and drew a very detailed picture of me beating the crap out of Val. I balled the paper and chucked it at her, hitting her right in the eye.

Her glaring eyes disappeared when she got a good look at the drawing. She went pale, and I couldn't help but smile. If these stereotypical bullies thought I would just cower back, they obviously didn't know me very well.

But the more I thought about it, the more I realized I'd hardly talked to Val all year. We'd been friends once upon a time. I'd been so wrapped up in Dylan that I hadn't paid attention to those around me.

Val opened her mouth, and suddenly Liam was standing right there. He smiled at her, and she melted. "Hey, Val, mind if we switch seats?"

With a stupid grin, she grabbed her things and squeezed by, her eyes never wavering from him. When he winked at her, she blushed furiously.

Liam plopped down in her seat and scooted the table next to mine, so they were touching. "You're not helping yourself."

I was fuming. I couldn't tear my gaze from Val, who was whispering to the girl next to her and pointing back at me. "What am I supposed to do? Just sit back and let them walk all over me?"

"Just a suggestion," he said, leaning back in his seat. "But maybe not threaten them? You're only making matters worse."

I turned to him. "Easy for you to say. No one's saying bad things about you."

He pulled the popcorn from his bag and set it on the desk, right in the middle of us. "Why do you care what they think, anyway? Tomorrow is the last day of the year. Summer will come, and everyone will forget all about it."

I popped some popcorn in my mouth and instantly relaxed. I hadn't noticed it was caramel. "This is my favorite."

His eyebrows went up. "Really? Mine, too. That butter stuff is for the unsophisticated."

A small smile came to my mouth, surprising me. Liam and the popcorn were somehow releasing all the tension I had burning inside. "Totally agree."

His eyes softened. "Then you should agree to forget about the whole rumor." His attention went to the boring movie, which should be banned from existence.

He was right. I should have just dropped it and moved on. But that wasn't in my nature.

CHAPTER 8

*D*uring lunch, I went to find Kaitlyn and Hayley in the cafeteria. I saw them sitting in the corner near a window, smiling and laughing. They were a sight for sore eyes. I'd only taken a couple of steps when my eyes were seared from an image that shattered my mood: Dylan and Raelynn were sitting at a table together. Their legs were touching, and he played with some of her hair. She giggled and pushed him in the chest.

It had been a couple days since we officially broke up, and he was already flirting with another girl. My appetite disappeared.

Dylan wiped a crumb from her nose, and then he leaned in and kissed her. He kissed Raelynn in the middle of the cafeteria, where anyone could see. Including me, who was standing there in frozen horror. So many eyes turned to me, looking back and forth between me and the disgusting display of affection. Dylan and Raelynn had no idea they'd created an audience.

The fact that he could do that to me left my blood boiling. Had Liam been right? Had Dylan been pining for

Raelynn for years, and I was too blind to see? It had only been days. DAYS. I wanted to vomit like the guy in Val's drawing, only in a spot where it would land on Dylan and Raelynn. Gah. Even their names together sounded like a sickeningly gooey celebrity couple. They were seconds away from being crowned Daelynn.

Both my hands tightened into fists. How dare he embarrass me like that in front of the whole school? We'd had such a good relationship, but the second we were done, it was like a switch flipped inside him. He'd moved on and started a horrible rumor about me, clashing with the guy I'd known. Maybe I'd been too blind to notice it before.

There was no way he was getting away with it. It would mean going against the rules I set for my kiss list, but I had to do something right then. My eyes sought out Brady until they landed on him a few tables away. His sad face was on 'Daelynn.' They were doing this to him, too.

I didn't have time for lip gloss. I needed to act. With a deep breath, I stormed over to Brady, my tennis shoes pounding against the linoleum. I took him by his thick bicep, yanked him up from his seat, wrapped my arms around him, put my hand on the back of his neck, and pressed his body against mine. Our lips met, and Brady didn't hesitate. He enfolded me in his strong arms, his lips moving feverishly on mine. My fingers slid up into his hair as his hands landed on the small of my back.

He tasted like ketchup, but I didn't care. It felt good to kiss someone besides Dylan. And honestly, the more I melted into Brady, the more I noticed he was a real good kisser. Raelynn was missing out.

When we finally released each other, my swollen lips pulsed with the heat of his. My fingers grazed my lips, surprised at how amazing that had been. Brady's eyes shined, and a smile spread across his face.

"I knew you wanted me," he said with a breathy voice.

My chest heaved in and out as I tried to calm myself. After a second, I realized it was silent in the cafeteria. I dropped my arms from around Brady and looked around. All the wide eyes of laughter had been replaced by eyes of intrigue.

Liam came into view, amusement in his eyes. He cleared his throat and spoke loudly. "So, Brady, how was it?"

Somehow, Brady's grin grew. "I have no idea what Dylan was talking about. Camille definitely knows what she's doing."

A smug smile tugged at my lips. I knew Dylan had been wrong. And Brady had just confirmed it in front of the cafeteria with most of the school watching.

"Please," Pete scoffed. He stood from his seat, flicking up the collar of his shirt like it added a cool factor or something. "Of course Brady would say that. Their exes were kissing each other moments before. Jealousy doesn't look good on either of you."

The smiles on mine and Brady's faces fell off.

I opened my mouth, but suddenly Hayley and Kaitlyn were there next to me, guiding me out of the cafeteria before I could do or say something stupid.

I wasn't sure who I wanted to hurt more: Dylan or Pete. All I knew was that they wouldn't be the ones getting the last laugh.

CHAPTER 9

The nice thing about having a mom who's too busy to notice me was that I was able to ditch the last day of school. There was no point in going back to humiliate myself more. I just needed to wipe eleventh grade out of existence and start fresh senior year.

I still had every intention of crossing the guys off my list. It was nice to be able to put a big red check mark next to Brady's name. I may or may not have put a ranking next to his name, too. It may or may not have been an eight and a half.

Which, now that I had something to compare it to, put Dylan at a measly six. But, unlike him, I wouldn't spread the word.

I watched chick flicks the entire day and didn't bother to change out of my pajamas. It was the best day I'd had in the longest time. I'd turned off my phone, so I wouldn't get any notifications from my friends or stupid people from school.

When the last movie finished, I rolled over onto my stomach and looked at my kiss list. Who was next? Mason was last, for sure. I had to pick between Isaac and Alejandro.

The guys couldn't have been more different if they tried.

Isaac was the sharp-dressed, pierced, rocking DJ who didn't bother with anything other than music or science. Alejandro was the sexy baseball player who had the perfect smile that charmed the panties off of every girl. I just wanted a kiss, though. My fear about him was that he'd want more. I would just need to be firm with my boundaries.

Brady's kiss had left my blood boiling to the point that I felt daring and brave. Which meant going for Alejandro next. Working my way into his life wouldn't be too hard. A simple social media search let me know he frequented the batting cages a few times a week. I'd played softball up until Dylan and I started dating. He found it boring and wouldn't go to any of my games, so I quit to spend time with him.

I hadn't missed it much, though. I'd rarely thought about it. But thinking about it now, getting a bat back in my gloved hands, the motion of swinging the bat and the vibration of connecting with the ball, would be the perfect form of therapy.

Since it had been a while, I needed to do a few practices to get myself back in the groove of things. Alejandro could have been one of those guys who wanted the flimsy girl who couldn't swing so he could show her how, but I had a feeling he'd be more impressed with a girl who knew what she was doing.

Since it was the last day of school, and a Wednesday, Alejandro wouldn't be there. Perfect time to practice. I rifled through my walk-in closet until I found my favorite softball bat and my perfectly worn-in gloves.

The second I slipped them on, the soft material hugging my skin, an overwhelming desire to be out on the field filled in a void I didn't know was there.

My bedroom door suddenly swung open, and my brother's voice boomed. "Camille! Where are you? The craziest thing happened at school today!"

I wandered out of the closet with my softball bat in tow. Seth was wearing the Lego Batman shirt I'd gotten for him for his birthday.

His face exploded in excitement. "Are you going to play softball again?"

Going into the middle of my room, and clear of any furniture and brothers, I took a few swings. My shoulders groaned a little in protest, but after some decent swings, they loosened up. "I'm thinking about it."

He flopped on my bed, his back hitting the comforter for a second before he bounced into the air and landed again. "Finally. I've missed watching you."

I lowered the bat and turned to him. "Really?" He'd kept wanting to play with me, but I hadn't been aware he enjoyed *watching* me play for a team. I'd thought he just wanted to focus on his technique.

He sat up on my bed and gave me his infamous 'duh' look, which involved narrowed eyes, a slightly dropped jaw, and a scrunched nose. "Camille, you're the best softball player, like, ever. I thought you were going to go pro, and then I could brag to all my friends that you're my sister." His shoulders drooped. "I've had to keep our relation a secret for the past year because, well, you became lame."

I pointed the bat at him. "I didn't become lame. I got busy."

He rolled his eyes. "Dylan does not equal busy. He equals you becoming an embarrassing, boy-crazy sister."

I had no idea Seth had thought that about me. "I thought you liked Dylan."

He threw out his hands with another 'duh' expression. "Of course I do. He's cool. But the two of you together are lame. You wouldn't hang out with me anymore."

Taking a seat on the bed, I tucked my leg under me and

faced my brother. "I'm sorry, Seth. I never meant to shut you out."

Had Pete been right about me being selfish? Pete was never right about anything.

Seth waved his hand. "No biggie." He pointed to the bat. "Now, are we going to sit and chit-chat like girls, or are we going to get you back into playing?"

A smile worked its way back onto my face. I'd forgotten how funny Seth was. I really needed to focus more on my little brother. "What was the crazy thing that happened at school?"

Scrambling from the bed, he jumped onto the ground and spread his arms and legs. "It ended!" He pumped his fists and threw his head back. "It was the greatest day of my life." He looked at me. "How was your last day of school?"

I smirked. "The best one yet because I didn't go."

His jaw dropped. "What? You stayed home from school and didn't invite me?" He folded his arms. "That's just rude, Camille. We could have pigged out and watched *Les Misérables*—all three versions that you own." His eyes darted to my nightstand. I tried to get there in time, but he saw the movies. "You watched them without me!" His eyes narrowed. "Where are the treats?"

I bit my lip and stared at the carpet.

"Where are the treats, Camille?"

When I didn't answer, he dove to the ground and checked under the bed. He pulled out an empty Oreo box and shook it out. "You didn't even save me some."

I snatched the box from his hand and tossed it in the trashcan. No point in hiding it anymore. "You shouldn't be watching *Les Misérables* anyway. You're not old enough." Good thing he really didn't understand most of it. He'd just liked hanging with me. Or maybe I'd never taken the time to ask him what he'd want to watch. "Come on. Let's go to the batting cages, and then we can grab a shake on the way home."

He perked up. "A shake before dinner?"

"Yep."

He pumped his fists. "This is officially the best day ever. School ends. I get my softball-playing sister back, and dessert before dinner."

I ruffled his hair and pulled him into a hug. "Come on."

It felt weird getting into the driver's seat of my car. It was an old piece-of-crap Hyundai that was literally being held together by white and pink duct tape. And I absolutely loved it.

Seth bounced in the passenger seat, sniffing around.

"Why are you acting like a dog?" I asked. I turned the ignition, and the car sputtered for a few seconds. I guess that was what happened when the car was left alone for months at a time. I drove it every now and then to keep the battery going, but that was about it. Dylan drove everywhere.

"Because it smells funny in here." Seth moved his nose up and down.

I breathed in my car. It smelled old and unused, like a shirt that you found in the bottom of your drawer. I'd really neglected a lot of things by being with Dylan.

"Well, that's gonna change," I said. With a determined breath, I tried the ignition again, and my car finally came to life.

We drove with the window rolled down and Maroon 5 blaring from the speakers. Seth rolled his hand out the window like waves. I couldn't help but smile while watching him. He hadn't been tainted by the world yet, and I hoped it would stay like that for a while.

CHAPTER 10

There was only one other batting cage being used when we arrived. Seth was out of the car the second I put it in park. As he ran to the wire fence to watch the guy inside, I got my equipment from the trunk.

After paying, I let Seth pick which cage he wanted to use. I placed a helmet on his head and slapped the sides.

"You remember how to do this?" I asked.

The Seth 'duh' look followed.

I pushed him into the cage and handed him a bat. "Let's see what you got, Slugger."

He whiffed on the first try and grunted, trying to sound tough, but it cracked, and I held in a laugh.

"Choke up on the bat, Seth. Plant your feet on the ground, shoulder width apart. Remember to bend at the knees."

He did as told, and when the next ball came at him, he swung hard, connecting with the bat.

"Nice!" I clapped loudly.

My brother grinned, something I hadn't seen in a long time. I missed it. When he'd done a few more swings, and had gotten into the groove of things, I claimed the cage next to his.

The first few swings were rough. It was crazy how easy it was to fall out of rhythm when you hadn't done something in a long time. I guess that was the meaning of 'practice makes perfect.'

I took my own advice and choked up on the bat, pushing my body into the ground. My knees bent, my gloved hands rubbing back and forth on the grip. The next ball sailed toward me, and I threw my weight into the swing. The vibration of the ball hitting my bat gave me a high, one I hadn't realized I'd been craving.

There was no better feeling than watching a ball soar in the direction I'd sent it. Each connection intoxicated me, and I wanted more. Sweat slid down my back and forehead. My head was hot underneath the helmet. I was soaked in it.

I wasn't sure how much time passed. I just kept on swinging, letting out all my emotions from the past few days.

Dylan being the first to call if off.

Wham.

Saying I was a bad kisser.

Wham.

Pete mocking me.

Wham.

Mom not being there for me to talk to.

Wham.

My body overheated with every blow. When I'd run out of coins, and the last ball had been knocked to its destination, I stood there in the batting cage, panting for breath and letting my smile explode.

It felt so good.

I stepped outside the cage and shut the door. Taking off my helmet, I shook out my sweaty hair, running my fingers through it.

"That. Was. Awesome," Seth said. He looked at me with so much awe and admiration that it made me blush. Thank goodness my cheeks were already red from the workout.

I held up a hand, and he high-fived it.

"Seriously, Camille. I've never seen you hit like that." He clasped his hands together. "Please tell me you'll start playing softball again."

I opened my mouth to say something when a rich, smoky voice sounded behind me.

"I agree."

I spun to find Alejandro Ramirez leaning against the chain-link fence, his arms and ankles crossed. He wore a tight-fitting baseball tee that showed off his muscles. His gaze traveled my body, and, despite the heat, I shivered.

Seth threw up his hands. "See. Even this random guy thinks so. My sister is so good. But she got all stupid over her boyfriend and stopped being cool." He glared at me, but it was in his adorable way.

I put my hand on my hip. "I did not stop being cool."

"Yeah, sure." Seth's tone was incredulous, almost a little snotty. When I ruffled his hair, he slapped my hand away and smoothed it out. "Don't mess up my game, sis."

"What game?" I asked.

Alejandro chuckled. "The guy has game." He winked at Seth, who beamed. "Camille, why aren't you playing for our school?"

Seth glanced back and forth between the two of us. "You know this guy?" He grunted. "Don't go all boy-crazy for him. I can't handle it. I just got you back five minutes ago."

Slapping my hand over my brother's mouth, I pulled him into my side. "Please stop talking." I looked at Alejandro and did my best not to melt at the sight of him. "What are you doing here?" I stopped myself before I could add, "After stalking you online, it didn't look like you came here on Wednesdays."

A sultry smile tugged at his thick lips. They were more than kissable, and just the thought of them on mine made me want to fan myself. He swept his bangs to the side. "My reward for surviving another school year." He quirked an eyebrow. "I didn't see you today."

Seth ripped my hand from his mouth, but still held onto my hand. "She ditched. She's a rebel like that."

"I needed a *me* day," I said.

Seth slumped. "Which didn't involve *me.*"

I hugged my arms around his throat and pulled his back into me. "I'll make it up to you, Seth. Promise."

"You better," he mumbled, his hands and chin resting on my arms.

Alejandro tipped his head toward the batting cage. "You were good in there. Come to summer camp. The baseball team always plays a couple games against the softball team." His gaze flitted to my lips for the briefest of seconds. "Things usually get interesting."

Seth tilted his head back to look up at me. "You should totally do that, Camille. You're totally going to be the star player."

"What position did you play?" Alejandro asked.

"Short stop." Why did I sound so out of breath? I cleared my throat. "I can pitch, but I prefer short stop."

"What position do you play?" Seth asked Alejandro.

He smiled at my brother. "Third base."

"Awesome," Seth said. "So does Kris Bryant. He's basically my hero."

Alejandro stroked his chiseled chin—so strong you could make a sculpture out of it. "Yeah, he's really good. He's no Jose Ramirez, but he's good."

"We can agree to disagree," Seth said.

"Do you just like him because you have the same last name?" I asked.

Alejandro licked his bottom lip. "Added bonus."

Seth bounced. "Are you related?"

"I wish." Alejandro pushed away from the fence and came closer, his musky cologne wafting toward me. "I better see you at summer camp." He took out his phone. "Give me your number so I can make sure you sign up."

I swallowed, trying to work moisture into my mouth. "Doesn't the team already have an amazing short stop?"

"She was a senior this year," he said. "There will be a battle for the opening, but it looks like you can handle yourself." He held his phone out to me, and I took it, trying to conceal my trembling hands.

I saved my number in his phone and gave it back to him.

"See you at camp," Alejandro said. He fake punched Seth in the stomach. "Keep on swinging. I watched you, too. If you work hard, you could be even better than your sister."

I laughed. "Good luck with that, Seth."

Seth flexed his tiny arms. "I got this."

We smiled and waved, parting ways with Alejandro. If I didn't have Seth with me, and hadn't promised him a shake, I would've stayed and watched Alejandro for a bit. He probably had the best form, and I could learn a thing or two from him. Or, I could just watch his backside.

While Seth sang at the top of his lungs as we drove to get our shakes, excitement tingled under my skin. Everything was going much better than I had anticipated. I'd already had interaction with Alejandro, and had just been given the perfect chance to kiss him: at summer camp.

I signed up as soon as we got home.

CHAPTER 11

*A*fter dinner, Seth and I helped Dad clean the kitchen. Mom still hadn't gotten home from work. I was anxiously waiting for her to come home so I could talk to her about the camp, and about Dylan. I still hadn't broached that subject with her because I hadn't had a chance.

Dad heard all about it the day after it happened. He did a terrible job of covering up his smile when I said Dylan and I were done. He followed that up by pulling IBC root beers out of the fridge and cheering to the single life.

"Tell me how you really feel, Dad," I'd said with a sigh that night.

Dad had beamed. "I'm ecstatic, thanks for asking."

He was even more excited when I told him about softball camp during dinner. He looked at me like a proud parent, and I swore I saw tears glistening in his eyes. For someone so tough, he could be a softy.

This childish part of me wanted my mom to have the same reaction, but I'd be lucky to get a reaction at all.

While I waited for Mom to get home, I stalked my kiss list members online. Alejandro's feed was full of smoldering selfies that would normally make me roll my eyes, but wow, he was hot. I had to reach over, grab a piece of paper, fold it in half, and use it as a fan, he was that sizzling.

Most of his followers were girls, no surprise there. It might be difficult to stand out from all the other girls, but I had to try. I commented on a few of his photos, just so he'd get my name bouncing around in his head.

Isaac's were all photos of him DJing, or him trying new experiments with inventions he'd created. The guy was a gorgeous genius. Who also had a lot of female followers.

The thing with both Isaac and Alejandro was that I'd have to be super bold with them if I wanted to stand out among the sea of girls swooning over them. They liked the aggressive type, which could get me in trouble. I was one to let things unfold naturally, but I didn't have time for that. I just hoped they wouldn't take my advances as anything more than what I wanted. I would have to tread lightly with them.

Which meant never being alone with either of them. The kisses had to be public—well, not too public if I didn't want to be labeled the wrong way—which could definitely work in my favor. Eyewitnesses were always key in these situations, especially if it showed Isaac and Alejandro being into the kiss. No way could they deny I was a good kisser if everyone saw their reactions.

Mason would be a slower approach, which was good since I wanted to save him for last. I'd have to gradually work my way into his life. He didn't have a lot of followers online, and the few females he had looked like his mom, grandma, and some other relatives. He was so cute with them that it made me happy he was on my list. I loved a guy who got along with his family.

After skimming through his photos, I saw he worked for a local movie theater, which was perfect. Hayley, Kaitlyn, and I were planning on going to the movies on Friday, like we did at

the end of each school year. It wasn't the normal theater we
went to, but I was sure I could convince them to try out a
new theater if it meant contact with Mason.

Giddiness swung on my nerves like a monkey in a tree. It
was latched on, having the time of its life. This kiss list was
looking obtainable, and I couldn't deny the fun I'd have
crossing off each name.

Mom's voice echoed in the hall. She was home.

Slamming my laptop closed, I scrambled from my bed so
fast that my legs tangled in the sheets. I lost my balance and
landed back-first on the floor, letting out a very audible, "oof."
Rubbing my back, I stood and hobbled to the door.

Mom's back disappeared into her bedroom as she closed
the door behind her. Normally, the closed door meant Mom
and Dad's room was off limits. But I could hear Dad
watching baseball in the front room, which meant Mom
was alone.

With a deep breath, I walked with my head held high—
hoping to build up some courage—and knocked on her
bedroom door.

No answer.

I knocked again. I could hear her shuffling around inside,
probably changing out of her work dress and into something
comfy. I waited a full minute before I knocked again.

"Mom?" My voice came out way quieter than I wanted.
Clearing my throat, I spoke up. "Mom? I need to talk to you."

Mom's voice sounded on the other side, so strong and
sure, getting my hopes up. But then I realized she was talking
on the phone.

Glancing over my shoulder like I was about to do something against the law, I turned the doorknob to see if Mom
had locked it. She hadn't. I pushed the door open a crack and
peered inside.

Mom sat on her bed, laptop in front of her, a Bluetooth

headset perched in her ear, her professional tone clashing with her baggy shirt and sweats.

She looked up when I came in, a smile on her face. Only, the smile was for the caller, so she sounded attentive. Her eyes were just a blue lake of tiredness.

Since she didn't motion for me to leave, I took a seat on the bed next to her, waiting patiently for her call to finish. After ten minutes, I almost gave up but decided to wait it out.

Another ten minutes passed before Mom finally ended the call.

"Hey, sweetie," she said, her eyes on her laptop. She pulled up her email and began clacking away at the keyboard.

"Do you have a few minutes?" I asked, watching her fingers fly.

"Uh huh." Mom erased her last sentence and tried again. "What's up?"

I flexed my hand like I was trying to wring out excess nerves. "Dylan and I broke up."

Her gaze finally flickered over to me. "What? When?"

"Saturday night."

Her eyes were already back on the screen. "What happened?"

I shrugged, even though she wasn't looking at me. "We just kind of fizzled out. It was overdue, but I'm still sad. He was my first boyfriend and first kiss, you know?"

"Uh huh." She swore under her breath as she read an incoming email. If I thought she'd been typing fast before, I was way wrong. If Olympic keyboarding were a thing, Mom would take home the gold by a landslide.

I tucked my legs close to my chest. "I mean, I know it will be for the best in the long run, but it hurts so bad. There's like a piece of me missing. I was Dylan's girlfriend for so long, I don't know who I am without him."

Mom reached over and rubbed my leg before her fingers found the keyboard again. "I'm sorry, sweetie. Things will get better. Just give it time." She scoffed. "Seriously, Carl? This is not what we just discussed."

Mom was yelling at an email. Poor Carl. He'd get the live version soon enough.

"I, uh, I signed up for softball camp," I said. "I think I want to get back into it."

"That sounds fun, dear," Mom said, her mouth in a frown as her eyes moved furiously back and forth, reading an email. She touched the side of her ear. "Carl? I told you my client won't settle. I don't know how you run things at your firm, but . . ."

I tuned her out, not wanting to listen to Carl get scolded like a little child. I slid off the bed and headed toward the door, giving my mom a last look.

She didn't look up at me. With a sigh, I closed the door so she could spend the next twenty minutes berating Carl.

CHAPTER 12

*a*t least Kaitlyn and Hayley were excited when I told them that I signed up for softball camp. Hayley said something to the extent of, "I'm so glad we got Dylan's claws out of you."

I honestly thought everyone was overreacting. I hadn't been *that* bad when I'd been with Dylan. I hadn't.

It wasn't difficult to get Hayley and Kaitlyn to switch theaters for our yearly ritual: a triple feature at the movies. Thankfully, it was the time of year when all the good movies were out, so it wasn't hard to find movies to see. Sometimes we had a hard time narrowing it down, which led to a double or triple feature on Saturday. When we were in school, we didn't get to the movies all that often.

We went all out. Popcorn, large soda, and tons of candy. Each. It cost a lot, but we'd been saving up for it, like every year.

Kaitlyn wore track shorts and a basketball T-shirt. Hayley had her holey skinny jeans and a shirt with her favorite band's logo on it. I'd opted for capris and a loose blouse hanging off my shoulder. It was something simple, which I thought

Mason would appreciate. He didn't strike me as the type who liked flashy.

"So," Kaitlyn said as we were in the concession line, "are you going to kiss Alejandro the first day at camp, or you gonna make him work for it?"

I pursed my lips and batted my eyelashes. "Work for it, obviously."

Hayley pulled her red hair back in a stump of a ponytail. "I bet he's going to be amazing."

"Oh, I have no doubt he will." A wicked grin rested on Kaitlyn's lips.

Hayley and I exchanged a glance before we looked at her.

"Experience?" I asked. She'd said before that she wanted to know what it would be like to kiss him, but she was acting like she knew.

She bumped me with her hip. "Not with him. But Amy did at Prom, and she won't stop talking about it."

I narrowed my eyes. "I thought he went with Jess."

Kaitlyn scrunched her nose like she was holding in a giggle. "He did."

My heart sank the smallest bit. I didn't want anything with Alejandro, just a kiss. But for some reason, the thought of him playing the field like that made a little bit of the spark I had for him disintegrate. I may have seemed hypocritical because I had a list of guys I wanted to kiss, but I'd never go to a dance with one guy, and then kiss another while we were there. A day buffer was required, at the minimum.

"The tricky thing will be that Mason will also be there." I'd forgotten he was on the baseball team until I'd perused his social media feed. "I'm going to have to keep them separate somehow."

"Next," the guy at the counter said.

"Speaking of Mason," Kaitlyn said under her breath.

Hayley adjusted my shirt so more of my shoulder showed,

giving me a wink. With a roll of my eyes, I put it back how it was, ignoring her scowl. That would have worked better on the other guys.

Hayley answered by pushing me toward Mason. I stumbled toward the counter, catching hold to keep myself from falling over.

"Are you okay?" Mason asked.

I straightened out my shirt. "Yeah, fine. Just clumsy." I meant to stare at the menu, like I always did, pretending like I didn't know exactly what I wanted to get, though I knew. But I couldn't take my eyes off his. Mason Payne had this adorable, sexy quality about him. He kept his blond hair a little shaggy, but not too much that it covered his green eyes.

A blush climbed up his neck to his cheeks. He shook out his hair, his eyes darting to the register. "What can I get you?"

I thought about biting my lip to draw attention to it, but he wasn't looking at me. "A bag of caramel corn and a large Dr Pepper."

His eyes briefly landed on mine before he stared at the soda fountain. "We only have Coke products."

I knew that; I just wanted him to speak again. He had a low vibrato that made me want to listen to him forever. "Cherry Coke will be fine, then."

"Ice?" He held a large cup in his hand, still not daring to look my way.

"Yes, please," I said. As he filled the cup, I spoke. "Have any big plans this summer?"

He licked his dry lips. The guy could definitely use the moisture from my lip gloss. "Just a family vacation to Hawaii."

I'd always wanted to go there, but Mom never took a day off work. "Awesome! Have you been there before?"

He set the cup and a straw in front of me. "Uh, no. First time." He hurried to get the bag of popcorn and set it next to my drink. "Anything else?"

I pointed at the glass container full of candy beneath me. "Licorice, Sour Patch Kids, and . . ." I tapped my fingers along the counter. "Junior Mints."

"Is this all for you?" he asked, his gaze sliding to the left. Hayley and Kaitlyn were probably watching the whole thing from the next cash register over. But if I looked at them, it would distract me.

I lifted my shoulder in a shrug. "We're seeing three movies. Oh, peanut M&Ms, too."

He rang me up, and I gave him the cash. As he was getting the change, I held out my hand.

"I'm going to need your phone as well," I said.

He paused, his hand hovering over the change in the register drawer. "Why?"

I leaned in like I was going to tell him a secret. "So I can give you my number. I want to hear all about Hawaii when you get back. If I can't go, I want to live vicariously through you."

His tone somehow dropped a notch. "Don't you have a boyfriend?"

How had he not heard? Maybe that would be a good thing for me. "We broke up." I reached my arm out, and he set the change in my hand. "And your phone."

He glanced around, probably looking for a manager, before he fumbled to get the phone out of his pocket and handed it to me. I entered my name and number, then took a selfie. I smiled at him. "Just in case you forget what I look like."

When I handed it back, he stared at the picture on his phone. "Pretty sure that's not possible." He stuffed the phone in his pocket. "Enjoy your movies."

I gathered everything in my arms. "Don't forget to call me, Mason. I'm serious."

He scratched the back of his neck, a small smile landing

on his thin lips. There wasn't much to work with, but I'd make do.

"Yeah, sure," he said.

With a wink, I sauntered away and found Hayley and Kaitlyn waiting for me off to the side. They already had all their food and drinks. Kaitlyn had gotten a hotdog, but I didn't trust those from a movie theater.

Hayley just rubbed the side of her neck—making the stars behind her ear move—rolled her eyes, and then handed the attendant her ticket for the first movie. Kaitlyn bumped her arm with mine. "Everything is just coming up Camille, isn't it? You've now made contact with three of the four guys."

I pressed my glossed lips together. "It's like it was meant to be."

CHAPTER 13

*a*fter the first movie, we went back into the foyer to refill our drinks and my friends' popcorn. The bad thing with getting caramel corn was that there weren't free refills. I hoped Mason would be at the counter, but he must have been on break. Some old lady was in his spot. She wasn't nearly as fun to flirt with.

I'd just thanked her and turned around when I bumped into someone.

"Hey, Cam-Lam," Liam said. He wore a Florida Georgia Line T-shirt that looked fairly new. The front was tucked into his jeans. "What are you doing here?"

"Um, seeing a movie?" Wasn't that obvious?

He chuckled. "I guess that makes sense." He pointed to my bag of caramel popcorn. "I'm getting the same thing. I just wish they'd give refills for it, you know?"

Yeah, I did. "They shouldn't punish people for having good taste."

"Right?" He grinned at the lady behind the counter. "You'll give me a free refill if I get some caramel corn, right?" Her narrowed eyes were enough of a response. Liam sighed.

"Fine. Can I please get a bag of caramel corn and a large Dr Pepper?"

"We only have Coke products," the lady said in a flat tone. I'd said the same thing at the same time, using a very formal voice in anticipation of her answer.

Liam snickered and pushed me away from him, the light touch making me blush, surprising me. "Fine. A Cherry Coke."

I just stared at him. What was happening? Since when did Liam and me like the same exact things?

"You can stop checking me out now," Liam said, his smug smile turning toward me.

He was insufferable. We may have had the same tastes in food, but it didn't make up for the fact that he drove me crazy. I had no idea why I was even still standing there. I had another movie to get to.

I whipped around to find Brady. He had his hands in his pockets and wore a sheepish smile. "Hey, Camille."

"Hey, Brady."

Liam's voice sounded over my shoulder. "Please tell me we're not seeing the same movie. I don't think I could handle the two of you making out the whole time."

I elbowed him in the stomach, and he grunted.

I knew it would be awkward the first time Brady and I talked after our kiss, but this was beyond anything I could have prepared for.

"Brady! Liam!" Kaitlyn bounded up, all smiles. "What movie are you guys seeing?"

When they mentioned they were going to the same movie we were, I stood on my tiptoes and gave Kaitlyn the cut-throat, but she didn't notice and invited the guys to sit with us.

"This is going to be so awkward," Liam whispered. I elbowed him again before we went inside.

My friends were usually good at picking up on hints, but for whatever reason, they were both completely clueless that day. They were chatting with Brady as we entered the theater. Hayley went down the aisle, followed by Kaitlyn, and then Brady. I stared at the aisle, not wanting to go next. Maybe I could go around and sit next to Hayley.

Liam batted his eyelashes. "Sorry, love, but Brady is all mine." He scooted past me and sauntered down the aisle, his hips swaying, making me laugh.

All the tension fluttered away, and I'd never been so grateful for Liam's silly ways. I plopped down next to him, took off my shoes, and tucked my legs underneath me. I wasn't thinking that moving my legs to the left would make me lean right, getting awfully close to Liam. But it would be too noticeable to switch.

Liam opened his bag of popcorn. "I'm so glad you got your own. You practically ate all of mine in class."

I threw a piece of popcorn at his face. "I did not." I totally had.

He picked the piece from his shirt and tossed it into his mouth. "Thanks, but that's not nearly enough payback. You'll just have to get me a bag for the next movie."

My eyebrows furrowed together. "You're seeing another movie?"

"Yeah, that new horror movie. I've been *dying* to see it." He laughed at his pun.

I pelted him with more popcorn. He caught a couple in his mouth. I ate some before I ended up throwing a bunch at him. The lights dimmed.

"We're seeing it, too," I whispered. "I had to practically beg Kaitlyn to go." I grimaced. "I agreed to go to that sappy chick flick with her tomorrow to make up for it."

"I'm so glad I'm not you," he said. "I'm not that nice.

Brady would be seeing the chick flick on his own. Which he's actually done a lot. They're his favorite."

I choked on the sip of Cherry Coke I'd just taken. "Yeah, but then you could make out during the whole movie with your *love*."

A wicked grin spread across his lips. "True. Maybe we'll join you guys tomorrow. Brady and I could snuggle." He turned to me, our faces inches from each other. "Is he a good kisser?"

I was grateful for the darkness so he couldn't see my blush. "I don't believe in spreading rumors about people's kissing abilities."

"So you wouldn't want me to tell everyone you were a good kisser?"

"Well, yeah, because you don't know if I am or not."

Liam stared at me for a moment like he was trying to read my face. "You're serious, aren't you?"

"Well, yeah."

He shook his head, turning back to the screen. It was another preview, so I didn't mind talking during it. Normally, I was a stickler for being quiet in movies.

"What?" I asked.

When he ignored me, I faced the screen, holding my popcorn close. What was he talking about? And why was he suddenly so moody?

The movie had just started when Liam's lips brushed against my ear. "Fourth grade. Timmy Clark's birthday party."

Heat rushed to my ears. My first kiss. I'd forgotten about it. Forgotten it was *Liam*. We played a truth or dare game, and Hayley dared Liam to kiss me.

It was my turn to lean into him, my mouth close to his ear. I made sure to keep my skin to myself, though. "That doesn't count. It was a peck on the lips and so long ago."

"Shhh!"

Popcorn came flying at me from the direction of Kaitlyn and Hayley. The buttery mess landed in my hair and on my shirt. I picked them all off and threw them on the floor.

"Pretty sure a peck counts as a kiss," Liam whispered. "And our lips lingered for a moment. Obviously, it meant nothing to you, but I actually enjoyed it. You had soft lips."

Instinctively, my hands went to my mouth. How did he remember that? And if it was true, why hadn't he stood up for me when Dylan told everyone I sucked at kissing? I couldn't concentrate for the rest of the movie. I shifted in my seat, creating a distance between us. How had I forgotten that Liam had once kissed me? Kissing was one of my favorite hobbies. I remembered all the kisses after that one, but for some reason, my brain had blocked it. I didn't remember hating it or thinking it was gross.

In fact, looking back, I think it was the moment I decided that kissing was fun.

All because of Liam Elliott.

CHAPTER 14

*T*here was something liberating about getting all dressed up for a night out, and doing it only for myself. I had no boy to impress. I could wear whatever I wanted, including my green maxi dress that fell to my feet. It hugged my curves, highlighting my wide hips and thick thighs. It was so comfortable, and the material was soft against my skin. Dylan hated it.

Kaitlyn opened the passenger side door of my car and grinned wickedly at me. "First, I *love* that dress." She plopped down in the seat and used both hands to shut the rusty door. Her long legs were pulled close, not having much room. "Second, I've missed this piece-of-crap car."

Hayley leaned forward from the backseat. "And Camille driving." She patted Kaitlyn's shoulder. "She's such a better driver than you are."

Kaitlyn stuck her tongue out over her shoulder. "I'm not *that* bad."

Smiling, I pulled away from the curb. "I'm used to having my brother in the car. Makes me pay closer attention." I patted the dashboard. "Also helps that the car shakes violently if I go over forty."

Hayley drummed her hands along the center console, playing the beat of the song on the radio. It wasn't a band I recognized, but one she loved.

I flashed a glance at her through the rear-view mirror. "So, I was thinking of adding a blue streak to my hair."

Hayley's eyes lit up. "Yes! Finally."

I'd been talking about doing it for months, but Dylan always talked me down. He said I'd look stupid and couldn't pull it off. I just wanted a pop of color in my blonde hair.

Kaitlyn raised her hand, wiggling her fingers. "Can I do it? Pretty please?" She did Hayley's hair all the time, and it always turned out great.

"I was going to ask if you would," I said.

She danced in her seat, throwing up her arms as high as she could without hitting the roof. "We're doing it tomorrow."

I shimmied my shoulders, dancing along. Hayley upped the sound of her drums and banged her head. I missed our random dance parties and sing-offs in the car. Dylan always made us stop.

Why did I keep thinking about him? Everything reminded me of him. But I was starting to realize that he'd taken control of my life, probably without meaning to. I let him make my decisions for me. I'd been so concerned about what he thought of me and wanted him to like me so badly, I'd changed myself.

Ugh. I hated myself for it.

We sang and danced until we arrived at The Shack. I had to find street parking a few blocks away. It was a nice night, so I didn't mind the walk.

We took a quick glance at the alley we had to walk down.

There was a slightly creepy vibe to it, like we were heading into a death trap.

"Maybe we should leave our purses in the car," Kaitlyn said.

"Good call," Hayley said.

We all got the cash we needed and tucked it into our phone cases. Then I locked the purses in the trunk so no one would see them before we set off. I was in the middle, with Hayley and Kaitlyn flanking my sides, both linked on my arms.

When I'd been stalking my kiss list guys, I'd noticed Isaac would be DJing at The Shack before the bands started. It was an added perk to the night. I just needed to get in a spot where I could catch his eye. And hope he wasn't mad at me for pulling the plug at his last job. I'd been trying to comment on his stuff, being slightly flirty in my responses. And by slightly, I mean aggressively.

Kaitlyn picked up the speed when we got closer, yanking us along. We struggled to keep up with her long stride.

"I don't even care if this band sucks," Kaitlyn said. "I'm just excited to get out!"

Hayley raised her nose in a snarl. "It's not like we're seeing Harry Styles. They aren't going to suck."

Kaitlyn flipped her curly hair over her shoulder. "I'm just going to pretend like you didn't say that."

"Still won't change the fact that I did," Hayley grumbled.

The Shack was an old, run-down building. The back of it didn't even have a wall anymore, leaving it open and breezy. They had string lights up, giving it a soft, cozy vibe instead of a you're-about-to-die feel.

They had plenty of security, too, most of which had looks that could kill.

We paid the entry charge and squeezed ourselves into the crowd. The three of us held hands as Hayley weaved us

toward the front of the stage. I was already sweating by the
time we found a decent spot, and I so didn't care.

DJ Ice had already started. We waved up at him, which he
returned with a nod. His smoldering eyes caught mine, and
the smallest smirk landed on his lips. I wasn't sure what it
meant, but I was curious to find out.

"He totally checked you out," Kaitlyn whispered in
my ear.

I bit my lip and stared up at him. "Did he?"

Hayley bumped my hip. "You know he did."

I lifted my arms in the air and moved my hips side to side
with the music. And Dylan said this dress would never make a
guy look twice at me. Groaning, I shook him from my head.
No Dylan tonight. Or ever again.

We danced until Isaac's set ended, and the roadies started
setting up for the band.

"I need a drink," I said, fanning myself with my hand.
"You girls wanna come with?"

Hayley shook her head. "No way I'm losing our prime
spot. And I need Kaitlyn in case someone tries to wriggle
their way into our space. But get us some waters, too."

Kaitlyn patted my shoulder. "Sorry, sweetie. You're on
your own. Do you think you can handle that?"

With a roll of my eyes, I pushed her hand away from me
and forced myself through the crowd, moving away from
their laughter. It was a pretty girly thing to expect them to
come with me. I hadn't done anything on my own in
forever.

I got in the long line for the concession stand, still
bouncing along to a beat in my head.

"What are you listening to?" Isaac's smooth voice came
from behind me.

I turned to find him checking me out, doing a toe-to-head
glance. "The last remix you did. Loved it."

A smile pulled at his lips. "It's a favorite of mine. Glad you liked it."

Sweat trickled down the side of my face. Normally, I'd be embarrassed. It always grossed Dylan out. Another reason I stopped playing softball. No way I could play and *not* sweat.

But I just used the back of my hand to wipe it away, and Isaac didn't even flinch or blanch.

"How come I haven't seen you here before?" he asked.

We moved forward in the line. I almost mentioned Dylan, but I stopped myself in time. The Shack wasn't his scene. I hadn't thought it was mine, either, but I hadn't had so much fun in the longest time. I really enjoyed all the music Isaac had played.

I stepped in close. "I didn't know you were looking for me."

His hand brushed along my arm. "I didn't know I was, either." He put his hands on my waist and pushed me forward in line. I eyed his full lips, wondering what it would be like to kiss him. "Want to take off?"

That had been my biggest worry about my kiss list. I didn't want to start flirting with guys, and then have them expect I would do more than kissing. Maybe that wasn't what Isaac was suggesting, but by the way he was pressing his hips into mine, I had a feeling he'd want more.

But I could cross him off the list. It would be so easy. My gaze flitted past him, catching my friends near the stage. They were both staring at me, a mix of hope and sadness in their eyes. They were probably happy for me but didn't want me to ditch them. It had been so long since they had me all alone on a weekend night.

I turned my gaze back to Isaac and pushed up on my tiptoes, our lips close. "I'm hanging with friends tonight, but maybe another time." I turned to the front of the line and ordered three bottled waters.

When I turned back around, Isaac had left.

I hurried back to my friends and handed them their waters. "Should I cancel the kiss list?"

They shared a surprised look before Kaitlyn spoke. "Why?"

Shrugging, I twirled the water bottle in my hands. "Maybe I was too rash."

Hayley narrowed her eyes. "What did Isaac do?" She cracked her knuckles. "Do I need to beat him up?"

"No," I said. "His body language was saying he wanted something way more than kissing."

Kaitlyn waved her hand. "He's a guy. Of course he does. But that doesn't mean he's going to get it. He needs to learn."

True. But did I want to put myself in a situation where I'd have to stop him? What was the point of that?

"Besides," Kaitlyn went on, "you've only crossed one of the guys off the list. You're so close to getting Alejandro. Don't give up yet."

I pointed my water bottle at her. "Weren't you saying the kiss list was a bad idea to begin with?"

"Well, yeah." Kaitlyn tucked her hair behind her ear. "But after watching you kiss Brady, I got excited for you. I wanted you to seize your moments. Take control of your life."

"Prove to the world that Dylan is a jerk." Hayley folded her arms and swung the star pendant back and forth on the chain.

Kaitlyn adjusted her dress, which was basically an oversized shirt. She had it cinched in the middle with a belt. "Forget about Isaac for now. You were both high on music. Wait for a calmer moment." Her tone turned seductive. "Just think about Alejandro." She said his name with an exaggerated roll of the tongue. "You've already laid the groundwork for that."

I held up a finger. "I actually just turned Isaac down for you guys."

Hayley wrapped her arm around my shoulder. "I feel so special. But don't expect to be getting any action here." When I rolled my eyes, she kissed my cheek.

The lights dimmed, and the crowd went wild. I took my friends' hands and, for once, focused on the moment and having fun.

CHAPTER 15

*I*t was almost two in the morning when we finally rumbled into my driveway. As soon as I put the car in park, I quickly turned off the ignition so it wouldn't squeal like it always did. I was way past curfew and didn't need my car shouting it to my parents.

Since we were so late, Hayley and Kaitlyn came home with me. They texted their parents close to midnight and told them they were staying over at my house. Out of all our homes, mine was the easiest to sneak into without getting caught. My parents were heavy sleepers, and Seth was easy to bribe.

As soon as Hayley's head appeared from climbing out from the back seat, I whispered over the hood at her. "Don't forget to lock the door."

"I can't believe this is how our parents lived before modern technology." Hayley made a show of locking the door, and then closing it. Then, as I had just done on my side, she pulled at the handle to make sure it was really locked.

My car was old, but I loved it.

"Our purses," Kaitlyn said, pointing to the trunk.

I used my key to open it, and we all went for our purses. Everything happened in the blink of an eye, but the next thing I knew, my keys were in the trunk, and Hayley slammed it shut. I would have made a remark about her waking up my parents with the noise, but all I could think about was the fact that my keys were locked inside.

Hayley stared at the closed trunk in horror. "Please tell me those weren't your keys in there."

"Those were my keys," I whispered. The key to the house was on the chain.

Hayley went to pound a fist against the car, but Kaitlyn stopped her in time.

The brief fear clenching my airways closed suddenly evaporated. I couldn't help the smirk that crossed my face. "Guess it's time for monkey Hayley."

Kaitlyn returned my wicked grin.

"No." Hayley folded her arms. "No way."

When Hayley's mom got sick, she used to sneak over to my house all the time in the middle of the night when she couldn't sleep. She'd climb up the tree outside my window, let herself in, and snuggle in with me. Sometimes she wouldn't wake me. It wasn't until morning that I realized she was there, but I never cared.

Hayley pointed at her tall, laced boots. "I can't in these."

"Take them off," I said.

She jutted her chin. "I'm not as nimble as I once was."

"Nimble?" Kaitlyn stifled a laugh.

Hayley answered by punching her on the arm.

"You're the one who locked my keys in there," I said. "You gotta fix this."

With a grumble, Hayley fumed toward the tree. She untied her boots and tossed them on the grass. "You two owe me." She rolled her shoulders—loosening her joints—and then jumped up, grabbing hold of the lowest branch and pulling herself up.

"Climb, little monkey," I said.

She flipped me the bird instead.

I think her anger fueled her. She flung through the tree with ease, bringing me back to her monkey days. Her hand reached out for the last branch before my window, her fingers grazing the branch, when she slipped, falling back. Kaitlyn and I gasped at the same time, both lifting our arms like we could actually catch her if she fell. At least with Kaitlyn's tall frame and long arms, it wouldn't be as far of a fall for Hayley.

The inside of Hayley's knees curled around the branch and stopped her from completely falling. But now she was upside down in the tree, head and torso dangling in the air, her skirt flipped, exposing her red cotton panties.

I was torn between being worried and trying not to laugh. Kaitlyn went into full-on warrior mode and hurled herself at the tree with a low growl, climbing up with an amazing amount of arm strength. Good thing basketball had her in the weight room a lot.

"Hold on, Hayley," I said. "Kaitlyn is almost there."

Hayley folded at the stomach, trying to reach up and grab the branch, and also push her skirt back into place at the same time. "Please, take your time. I'm totally fine here."

Kaitlyn was almost to her when she made the mistake of looking down. She was afraid of heights. She wrapped both her arms and legs around a tree branch, hanging on for dear life. Her dress had ridden up, showing even more of her incredibly long legs. "We're going to die."

"We aren't that high up," Hayley muttered with a strained voice. She was still working to pull herself up, getting a nice abs workout in the process.

"Guess it's up to me." I took off my shoes, stretched out my neck, and went to climbing, not being nearly as graceful as my friends. The bark rubbed against my palms as I ascended, and I had to bite back a yell. Problem was, when I was finally in arm's reach of them, there was no room left for me to join them. There wasn't a branch near enough that I could latch onto and help them out.

Maybe I could get a ladder from the garage. But I'd have to get in the house to get access. "I'm going for the window," I said. "Once inside, I'll go get a ladder to rescue you."

"We'll be dead by then!" Kaitlyn shouted.

"Shhhhh!" I hissed.

"Could you just call the fire department?" Hayley asked. "Get some hot firefighters to rescue us instead?" Then she took in her exposed underwear and shook her head wildly. "Scratch that idea."

I shimmied across a branch, working my way to my window. The closer I got, the lower the branch sagged. "Okay, maybe this isn't going to work."

"Need some help?" My dad's voice cut through the night.

All three of us screamed.

Dad leaned out my window, folding his arms along the sill. "You should really make less noise if you want to sneak back in."

"Don't look at me!" Hayley screamed, putting all her effort in holding her skirt over her underwear.

Dad sighed. "Fine." He disappeared inside and shut my window.

"Dad!" I screamed. He was seriously going to leave us?

A minute later, his voice came from below, making us scream again.

He'd brought the ladder. He helped us down one by one until we were all safely back on the grass.

Suddenly, the front door opened, and Seth came roaring out like a gladiator, holding a bat high above his head.

"What are you doing?" Dad asked.

Seth froze, bat hovering above his head, and frowned when he saw all of us. He slowly lowered the bat. "I heard screaming. But apparently, no one needs to be saved." With a dramatic sigh, he slumped his shoulders, lowered his chin to his chest, and sulked back into the house, the bottom of the bat dragging along the ground.

Our attention turned back to Dad.

"What were you doing out so late?" His eyes narrowed at me like he was switching to interrogation mode. Having a dad in the military sucked sometimes.

"We were at The Shack," I said. "We were dancing and lost track of time."

Dad didn't say anything for a bit. The silence stretched on. Both Kaitlyn and Hayley shifted next to me, probably as uncomfortable as I was. But then Dad spoke. "Was it just the three of you?"

I pulled back in surprise. "Yeah."

He nodded, satisfied with my answer. "Good. Just making sure." He looked down at the grass, setting his hands on his hips. Not in his usual tough military stance, but in a way that said he didn't know what to do with his hands. "I, uh, I thought that maybe you had a relapse."

I blinked a few times, trying to process his words and a response at the same time. He thought I'd been out with Dylan. "Dad, Dylan's not a drug!"

"Eh," Hayley squeaked out. "That's actually a perfect way to describe him."

Kaitlyn shifted her weight. "It really is."

I wanted to argue with them, but they were kind of right. I'd needed some major mental rehab thanks to the guy.

"Since you were out with just these two," Dad said. "I'll let it slide this one time. All of you, in the house and up to bed."

"Thanks, Mr. Collins," Kaitlyn said.

Hayley saluted him.

"Thanks, Dad!" I grabbed both my friends' hands and rushed inside before he could change his mind.

CHAPTER 16

a part of me hoped that Mason would call before he went on his trip, but he didn't. It was basically radio silence on his end. He hadn't even gotten on social media, so I couldn't connect with him that way, either.

I continued to go to the batting cages with Seth almost every day now that school was out and we had the summer hours to fill. We ran into Alejandro a lot. For some reason, adding a simple blue streak to my blonde hair upped my confidence. I just felt more like . . . me.

Alejandro spent some time giving Seth pointers, and even more time flirting with me. Luckily, for the most part, Seth didn't seem to notice the flirting. He was too wrapped up in thinking Alejandro was the greatest baseball player ever and making sure Alejandro remembered him when he went to the major leagues.

"Just remember, I'm your number one fan," Seth said as we were walking back to our cars one day.

"Pretty sure my mom has that spot," Alejandro said with a grin.

Seth pursed his lips. "Yeah, pretty sure it's me. No offense to your mom, but I don't see her out here every day."

Alejandro stopped at the driver side door of his car. "Well, you see, she has this thing called a job."

Seth did his best job snapping his fingers. "I've heard of those! My mom has one, too." He opened the passenger side door of my car and hopped in. "Bye, Alejandro!"

"Bye, Seth." Alejandro leaned his forearms against the side of my car and stared over the hood at me. His black hair looked gorgeous in the sunlight. Well, all of him did. "Hey, Camille, this Saturday a bunch of us are getting together for a baseball game before the camp starts. It's for anyone who wants to come." He tapped the hood of my car and backed away. "I better see you there. Noon at the school."

He waited for me to nod before he got in his car. I wasn't sure what thrilled me more: spending more time with Alejandro, or getting back out on the field. I hadn't played an actual baseball game in almost a year. I couldn't believe that much time had passed.

Just the thought of being out on the dirt, smelling the chalk and sweat, gave me a high nothing else could.

Not even kissing.

That night at dinner, Seth and I set the table as Dad finished preparing dinner. He was making his famous lasagna, and my mouth was drooling from the smell wafting from the kitchen. I loved when Dad cooked. He'd taught me some of his recipes, but I hadn't mastered them like he had.

"Hey, Dad," I said, placing a plate on the table.

He was wearing his US Navy apron that Seth and I had

given him for Father's Day once he had to throw in the towel after his injury. He currently worked at a local gun range.

"Yeah, sweetie?" He pulled the lasagna from the oven and set it on the stove.

"Next time you make this, will you show me how? I should've asked today, but we got back too late from the batting cages."

Dad beamed. "Of course." He slipped off the oven mitts. "I miss the days of teaching my little Camille how to cook. I looked forward to them."

I rolled my eyes. "It hasn't been that long since I've cooked with you."

"Yes, it has," Seth said. His face twisted to the side as he lined up the forks perfectly parallel to the plates.

I thought back, trying to remember the last time, and I couldn't think of it. Where had I gone the past year? Oh, yeah, into Dylan's mouth.

"I think Camille should promise not to have another boyfriend until she graduates high school." Seth put the last silverware in place with a satisfied nod.

Dad brought the salad and garlic bread into the dining room and set them on the table, leaning a little on his good leg. "I like that idea. In fact, maybe she should wait until she graduates college."

Seth nodded. "Good call, Dad."

I put my hands on my hips. "I'm not promising anything." I really didn't want another relationship. At least, not yet. I just wanted some decent make-out sessions. No strings attached.

Dad checked the clock hanging in the kitchen. "Why don't we get started?"

Seth frowned. "Mom isn't home yet."

"I know, buddy," he said, removing his apron and hanging it up in the pantry, "but she's working with a client today, and

I don't want this to go cold."

I hated that Mom wasn't there, but sometimes I had to push that aside for Seth. I sat down in my seat and dished myself a huge piece of lasagna. "What do you think Mom would do if she got home and *all* the lasagna was gone?"

Dad snatched the spatula from me, taking a large section for himself. He rolled his neck out. "I accept your challenge."

Seth's frown was quickly replaced by a smile. "Oh, man, she'd be so shocked!" After he got himself a piece, we all held up our forks and clinked them together.

By the time Mom finally got home, there was only one tiny section left. All three of us were slumped in our seats, completely full. The good kind of full, like you'd just had the best meal of your life.

Mom didn't look up from her phone when she came in the kitchen. "Smells good in here."

Seth snickered, covering his mouth with his hand.

Mom glanced over her phone at him. "What's so funny?"

"Nothing." He cackled, throwing his head back.

Mom's narrow eyes took in the lasagna dish, and she put a fist on her hip. "That's what you left me?"

Dad stood from his chair and rubbed her back, pulling her close to him. "You know food goes fast in this family, babe."

She kissed him on the lips before she took a seat at the table. "Sorry I'm so late. Court went long." She grabbed the pan of lasagna and set it in front of her, eating straight from it. "It's been way too long since we had this."

"Hey, Mom?" I asked.

She took another bite, and then wiped her mouth with a napkin before she finally looked up at me. Her eyes went wide. "When did you add blue to your hair?" A frown rested on her lips. Total opposite reaction my dad had given me. He'd loved it. He used to dye his hair all the time before he joined the Navy. Once he retired, I tried to get him to color his hair, but Mom wasn't having it.

I stole a glance at Dad. Seriously? She was just now noticing? "On Sunday." I'd tried to show her when I got home, but she was occupied with her phone. I needed to change the subject before I completely lost it and either blew up at her or broke down crying. Neither options were tempting. "I was wondering if we could go shopping on Saturday early evening. I want to get new cleats for softball camp."

She furrowed her light eyebrows, her gaze lingering on the blue in my hair. "What softball camp?"

Dad stood, removing empty dishes from the table, and not doing a good job at hiding his disappointment.

"I told you about it," I said. "Like two weeks ago."

She twisted her lips to the side. "Huh." Her phone vibrated, so she checked it.

"So, can we go?"

"What?"

"Shopping? On Saturday? To get new cleats."

Mom finished off the lasagna in the pan, staring at her phone the entire time. She licked her lips. "Have your dad take you. Looks like I got a new case." Her fingers flew across her phone as she stood and walked into the downstairs office, shutting the door behind her.

Dad took my plate. "Of course I can take you. Maybe we should get you some new batting gloves while we're out. I noticed yours are starting to fray."

"Yeah," I said, trying to conceal the sadness from my voice. "Sure. That sounds good."

Dad kissed the top of my head. "I'm sorry, Camille. She's just really . . ."

"Busy." I stood from the table with a little too much force, sending my chair flying backward. "Like always. I'll be in my room if anyone needs me." I left without looking at my dad or brother. Seeing their anguish would only make things worse.

Just once, I wanted my mom to be there for me. I had Hayley and Kaitlyn, but sometimes a girl just needed her mom.

CHAPTER 17

Kaitlyn was excited when she found out about the baseball game and wanted to join. After some begging, Hayley finally agreed to at least sit in the stands and watch. I think she was looking forward to heckling the other team.

The sun sat high in the blue sky, with only a couple of fluffy white clouds to join it. It was the perfect day for a game.

"We better be doing something fun tonight," Hayley grumbled, kicking her boots along the concrete as we took the path toward the baseball field behind the school. Her tall black combat boots covered up most of her legs.

"My dad's taking me shopping for some new equipment," I said, "but I'm free after."

Kaitlyn held out her arms. "This is amazing. We are getting our Camille all to ourselves on a Saturday night." She had her curly hair in a messy bun on top her head.

I adjusted my softball bag on my shoulder. "You've had me the past couple Saturdays."

Hayley paused near the bottom of the bleachers. "Yeah, and you still have about a year's worth to make up."

Kaitlyn wrapped her arms around me, setting her chin on my head. "We're just glad to have you back."

"I haven't been anywhere," I said.

Hayley clucked her tongue. "Tell that to the back of Dylan's car."

With a roll of my eyes, I jogged out onto the field. Kaitlyn and I immediately tossed down our bags and went to stretching. I breathed in the smell of dirt and grass, and I immediately sank into a tranquil place.

"I've missed this," I said.

Kaitlyn sat down and straightened out her legs, bending to touch her hands to her feet. "I know you're sick of us saying stuff, but honestly, I've missed watching you. I hate that you quit."

I took a seat next to her and tightened my high ponytail before stretching my calves. "I hate it, too. I honestly didn't realize I'd lost so much of me when I was with Dylan."

"He was cute and fun," Kaitlyn said with a one-shoulder shrug. "Any girl would have done the same."

"It's still stupid," I mumbled.

"Well, yeah, it's crazy stupid."

I pushed her so hard that she fell on her side, causing her to laugh.

"You ladies ready to lose?" Alejandro appeared above us, his sexy smile greeting us, and his excited eyes taking in my outfit.

I may have put on the shortest, tightest shorts I could find, and a form-fitting tank top to show off all the muscles I'd been gaining back. It wasn't the most practical outfit for a baseball game, but I thought it could be a good distraction for Alejandro.

Shielding my eyes with my hand, I looked up at him. "We haven't picked teams yet."

Alejandro squatted down so I could see him better. "I only like to compete against the best, because it makes the victory that much sweeter."

I placed my hand against my chest. "Why, Alejandro, I do believe you are complimenting me."

"I call it as I see it," he said. "You've got more talent than most people on this field. But please don't take it personally when I win."

I stood, brushing off the back of my shorts and making him look up at me. I ran a finger along his firm jawline. "You should be more worried about your own feelings when you get creamed." With a wink, I left him squatting there.

"Everyone gather up!" Liam stood on the mound, his hands cupped over his mouth.

I jogged over to him. "What are you doing here?" I didn't think he played baseball. He'd played volleyball and soccer for a bit, but that was it.

Liam lowered his hands. "Hey, Cam-Tam. Alejandro asked me to ref. Gotta make sure no one tries to cheat." He smiled at the blue in my hair. "Love it. Very fitting on you." Then he eyed my outfit. "What kind of baseball league is this?"

I suddenly felt very exposed, but I wouldn't let it show. "You like it."

He lifted a shoulder in a shrug, and then shooed me away with his hands. "Stop monopolizing my bod. I have a game to run."

Folding my arms, I stepped back until I was next to Kaitlyn. All the players were circled around the mound.

Liam rubbed his hands together. "Alright, Alejandro and Camille will be the captains."

My eyes sought out Alejandro, who puckered his lips at

me. I hadn't known they'd want me to be captain. At least I'd get to pick my power team.

There were a few of my old softball mates there, but none of them made eye contact with me, even when I selected a couple to be on my team. I tried to let it roll off me. Maybe I was reading too much into it.

Alejandro and I went back and forth until all the players were chosen. I ended up with a pretty decent team, despite one of them, Izzy, who looked like she'd sacrifice her pitching arm to be on the other team. We did a coin toss, and my team would be up to bat first. A small setback, but one I could handle.

My adrenaline spiked as I stepped up to bat. I tapped my bat against the base and breathed in the scent of the dirt. It had been a while since I'd hit from a pitcher. The batting cages and an actual person were way different. Which was probably why I struck out.

"I'm embarrassed for you," Alejandro shouted from third base. He held his arms in the air. "I can already smell victory."

Izzy did a horrible job at trying to hold in a laugh. One directed at me for striking out. She had her strawberry blonde hair in a bun on top of her head, and a few blue skinny headbands holding back the strays.

I ignored her and pointed the bat at Alejandro as I walked back to the dugout. "It's only the first inning. Watch out."

My second time up to bat, I hit the ball right to Alejandro. I sprinted to first base, but he was able to throw it in time to get me out. In fact, it hadn't been close. Frustration ate at me. I was better than this.

On my walk back to the dugout, Hayley hopped down from the bleachers and wrapped her fingers around the chain link fence, shaking it a little like she wished she could do the same to me. "Camille, get out of your head."

I approached her, leaning against the fence that separated us. "I'm rusty."

"You're better than anyone else out there," she said. "Stop over-thinking and find that peace." She pounded her palm against the fence. "Crush them!"

With a grin, I ran back to the dugout. I could do this. I never felt more at ease than when I was out on the baseball field. I just needed to get back in the zone.

By the fifth inning, I'd found my groove. I pushed aside all my doubts and focused on the moment. Relying on my instincts had taken me far when I played softball. I went through the motions, my body taking me exactly where I needed to be.

Alejandro stepped up to bat, pointing his bat to the outfield. "Might want to scoot back. This one's going far."

He may have been being cocky, but I couldn't deny his talent. I motioned for all the outfielders to back toward the fence.

His first two swings were fouls, thanks to Izzy's excellent pitching. When I tried to compliment her on it, she scowled at me, her disgusted glare taking in my barely there outfit. What had I done to make her so mad? I needed to shift my focus so I wouldn't lose my concentration.

"Wow, I'm super impressed, Alejandro," I said from short stop. I shifted my weight and folded my arms over my chest, looking like I was bored. "You play like my mom."

Kaitlyn, Hayley, and Liam all broke out in laughter.

Alejandro narrowed his eyes. "What am I missing?"

Liam grinned from behind the catcher, who was another old softball mate, and didn't seem to be as mad with me.

"Her mom is the worst," Liam said.

"No athletic ability whatsoever," Kaitlyn said.

Alejandro did a few warm-up swings. "I'm about to prove how little you know your mom."

I grimaced. "I don't like the sound of that."

When the pitcher threw the ball, Alejandro was ready for it. His bat connected, and the ball went soaring way over my head. The left and center fielders raced toward the ball, which looked like it was headed barely over the fence. The center fielder jumped up, his back against the fence, and his glove in the air. The baseball grazed the top and landed on the other side.

The other team hollered as Alejandro ran his victory lap around the bases. When he passed by me, he pecked me on the cheek, making my blood boil for two different reasons. Stomping out the part of me that wanted to swoon, I focused on the side that would never let him win and used it to fuel me.

Problem was, we were down by two with only one inning left. The first two up to bat were easy outs, followed by a single and a double.

Then it was my turn at bat, and there was only one out left. With players on third and second base, we had a chance to tie the game. I just needed to hit the ball deep between center and right field. The players were spaced oddly apart, so it would take them longer to get to the gap. Plus, no offense to the right fielder, but he kind of sucked. I'd have to watch out for the center fielder, though—she was good.

My first swing sent the ball flying behind me. Hayley caught it in the stands and screamed like a fangirl. "OMG! Can I keep it?"

A laugh bubbled up inside me. Acting like that so didn't fit her.

Liam motioned for her to throw the ball back.

Hayley snarled at him. "I'll never forget this, Elliott." She chucked the ball over the fence, and Liam caught it. She gave him the finger before he turned his back on her, which he returned by blowing her a kiss.

I bent down and rubbed some dirt in my hands. This was my home. My place of comfort. I needed to breathe it all in and focus. Closing my eyes, I took a couple practice swings.

"Should we leave you alone?" Liam asked from behind the catcher. "Looks like you're having an intimate moment with your bat."

I glared at him. "Don't ruin this for me, Liam. I need to concentrate."

He held up his palms in an apology.

Taking some deep breaths, I went back to my happy place. The bat was a part of me. I knew how to use it, where it needed to connect with the ball, and my instinct would move my body into the proper place once I saw the pitch.

I tapped home base and got into position. I kept my eye on the ball, following its path toward me, and swung at the perfect moment. The ball smashed into my bat and flew right where I wanted it to.

As I took off running, the center and right fielder ran for the back of the field, where my ball was heading. My team cheered as I rounded first base and the other two players crossed home plate. Now we were tied with the other team.

I rounded second, my eyes darting to the outfield. My ball had smacked into the fence. I tried not to think about the fact that if I'd lowered my bat just a fraction, the ball would have gone over.

I headed for third base. If it had been a real softball game, I would have stopped at third. The game was now tied, and since we only had one out left, I could have given the next person up to bat a chance to send me home.

Problem was, it was Izzy, and she wasn't the greatest hitter. Aside from her amazing pitching, she hadn't been having a decent game at the plate. And since I wanted nothing more than to beat Alejandro, I went for it, passing third and sprinting home.

My team jumped up and down from the dugout, cheering me on. The catcher had her glove open, ready for the ball as it came toward her. Liam was squatting and positioned where he'd have the best view.

Shoving back the knowledge it was going to hurt since I was stupidly wearing shorts to impress a guy, I dropped into a slide. Out of the corner of my eye, I saw the ball inches away from the catcher's glove. My feet and legs connected with home plate, and the catcher's glove touched my back a second later.

We turned to look at Liam. With an intense gaze, he threw out his arms, signaling safe.

My team ran out of the dugout and congratulated me—except Izzy. I hadn't felt that high in a long time. My adrenaline was pumping, my body hot with hope. I didn't even care that my leg stung from the slide.

Izzy ignored us, stomped to the plate, and ended up striking out.

"Don't worry about it," I said to her as she walked back in the dugout. "Just get out there and show them what an amazing pitcher you are."

She opened her mouth to say something, but then snapped it shut, grabbed her mitt, and ran out onto the pitcher's mound. I hoped her surly attitude wouldn't mess with her pitching, but I wasn't about to hold my breath.

Alejandro's team now had one last chance to either tie the game or win.

The first batter hit a pop fly to centerfield, which the player caught. Easy out. The second hit a single.

Two outs left. Alejandro was up to bat. He carried himself with such confidence, like there was no pressure on him. He'd easily hit it out of the park, or at least get on base. Their next batter was good, too.

Alejandro pointed toward the outfield again, but this time

I didn't motion for my team to move. I felt just as confident as he did.

He connected on the second swing, the grounder speeding right toward me. I scooped up the ball and moved to throw it to second base, but the second baseman had moved far enough away that he wouldn't get there in time. I rushed to second base, tagged it, and chucked the ball toward first. Kaitlyn had her foot planted against the base, her body turned toward me, long arm extended, glove open and waiting for the ball.

Liam had rushed up behind Alejandro so he could see. The ball landed in Kaitlyn's glove a second before Alejandro's foot touched down. Liam signaled out, and my team rushed the field.

We jumped up and down, yelling like we'd just won the World Series. To me, it almost felt like it. It had been way too long since victory had coursed through my veins. Even Izzy was celebrating.

Alejandro approached me once my team had calmed. He clapped my shoulder. "I'm way impressed, Camille. I hate that I lost, but winning looks good on you."

If my face hadn't already been hot from the exercise, it would've flared. "Thank you. This is the best feeling."

"Such a high," he said.

I nodded in agreement.

He stepped in close, keeping his voice low. "Want to do something tonight? We could celebrate your win." The smolder in his eyes almost made me melt. I wanted to say yes. I could cross him off the kiss list by the end of the night.

But then I looked over at Hayley and Kaitlyn, who were talking and laughing. I'd promised them a night out, but they'd understand. It was Alejandro. A chance to make a move.

I turned back to Alejandro and opened my mouth, ready and wanting to say yes.

"Camille!" Kaitlyn wrapped me up in her arms. "I can't wait to celebrate." She grinned at Hayley, who joined in our hug. "Girls night!"

Holding in a sigh, I smiled over my shoulder at Alejandro. "Rain check?"

A slight disappointment ran across his face, but he covered it just as quickly. "Rain check."

CHAPTER 18

*S*ummer camp couldn't come soon enough. Mason never got back to me, and after some slight social media stalking, I saw he'd already gone to Hawaii. I thought about messaging him online, but I didn't want to completely scare the guy off. I'd see him at camp, anyway.

Isaac had called me a couple times, but I'd sent every call to voicemail, and he didn't leave a message. Kissing him would be a sticky situation, so I needed to be very careful with him.

Besides, Alejandro was my current focus for a kiss. For Mason, the camp would be more about getting on his radar than anything else.

We were loading up the buses, getting ready to go. Mom couldn't come since she had to be in court, so Dad and Seth saw me off.

"Work hard." Seth wore his serious mask and tone that matched with his Batman shirt he was wearing once again. "You need to let them know how amazing you are." He had one hand on his hip, the other held out toward me. "Listen,

Camille, this is your chance to shine. You only have one year left of school, and you've wasted a year on a boy . . ."

"Hey." I slapped the back of his head.

He didn't even flinch. "You want colleges to notice you, so you have to take this seriously. No goofing off. No boys. No staying up late. You need to be well rested." He'd been spending too much time around my dad, because he was starting to sound and look like him.

Dad rubbed his chin. "He's taking all the words right from my mouth."

I rolled my eyes. "Yeah, so not going to miss the two of you."

Dad wrapped his arms around me and pulled me against him. "You will." He kissed the top of my head. "You'll be great, sweetie."

"Just make sure to listen to your intelligent brother," Seth said, using his "Dad" voice that was eerily spot-on. He joined in our family hug.

I really would miss them, but I was going to keep that to myself. No need to fuel their egos.

"Seth, my man." Alejandro jogged over to us and held out a fist. Seth tried to act cool as he gave him a fist-bump and a small nod.

Dad narrowed his eyes at Alejandro. "You must be the future major league player my son keeps rambling on about." He held out his hand. "I'm Lieutenant Commander Collins." Dad loved pulling his rank card to intimate people, especially guys my age.

Alejandro didn't even flinch at the name and firmly shook his hand. "Nice to meet you, sir." His smoky gaze flitted over to me. "Just your son has been talking about me?"

"Is there another child of mine that should be?" Dad asked, standing tall. He stretched his neck from side to side like he was cracking it.

The smile on Alejandro's face faltered for a second. "No, sir."

Dad broke out in a grin. "Just messing with you. But, no, Camille hasn't mentioned you."

Alejandro winked at me. "We'll fix that during camp."

Dad's smile fell off his face. I swore I heard it hit the asphalt. "How about you not? She just got over a breakup."

"How about you two stop talking like I'm not here?" I folded my arms, my weight resting on my left leg. "Besides, Seth has already declared the 'no boys' rule."

Seth puffed out his chest. "That's right. She needs to remain focused." He slapped Alejandro on the arm and switched to his rumbly Batman voice. "Make sure she does. I'm counting on you."

"Anything for you, little man," Alejandro said.

Seth beamed. He and Dad gave me another hug before they left.

"No boys, huh?" Alejandro pouted. "That's too bad."

I sauntered up close to him, tilting my chin up. "Seth wants you to keep the *boys* away from me." I bumped him with my hip. "He didn't say anything about *you* staying away."

His strong hand brushed my waist. "Well, then, I'll have to stay really close to make sure no boys come your way."

"Looking forward to it." With a bite of my lower lip, I sauntered away.

I missed flirting. It had been way too long because of Dylan. I thought I'd be rusty, but it was surprisingly easy, especially when you had the right target.

Before we got on the bus, I quickly texted Hayley and Kaitlyn to let them know I was leaving. Our softball coach had a strict 'no phone' rule at camp. We were only allowed to call our parents at night, and that was it. The rest of the time, she kept the phones locked up in her room.

"Hey, Cam-Wham." Liam looked over my shoulder. "Texting about me?"

I hit send and tucked the phone in my back pocket, turning to face him. "What are you doing here?" I swear, the guy was showing up everywhere, like a fly searching for food.

On his shirt, he had one of those movie clapperboard things with his name on the director's line. "Coach Barnes needed some volunteers." He had his hands stuffed in his pockets, and he rocked on his heels, bringing my attention to his black and white checkered Vans. "Counts toward my community service hours." He glanced over his shoulder at the parking lot. "I saw your dad and brother. How are they doing?"

"Good." I'd forgotten he'd met them before, back in middle school when we did a school project together.

"Mom couldn't make it?"

Heat crawled up my neck, inching toward my ears. I only talked about our relationship with Hayley and Kaitlyn. Not even Dylan knew my true feelings about my mom. How it hurt to have her ignore me day-in and day-out. I fiddled with my fingers. "She had to work."

Something flashed in his eyes, maybe sorrow, but it left just as quickly. "I get that. My dad's a workaholic."

"Construction, right?"

He nodded. "Yep. Working on the remodel downtown."

My eyes lit up. "It's looking great. I can't wait until they finish. I hear there's going to be lots of shopping, eating, and an outdoor area for bands to play."

Boredom consumed his posture and his voice. "I know. I know. I hear about it every single day."

I held back a laugh. "Sorry. I kind of sounded like an ad, didn't I?"

"It's everyone's reaction." He shrugged it off. "So, I guess I'll be seeing you around at camp. Good luck." He rocked on his heels again. "I, uh, I mean, you looked great at the game the other week. I forgot how good you are."

I pushed him on the arm. "Why, thank you, Liam. I just hope I can keep it up. I'd forgotten how much I missed playing."

"Weird how we can lose ourselves over someone, right?"

I stepped back in surprise. "What?"

He cleared his throat. "Nothing. See ya." He took off at a jog.

What had he meant by that? Was he referring to Dylan and me? Or was he talking about himself and a relationship he'd had? I tried to remember whether he'd dated anyone recently, but I hadn't paid close attention to his love life. Or his life in general.

"Let's load up!" The softball coach, Coach Wilkes, cupped her hands over her wide mouth. "We're leaving in T minus five minutes!"

I knew some of the softball players from when I'd played before. But like most people in my life, I'd cut off ties when I'd started dating Dylan. It was never on purpose, I'd just been too busy to do anything with them until we'd stopped talking all together.

I hopped up the stairs and onto the bus. The chatter cut off, and all heads whipped toward me. Coach Wilkes held out a basket filled with cell phones. I couldn't believe she was already taking them. Having them for the ride to the camp wouldn't be a big deal. It would give me something to distract myself. At least I'd remembered to pack an MP3 player in my backpack. I set my phone in the basket with the others.

With a smile, I headed for the back of the bus. Halfway down the aisle, I saw Val. The girl from my science class. She played softball? I took in her tiny frame. With what muscles? Maybe she was really fast or something.

"Hey, Val." I tried to plaster on a natural smile, but with her sneer, it was difficult.

Her brown eyes narrowed as she stood to get closer. "Don't think you can just walk back on the team."

It was then that I remembered she'd been the student athletic trainer for our team. I'd never needed her, so we rarely spoke when I was on the team. I was starting to realize all these things about myself, and I didn't like any of them. Had I been that self-absorbed even before Dylan?

I'd been rude to her in class, and Liam had mentioned not threatening anyone, so I thought I'd try a different tactic. I spoke softly. "I'm not trying to do anything. I just wanted to come to camp." I pointed to her dangly earrings. They were round hoops with yarn stretched in the middle to create a fun design. "Did you make those? They're amazing."

The snarl on her face slowly lessened. "No one asked for your opinion."

Instead of snapping back, I left and found an empty bench in the back. It was a small step, but hopefully, she'd soften, along with the rest of the team, so I could survive camp.

PART 2: THREE STRIKES & YOU'RE OUT

CHAPTER 19

$\mathcal{I}$ ended up falling asleep on the ride with my earbuds in, Maroon 5 blaring. The bus jerked to a stop outside the university dorms. Coach Barnes had a relationship with a university about five hours away from where we lived. They let us stay there for a week during the summer and use their facilities. I'd gone the summer before sophomore year and absolutely loved it.

I waited for everyone to get off the bus before I did. It wasn't until I stepped off that I realized I desperately needed to pee. And I was starving. I went to check my phone for the time, but I didn't have it. So, I checked the actual watch on my wrist. How had so much time passed?

Coach Wilkes clapped her hands. "Listen up! Val has the room assignments. Everyone needs to drop their stuff off in their room, and then we'll meet up right outside the dorms and take a tour of the facilities."

I crossed my legs, squeezing my thighs together. I *really* needed to go. My stomach rumbled. I couldn't believe they didn't stop for lunch. How long were they going to make us wait until dinner? No. I wasn't going to think that way. I was going to be positive. I was here to have a good time and improve my softball skills.

Val went to work, pointing to each girl and giving them her room number, the baggy sleeves of her thin sweater flapping around with the motion. The bus driver opened the cargo area so we could get our bags.

I hurried up to Val, bouncing a little where I stood. "What's my room number?"

She clenched her jaw. "I'll let you know when I get to it."

"Can't you just tell me now?" My bladder could explode at any moment, which would be disastrous.

She put her hand on her narrow hip. "You don't get special treatment, Camille."

I danced. "I don't want special treatment. I just want to pee."

Val smirked. "Too bad." She cupped her hand over her mouth and called over another pairing.

I ran over to the bus and searched for my bag. I found it buried in the back of some others. All the movement took my mind off my bladder, so I grabbed the bags one by one and set them outside of the bus.

"Wow, what service." Izzy bent down and picked up her bag. As usual, she had her long, strawberry-blonde hair wrapped up in a high bun on top of her head. "You think this will make people like you?"

"I just want my bag." I plopped another bag on the ground, and then wrapped my hands around the handle of the bag in front of mine.

Ava, the first baseman, ripped the bag from my hand. Her blue and tan UCLA trucker hat covered up most of her blonde hair, which she had in double Dutch braids. "Don't touch my things."

I held up my palms. "Sorry."

She rolled her soft, blue eyes. "You haven't changed. So impatient and wanting everything your way."

I scrunched my eyebrows in confusion. "What are you talking about?"

Izzy and Val flanked her sides. Ava took a deep breath, annoyance bouncing in her eyes. "I know you got away with a lot sophomore year, but things have changed. You can't push people around anymore and call the shots."

A frown formed on my lips. Had I been that bad? "Listen, I'm really sorry. I didn't mean anything . . ."

Izzy pointed a finger into my chest. "How about you just stay out of everyone's way, okay? Stop interfering. Stop being controlling. Stop demanding attention."

I had no idea how to respond. I didn't realize they all hated me *that* much. Plus, it was hard to focus when my bladder was burning. I shifted back in forth in an awkward dance.

"What's wrong with you?" Ava asked.

"Have I not mentioned I have to use the bathroom? Because I do." My legs were squeezed together so tightly, my muscles were on fire.

The three of them shared this weird look that made me squirm. The next think I knew, Izzy and Ava had me pinned to the bus.

"What are you doing?" I tried to wriggle away, but they held on tight.

Val arched a sculpted eyebrow as she tucked her clipboard under her armpit. "Doesn't she have an incredibly ticklish spot?" She tapped her chin, her eyes looking like they were flipping through memories. They finally lit up when they found the right one. She moved toward me, slowly and deliberately.

"I'm sorry," I said through clenched teeth. "Please don't do this."

With a smirk, she tickled my soft spot on the left side of my stomach. It made me loosen my muscles enough for Izzy and Ava to pry my legs apart before their hands held my arms again. Seconds later, my bladder released, not wanting to hold it any longer. The warm urine soaked my shorts and travelled down my legs, my socks absorbing it.

Izzy and Ava finally let go of me, and the three of them laughed to the point of tears. I'd forgotten that Ava had the loudest and most annoying laugh—almost like a cackle. Val pulled a phone out of her pocket and snapped a picture of me.

"How do you have a phone?" I asked, frozen in place. I hadn't peed myself since I was a kid, and it was just as horrible now.

She tucked her phone in her bra. "Special perk of being a trainer." She pointed her thumb over her shoulder at Jordyn, the catcher. "Oh, and you're with her. Room 308." She held her clipboard close to her chest. "Good luck." The three of them snickered and took off. I wanted to run myself, but I also wanted to hold onto any pride I had left.

I might not have remembered a lot, but I did remember that Jordyn snored incredibly loud.

All I wanted was to get in my room, grab some fresh clothes, and take a long, hot shower. I pulled my bag out of the bus and trudged over to Jordyn. She had her black hair slicked back in a ponytail, all her hair past the hairband bunching out in extreme curls. She wore shorts and a tee like most of the girls there.

"Hey, roomy," I said, hoping she couldn't smell my pee. "Ready?"

She grunted, her dark brown eyes less than enthusiastic.

That was it. What did that mean? Yes? No? I hate you, and I'm going to kill you in your sleep?

"Well, I'm heading in." I shifted my bag on my shoulder. With my backpack and the overstuffed bag, I was about to fall over. Jordyn answered with another grunt. I walked as fast as I could to the dorms. Izzy had gone in front of me, not bothering to hold open the door. I rushed to get there before it closed, but it ended up hitting me on the back before I could get fully inside. With a sigh, I pushed the door away from me with my back and shuffled inside.

Some of the girls were already on their way back down from their dorm rooms. Coach Wilkes pointed at me. "Run that up and get back down here in the next minute."

Jordyn grunted behind me, making me jump. She'd come out of nowhere.

"I'm going to need more time," I said.

Coach Wilkes' gaze landed on my wet shorts. She rubbed her forehead. "I didn't realize you weren't potty trained yet."

I opened my mouth, ready to lash out and point the blame, but my three assailants stood behind the coach, all giving me threatening looks. With a deep breath, I stared at the elevator. Waiting for it would take too long, so I ran for the stairs, taking them two at a time. Without food, I was running on empty, but the need to wash off pushed me along. When I finally found our room, I threw my bags on the floor, grabbed a fresh pair of shorts, underwear, and socks, plus a towel and some soap, and then booked it down the hall to the community bathroom.

Coach Wilkes did not look happy when I got back downstairs.

"I said you had a minute." She wore a snarl that was definitely new. She hadn't been this ornery when I was on the team. Apparently, a lot had changed since then.

"I'm sorry," I said. "It won't happen again."

She snapped her fingers. "Let's go. We're already behind schedule, thanks to Camille."

All the girls turned glares on me, including Val, Izzy, and Ava, like it had been my fault. I couldn't let them get to me, no matter how hard it was.

We followed Coach out, keeping close behind.

My stomach rumbled, and I placed a hand over it. "I'm starving."

Jordyn stomped next to me, her curls bouncing with the movement. "You shouldn't have slept through lunch."

"What?"

She scratched her thick nose. "You were sound asleep when we stopped."

I almost stopped walking, but I didn't want to fall behind. Coach was moving at lightning speed. "What? When?"

"A couple hours ago." She hacked and spit on the ground.

Anger boiled inside me. "How come no one woke me?"

Jordyn scoffed. "Are you serious, princess? You bite people's heads off if they interrupt your beauty sleep."

I wanted to deny that fact, but that much I remembered. I still hated my sleep getting interrupted. Seth and my dad knew better than to wake me on the weekends. It kind of irked me that my teammates seemed to remember so many negative things about me. I had to have some good qualities. I just needed to remind them of that.

The guys were waiting for us when we arrived outside the locker rooms.

"What took you so long?" Coach Barnes asked, a gruffness in his voice. Why were they all in such a hurry? He tapped his watch. "We're already off schedule."

All the girls' heads turned toward me. Liam chuckled when I clenched my fists at my side. I wasn't used to so many people hating me. Or maybe they always had, and I'd never noticed.

Both coaches snapped at us to follow them. I stayed in back, trying to calm myself. Anger would get me nowhere.

Liam bumped my arm with his. "Did you have to freshen up your makeup?"

I turned to him. "I'm not even wearing makeup."

His eyes traveled my face. "Huh. Look at that. You're not." He pulled a pad of paper out of his pocket and wrote something down.

"What are you doing?" I asked.

He tucked the pad back in his pocket. "Making note of this historic occasion."

I rolled my eyes. "I've gone outside without makeup before." Hadn't I? Dylan didn't like me without it, but I'd gone without makeup before. Maybe some time back in middle school, before I'd started wearing it.

"Keep telling yourself that, Cam-I-Am." His eyes widened, and he whipped out his notepad again. "That's the best one yet."

I rubbed my arms. "Why are they in such a hurry anyway?"

"We have a schedule," Liam said, trying to impersonate Coach Barnes and doing a terrible job.

Even though I was beyond irritated, and crazy hangry, a smile found its way to my face.

Alejandro fell back, so he was walking on the other side of me. "You know I'll be getting payback from the last game, right?" He grinned at me, a wicked glint in his eyes.

"I wouldn't expect anything less." I scanned the sea of baseball players until I spotted freshly cut blond hair and a shy smile—Mason Payne. I'd have to find time to talk to him without Alejandro around.

It would be kind of hard to flirt with both of them without the other noticing. I'd have to be subtle about it.

With Mason, subtle would be easy, with how quiet he was. Alejandro? He didn't know the meaning of subtle.

Izzy and Ava looked over their shoulders at me, whispering away. They weren't going to make things easy, either. I really hoped I hadn't made a mistake by going to camp.

CHAPTER 20

*V*al was trying to make my life difficult by forcing me to share a room with Jordyn, but as I'd proved the day before, I could sleep through anything. I popped in my earbuds and fell asleep to Adam Levine's voice, so really, the joke was on her.

I bounded into the mess hall in the morning, ready for breakfast. I ignored the shared looks of disappointment Val, Izzy, and Ava wore. They were expecting me to be all sleepy-eyed and upset, but they were wrong.

I'd just got in the food line when Liam clapped me on the shoulder and pulled me close to him so he could talk quietly.

"Bad news, Cam-I-Am."

I looked up at him, fake shock and horror on my face. "They found out you weren't actually a baseball player?" Then I took in his royal blue shirt that said, *'The only way to ball is bocce.'* "Oh, wait, it's because of the confrontational shirt you're wearing. Pretty ballsy to wear it here, if you ask me."

He lowered his hand and stared at the ground. Liam normally loved a good pun. Had I upset him by my comment?

That didn't seem likely. Something else was eating away at him.

"What?" I set my hand on his arm, hoping to let him know he could tell me anything.

He licked his lips. "You have another rumor going around."

My whole body deflated, like all the air had been let out. Val. It had to be. I cupped my elbows, pulling my arms close. "A picture?"

He nodded. "It was uploaded last night, but no one knows by who."

Val. She'd taken the picture of me in my pee-stained shorts. Obviously, she uploaded it. I glanced over my shoulder, seeking her out. She sat at a table with the other softball players, all of them huddled around her phone and laughing, a few looking up at me.

I scooted forward in line. "Great. Not only am I a terrible kisser, I wet myself. That's just great." I reached the front of the line. "Just load me up with whatever." The worker—probably a college student taking summer courses—arched an eyebrow, but didn't say anything as she plopped food onto a plate.

Liam stood close, so our arms were touching. "What happened?"

"Exactly what it looked like."

"So, like, you didn't spill water on yourself or . . ."

I bit my lip and shook my head in anger. I could lie, but what would be the point in that? It was me against them. And it totally just blew a shotgun round through my kiss list.

"I had to pee, they knew it, and they also know my ticklish spot, and Val happened to have her phone, and apparently the whole team hates me, and so does the universe, and why did I come here again?" I took the plate from the worker, giving her a short but thankful smile.

Liam blew out a long breath. "Tough break."

"Totally ruins my plans," I muttered. I stopped short when I realized I'd said that out loud. I'd been talking to him like I would Kaitlyn or Hayley, which was just downright crazy. I shakily took a seat at an empty table.

"What plans?" He sat down across from me at the empty table. His plate was piled as high as mine.

No way I was telling him about my kiss list. "World domination." I stuffed some scrambled eggs in my mouth. "What else?"

He laughed at my chipmunk cheeks, and probably because I sounded funny with food in my mouth. It was nice sitting with Liam. I could be myself and not have to worry about being pretty or proper.

The bacon was perfectly crispy. I eyed the French toast and pancakes, not sure which one to start with. So, I just dumped a ton of syrup on the plate and dove in.

"You should be glad you came," Liam said. "You belong here."

I stopped chewing and stared at him. He was right. Again. Gah. Why was this becoming a thing—him being right? But I did belong there. Softball was my high. The one thing that gave me an infinite amount of pleasure.

The bench jostled as someone sat down next to me. I turned to find Alejandro, looking as sexy as ever with his baseball hat and the smallest hint of stubble. My cheeks were still stuffed with pancakes and French toast.

"Did you see?" Alejandro asked, a sympathetic look in his eyes, which was the exact opposite of sexy. I didn't want sympathy. I wanted understanding.

I swallowed my food. "I thought there was a no-phone policy. How is this possibly spreading?" And was there a way for me to wipe the memory from Alejandro, Mason, and Isaac's minds like they never found out it happened?

Liam chuckled. "You don't really think everyone turned in their phones, right?"

I did. There was no way Coach Wilkes would have let me keep mine. Maybe if I had been a favorite of hers, I could have, but those days were long past.

As if to prove his point, Liam took his phone out of his pocket and wiggled it at me.

"You're a volunteer," I muttered, "so you can have one." Just like Val could. She's a trainer, not a player..

Alejandro showed me his phone as well. "We all snuck into Coach's room while he was asleep and got them back."

As I glanced around, I noticed almost everyone had their phones. "That's just great. Really. So freaking great." No way would Alejandro be kissing me now. Who wanted to make out with the girl who wet herself? That was as far from sexy as possible. I stared at my food, not sure if I could eat any more.

Val sauntered up to the table and leaned toward me. "Did you remember your diaper today?"

I expected Alejandro and Liam to laugh, but they both shot her angry glares. She was too busy waiting for my reaction to notice theirs. My hands balled into fists. I'd tried the 'not responding to it' approach, and that hadn't worked.

But Val just stood there, hand on her hip, sporting a triumphant look, and I couldn't take it anymore. I picked up my half-eaten plate of food and shoved the syrupy mess right into her face. I turned the plate back and forth, making sure it really dug into her.

Her shrieks were muffled by the plate and food. Her lanky arms flailed around, and for the briefest moment, satisfaction ran through my veins.

"COLLINS!" Coach Wilkes' voice boomed through the room.

My high vanished. I removed the plate from Val's face and

set it on the table. Val's arms were spread wide as she leaned forward, the syrup and remnants of my breakfast dripping down her face and onto the tiled floor. What a waste of perfectly good food.

Coach Wilkes' eyes were practically popping out of her head. She took in the scene, her angry gaze finally landing on me. "I will not tolerate this behavior. If we weren't so far away, I'd send you back home."

Ava and Izzy escorted a crying Val out of the mess hall, but not before shooting me dirty looks.

"First," Coach Wilkes said, "you're going to clean up this mess. Then you can run five miles around the track and think through your actions." She stepped in close to me. "I know it's been a while, Camille, but I expected more from you." She rubbed her large forehead and muttered something under her breath that I couldn't quite make out.

"I'm sorry, Coach," I said. "I shouldn't have overreacted like that."

She dropped her hand. "Overreacted to what?"

All the softball and baseball players stared at me, an urgency in their eyes. They didn't want me to rat them out for having their phones. The thought was awfully tempting. I was the only one without a phone. All of them had seen my picture and laughed about it.

But if I wanted back on their good sides, tattling wouldn't get me anywhere. I stared at the mess on the ground. "Nothing. It's nothing. I messed up. It won't happen again."

She held up two stumpy fingers. "That's the second time you've said that to me since we got here. If you want even a sliver of a chance to get back on the team, you better change your attitude." She switched to one finger. "You have one more try. If something like this happens again, that will be strike three. I'm sure you remember what that means."

I sighed. "I'm out."

She pointed at the ground. "Clean it up. Then five miles. You can join us when you're done."

When coach had walked away, Liam hurried over to me. He held up his phone, showing me a video of me rubbing my plate in Val's face. "Say the word, and I'll post it."

I took the phone from him and pressed "delete" before I handed it back. "No. I don't want to play that way." I rubbed my eyes with my thumb and forefinger. It was nice not having to worry about smearing makeup. "All I wanted was one good piece of my life back. One. Now I'm not even sure if that's possible."

Mom certainly wasn't going to start being a mom again. I wasn't getting Dylan back, not that I really wanted him. I'd lost my chance at kissing Alejandro and probably Mason. Isaac, too, when he saw the picture—if he hadn't already.

Softball was one thing I thought I could get back.

At least I still had Kaitlyn and Hayley. Too bad I couldn't call them and hear their voices. I could sneak into Coach's room and get my phone back, but I wasn't taking any chances. It was staying there until she handed it back.

"Want help?" Liam eyed the floor.

"No, thanks. I need to do this on my own."

Four days. I just had to survive four more days. And somehow make Alejandro and Mason forget about what happened so I could resume my kiss list.

CHAPTER 21

*B*y Wednesday night, every muscle in my body was aching for relief. Coach wasn't the least bit gentle with us, especially me. The only peace I had was that everyone was keeping a large distance from me. It didn't stop the stares and the laughter, but it beat new things happening to me. I'd taken every opportunity I could to flirt with Alejandro, trying to remind him of the non-wetting version of myself.

After dinner, I took a long, cold shower. I wanted to ice my body, but that would mean going to Val for help, and that wasn't going to happen. Not that I didn't want to ask for her help, I just worried she'd do something else to me.

I hobbled down the stairs and over to the mess hall. Maybe there was ice in the kitchen.

"Hey, Camille."

I slowly turned to see Mason. He'd cut his blonde hair to a short length, styled and gelled perfectly. He wore a white baseball tee with blue sleeves that said *'Team Read'* on it, looking hotter than ever.

If I hadn't been in so much pain, I probably would have

been happy to see him. I hadn't had much time to interact with him at camp, aside from the casual smile and wave. I'd thought about approaching him a few times, but Mason struck me as the type who'd come to me when he was comfortable. The last thing I wanted to do was scare the guy.

"Hey, Mason. How was Hawaii?"

He rubbed the back of his neck and stared at the cement. "Fun." His green eyes met mine. "I meant to call you, I just..."

"Don't worry about it. I'm not really high on the list of people's favorites right now."

When he scrunched his light eyebrows in confusion, I just shook my head and moved toward the kitchen. Mason's dreamy eyes were such a distraction, I worried I'd say something stupid.

He jogged to catch up with me. "Where you going?"

"Hoping to find ice."

"Why don't you go to the trainer?"

A laugh escaped my mouth, but it cut off when I saw he was serious. "Yeah, sure, let me go to Val. I'm sure she's dying to help me."

"Well, it's her job." His tone told me he had no idea why I wouldn't want to face Val. "She's really nice."

I stopped and turned to him. "I know. We just aren't on good terms right now. I'm tired. I'm sore. I just want some freaking ice."

A smile tugged at his lips. "I'm sure the baseball trainer would be willing to help you out."

"Do you know where he is?"

"Follow me." He took off at way too fast a pace for my sore body.

"You're going to have to slow down if you want me to keep up." Hitting up the batting cages every day hadn't been enough. I should have been focused on cardio as well. It had been way too long since my body had that kind of exercise.

Mason slowed down until he was at my side. "Seen any good movies lately?"

I shook my head. "Unfortunately, I haven't made it back to the theater since the last time. Life and friends have kept me busy." I lifted my left shoulder in a shrug. "Money is also a factor."

"I could probably get you in for free." His cheeks reddened. "I mean, if you wanted."

Maybe Mason hadn't seen the picture of me. But it would be almost impossible for him to not have heard about it. Everyone was talking.

"Do you have your phone?" I asked.

"Coach does."

Mason was one to follow the rules. I respected that.

"That's right." I inhaled sharply. My thighs, shins, and calves were killing me. Plus, my shoulders, arms, and back. Oh, and my feet. "Don't you feel like your body is about to combust?"

He laughed, the sound light and airy. "Not really. But I'm used to Coach pushing us like this."

Right. Most of the people there probably were.

We entered the gym and looked around for the baseball trainer, but he wasn't there. No one was. They were probably all relaxing for the night.

"Maybe he headed back to the hall for game night," Mason said.

I looked up at him. "Game night?"

His cheeks went red again. "Yeah. Everyone's meeting in the rec hall and playing board games. I was coming to find you since you weren't there." At my frown, his eyes went wide in slight horror. "You didn't know about it?"

No. Great. That meant I had to walk all the way back to the kitchen in hopes of finding ice. I was on my own. My new theme song. Ugh. That made me Éponine, Dylan was Marius, and Raelynn was Cosette. Éponine died in the arms of Marius.

Except, I wasn't pining for Marius, aka Dylan. I just wanted to make out with some of Marius' buddies. And most definitely not die.

"Thanks for coming to get me, Mason." I squeezed his arm, my hand lingering a little too long when I felt the muscle. "At least one person doesn't hate me." Dread crept in. "Unless this is some sort of prank . . ." I glanced around the empty weight room, expecting to see some people jumping out or throwing food at me.

He quickly shook his head. "What? No. It's not a prank." He scratched the side of his head. "How come no one told you?"

"Do you seriously not know what's going on?"

"No."

I almost sighed, but then stopped myself, taking in my situation. I was alone with Mason. He knew nothing about the picture, or what I did to Val afterward. There was a good chance he hadn't heard the bad kisser rumor, either. I had a golden opportunity to make a move. But I hurt so bad, and I'd probably frighten him. The situation wasn't romantic at all.

"Go ask anyone here. They'll be more than happy to tell you all about it." I moved toward the door. "Okay, I really need ice and to lay down. Thanks for your help, Mason. Have fun at game night." I pushed out the door and hobbled my way back toward the kitchen.

Mason caught up with me again. "You sure you don't want to play?"

Why was he so nice? It made it hard to concentrate. I sat down on a bench, needing to relieve my body of the pain. He sat down next to me.

"I'll give you the condensed version." I rubbed my forearms. "No one here likes me all that much, especially the soft-ball players. They didn't invite me to play because they don't want me there."

He leaned forward, resting his arms on his legs. "Why don't they like you?"

"Spoiler alert: I'm not that great of a person. Apparently, I'm shallow, self-serving, bossy, rude, and a bunch of other things." I moved on to rubbing my calves, hoping to work out some of the pain, and block out the fact that I'd just revealed all of that to Mason. What was wrong with me? That was definitely not in the manual of how to woo a guy.

"Let me help." Mason got down on his knees, his warm hands landing on my calf. My breath caught in my throat at his touch. The boy really knew how to use his hands. It was my turn for my cheeks to warm. He cleared his throat. "I don't think you're all those things. You've always been nice to me."

"You make it easy." I thought of the salty glares all the girls had given me. It made it hard to want to like them. But it didn't make them bad people. They just misunderstood me. I needed to fix their perception of me, and everything I'd been doing had only made it worse.

Mason moved on to my other calf. My right leg was already feeling better.

"Okay, I think I'm going to hire you as my personal train-er," I said. "I can't pay, though. You'll just have to suffer through my personality."

He chuckled. "I actually want to be an athletic trainer. That's what I'm going to school for."

"Not baseball?"

His hands worked through my sore muscles, relaxing them. "Nah. I just play it for fun. It's not my passion. I prefer to help players."

"That's awesome." I bit my lower lip when he dug deep into a tightened muscle. "You're a natural at it."

A blush rose from his neck to his cheeks. "Thanks."

I stared up at the blue sky. The sun was close to setting. "You're missing game night."

He let go of my leg. "Where else hurts?"

I pointed to my arms and shoulders. Mason sat back down on the bench and took my right arm.

"Is it weird that I'd actually rather be doing this instead?" His voice was barely audible.

"Not really. It's nice and quiet out here." Even if I had been invited to play games, I wasn't in the mood for loud voices and talking. I hadn't had this much peace in the longest time.

Mason grinned. "And Ava's laughing."

I snorted, and then covered up my nose in embarrassment. But Mason just broke out in a warm laugh that made me join in.

"It's so loud," I said through my laughter.

"It reminds me of a hyena."

My laughter grew, and I didn't hold back.

Mason got up and sat down on the other side of me so he could work on my left arm. "Your laugh is much better."

With him so close, I had a chance to take him all in. His blond eyelashes were long. He had a few acne scars, but so did I. It always made someone more human to me when I saw that. I'd always felt the need to cover them up with Dylan.

Mason smelled like Irish Spring soap. A small ladybug landed in his hair, and I smiled. Instead of flicking it away like Liam would have done, I reached up, gently removed it, and held it in my hand. It crawled over my thumb and toward my wrist.

I was smiling big at it when I looked up at Mason. He'd stopped rubbing my arm, and his eyes were on my lips. He locked eyes with me, and when I didn't back away, he slowly moved forward, his eyes on my lips again.

It was the perfect moment. We were all alone on the bench. It was a nice evening, the sun having just set, the pink and orange hues fading.

In a matter of seconds, I could have Mason crossed off my list. At the thought, I quickly stood and rubbed my arm where he'd been holding it. For some reason, I couldn't just kiss him. Mason wasn't like the other guys. He was relationship material. I wasn't ready for that, and it wouldn't be fair to lead him on.

"I think I'm going to head up to bed." I couldn't get myself to look at him. I worried his reaction could shatter my heart. "Thank you so much for helping. My sore muscles appreciate it."

He quickly got to his feet and shoved his hands in his pockets. "Yeah, sure. Anytime."

I forced myself to look up at him, and my heart melted. There was a mixture of hope and sadness mixed in his eyes. I smiled softly. "Thanks for keeping me company, too. It's nice to talk to someone and not have them yelling at me or criticizing me." I turned to walk away but stopped at his voice.

"Camille? Don't let them get to you. They aren't worth it."

No, they weren't. And Mason didn't deserve to have his heart played with. What had I been thinking?

All I'd wanted were a few kisses, but suddenly, it didn't seem as charming as it once had.

CHAPTER 22

*T*he next morning, my muscles weren't as sore as I thought they'd be. Whatever Mason had done had helped a ton.

Before I got breakfast, I wanted to seek out Alejandro and make contact. He was sitting in the middle of a long bench in the mess hall, chatting with his friends. I worried that Mason might see, but his back was to us, so I could easily do some light flirting with Alejandro. It was a risky move, but I needed to move things along.

First, though, I had something more important to do. If I wanted my kiss list to go smoothly, I needed to make nice with my former softball friends. They kept doing things that hurt my chances of ever getting kissed again.

I found Val with the others at a table in the corner. Her face darkened when she saw me. I held up my hands in a peace offering. "I just came to apologize. I'm sorry for what I did."

"Well, I'm not sorry for what I did," she snarled. Her homemade earrings trembled with her fuming body. "You deserved it."

I wasn't sure anyone deserved to be forced to pee their pants and have the evidence uploaded to social media, but I bit my tongue. They obviously thought it was a fair trade. "I'm sure I did. Can we just call a truce?" I held out my hand.

She swatted it away. "I'm not sure what you're up to, but I'm not falling for your games this time."

I lowered my hand, my head flinching back in confusion. "What are you talking about?"

Ava, who was sitting next to her with her double Dutch braids under her hat, scoffed. "You seriously don't remember what you did sophomore year, do you?"

I slowly shook my head as I racked my brain, trying to think back. Had I humiliated her somehow? Why couldn't I remember?

Val scrambled to her feet and stepped back from me. "If you don't know what you did wrong, then you haven't changed."

"Please," I said, "just tell me what I did so I can apologize . . ."

Izzy stood and put her arm around Val. She had her straw-berry-blonde hair in a long braid down her back instead of her usual bun. Her sweet, soft face clashed with the harshness in her tone. "So, it's not worth apologizing until you know what it is?"

I stepped forward, causing them to step back. "That's not what I meant. I feel bad that I can't remember. I'm trying here. Can't you help me out?"

Val wiped at a tear that had escaped down her cheek. "Forget it. Just stay away from me." She stormed off with Izzy and Ava at her heels.

"Man, you just make everyone cry." Liam was suddenly at my side with his stupid grin.

I shoved him away and ran out of the mess hall. What was wrong with me? Why couldn't I remember what I'd done? I wished I could call Kaitlyn and Hayley. Maybe they would know. I told them everything.

At least, I thought I did. Now I wasn't sure about anything.

"Camille, wait!" Liam's voice bounced as he ran after me.

I stopped near an oak tree and folded my arms, trying to hold back the tears. I wouldn't cry. Why was I even letting them get to me?

"What's going on, Cam-I-Am?" Liam asked when he caught up with me.

I stared at my neon-blue sneakers. They just happened to match the blue in my hair, which normally would have made me smile. "I have no idea why I came to this stupid camp."

He folded his arms to match me. "Um, I don't know, maybe because you're extremely talented and belong on the team?"

I kicked at a root protruding from the grass. "Unfortunately, talent doesn't get you far on a team. It helps if your teammates, you know, like you." I rubbed my forehead. "I should've known better than to come."

"What did you do to piss off your teammates, anyway?"

"I have no idea. It was something from sophomore year, I guess. I've been trying to remember, but it's like my brain has blocked out all the memories before Dylan." My hands tightened into fists. I hated that I couldn't remember who I was before him. How had I lost myself completely?

Liam tapped my arm. "There's nothing in this life that isn't fixable." He shrugged. "Except for killing someone." When I rolled my eyes, he chuckled. "Want me to ask around and see if I can figure out what you did?"

I played with my fingers. "You wouldn't mind?"

"Are you kidding? This is like some sort of top secret mission, just like the old days."

A smile pulled at my lips. There was something I actually

remembered. Liam and I would assign each other missions when we were in elementary school. I once had him get a piece of toilet paper from the girls' bathroom. He had me take an eraser from Brady's backpack. Just silly things like that.

I twisted my lips to the side. "Yeah, not sure if you could handle this one."

He bumped my arm. "Please. If I could put a tiny piece of paper in Mrs. Jenkins' curly hair without her noticing, I can handle getting some information from the softball team." He wiggled his eyebrows. "All I gotta do is turn on my charm, and they'll be spilling their deepest, darkest secrets to me."

"Seeing how Sadie was fawning over you at Brady's party, I think you may be right."

Liam placed his hand over his heart. "Oh, do I detect a hint of jealousy? Don't worry, Cam-I-Am. I'll always be your partner-in-crime."

He did it once again. He took my sour mood and turned it into something sweet. We stood there in this contemplative silence, both looking at each other. I'd missed having him as a friend. I'd always thought he was annoying, but really, it was my attitude, not his. He was just a fun-loving guy.

Liam broke the silence. "You need to do something to make them like you again."

"Like what?"

Baseball and softball players were trickling out of the mess hall, heading to practice. It meant I'd missed breakfast, which sucked, but I'd survive.

He glanced over his shoulder at everyone, and then back at me. "Don't take this the wrong way, but from what I can tell, it almost seems like they felt abandoned by you. They're probably expecting you to do it again."

"I won't." I never wanted to lose myself over a stupid boy again.

He pointed his thumb over his shoulder. "They don't know that. You need to prove to them that you're a part of the team. Let them know you care."

I picked a piece of lint off the top of his shirt, and then smoothed out the material. "When did you become all wise?"

He'd frozen in place, his sure smile nowhere to be found. I waited for his witty remark, but it never came.

"You feeling okay?" I asked.

Liam licked his lips and ran his fingers through his hair. "Uh. We should get going." He took off toward the field at a brisk pace.

Thanks to Mason's magic hands and my loose muscles, I was able to easily catch up with Liam. It was weird to see him without his usual confidence, but I didn't want to push the issue.

"Have any brilliant ideas?" I asked, trying to keep up with his speed walking. "I have no food on me, so that's out of the question."

His smile came back, relieving me. "You're really bad at coming up with ways to make people like you. I mean, ways that would actually work."

The sun was shining brightly that day, making me glad I'd put on a baseball hat. It was my vintage Dr Pepper one that my mom had bought me when I was twelve. It was falling apart, but it was one of my treasures. She'd just randomly come home with it—it was also the last time she'd randomly bought me something.

We walked onto the grass, heading toward all the players warming up before practice. I scanned the baseball players, searching for Alejandro and hoping to at least make eye contact since I didn't get a chance to talk to him, but he wasn't looking in my direction.

"Obviously, my words can't convince them," I said,

scratching at an itch on the side of my arm. "I need a grand gesture."

Liam stopped me by putting his hands on my shoulder. "It doesn't have to be grand. It just has to confirm your commitment to the team."

I nodded. "Right. Got it." I rubbed my hands together. "Let the fun begin."

With a grin, Liam took off toward Coach Barnes to assist him.

A gesture of commitment. If I could do that for Dylan for over a year, I could handle that for the softball team, right? Maybe then, my kiss list would be back on track.

CHAPTER 23

$\mathcal{C}$oach Wilkes wasn't the least bit gentle with us during exercises. She pushed us as far as we could go, and then a little bit farther. We'd be playing the boys the next day, which was the last day of camp, and a perfect time for some fun flirting with the guys.

Unfortunately, when your team doesn't like you, there isn't a lot of trust to be found. Every dropped or overthrown ball made the swears fly from Coach Wilkes like it was the only language she knew. It also didn't help that I was off my game. I couldn't shake the glares being thrown at me. I tried to think about Alejandro's sultry smile or Mason's gorgeous eyes instead, but that only caused more of a distraction.

"Camille!" Coach shouted. "Are you aware of how tall Ava is?"

"Yes, Coach." I adjusted my hat, wiping some sweat from my forehead in the process.

Coach had a fist on her hip, her legs spread shoulder-width apart, whistle hanging from a string around her neck, and resting a softball bat on her shoulder. "Really? Because it seems to me like you think she's eight feet tall."

Izzy snickered from the pitcher's mound, but I tried to push the sound away. I didn't need all of them getting in my head. I was good at softball. I was good at my position. I needed to remind all of them, and myself, of that.

I punched my fist into my glove and nodded at the coach, telling her I understood.

Coach was at bat, sending balls in different directions. The next ball she hit headed straight between me and the third baseman, Tamara. From where I stood, it looked like I had the better angle, so I shouted, "Got it!" and sprinted toward it. We only had seconds to react, and in that amount of time, both Tamara and I ran for the ball, Tamara ignoring my declaration. We reached the ball at the same time, my right side colliding with her left, sending us both to the ground, dirt raining down around us.

A slight pain tore through my shoulder, but it was nothing major. I sat up, rubbing my shoulder and staring down at Tamara, who was doing NBA-worthy squirming on the dirt. Val rushed to her, the medic bag slung over her shoulder, bouncing against her tiny frame. She fell on her knees next to Tamara and put her hand on Tamara's leg where she was holding it.

"What was that?" Coach snarled as she stomped toward us.

"I called for it." I rotated my shoulder around, trying to work out the pain.

"I did!" Tamara screeched. If she had, I didn't hear her. I had no idea if she was lying or not. She hadn't been on the team during sophomore year, so I hadn't had any interaction with her until the camp. There was a good chance she believed all the things the others had said about me.

I licked my lips, wishing I'd remembered to put some lip balm in my pocket. "Sorry, Tamara. I didn't hear you."

"I did," Izzy said, glaring down at me, her braid resting over her shoulder.

"So did I," Ava put in. She adjusted her hat, stuffing some loose hairs back under it. "And I didn't hear anything from Camille."

I turned to her. She'd been at first base. No way could she have heard it so crystal clear from there, unless she had Daredevil-level hearing.

Tamara writhed on the ground like a hurt puppy. She held onto her leg, whimpering in pain. Val fussed over her.

"Where exactly does it hurt?" Val asked, her tone soft and motherly. I held in a gag.

Tamara pointed to her right calf. "Right here."

We'd collided on her left side, but I kept my mouth shut. I needed to be careful of what I said.

Coach pulled me up by the arm until I was on my feet, and dragged me away from the others. "You don't have to get every ball, Camille. Let the other girls play, too."

I watched as all our teammates huddled around Tamara, cooing over her and basically coddling her like a baby. "I'm sorry, Coach. I honestly didn't hear her say anything." I wasn't sure she even had. "I thought I had the better angle, but obviously, I read the situation wrong."

Coach's jaw tightened as if she was trying to figure out something to say. She must not have expected me to apologize like that. She glanced at the others. "If she's seriously injured, we'll have to switch some players around. No one can play third base like Tamara can."

"I know, Coach," I said. "But we didn't hit too hard. I'm sure she'll be okay. Val's good at what she does. She'll get Tamara all fixed up."

"Well." Coach huffed. "You better hope so."

As if they'd heard my declaration, Izzy and Val helped Tamara to her feet, and she hobbled off the field. She had to be overreacting, but I had no way to prove it. Every single girl snarled at me like I'd done it on purpose. So much for getting them to like me.

I walked to where the rest of the team was huddled, obviously talking about me. The chatter shut off when I approached.

"I'm sorry, everyone," I said. "I didn't mean for that to happen. I'll be more careful from now on."

Ava wiped a tear from her eye. Wow, they were really laying on the theatrics. "What if she can't play this season because of you?"

I pulled back in surprise. "It was a small collision. There's no possible way for her to be *that* injured."

Jordyn had her catcher's mask resting on top of her head. "Not everyone is as muscular as you, Camille. She can't take as big a hit." She wiped the side her nose on the sleeve of her baseball shirt, her glove still on her hand.

I hadn't expected Jordyn to side with me, but I hadn't really expected her to side with the team, either. We hadn't talked much as roommates, but there hadn't been any arguments. I threw up my hands. "What do you expect me to do here? It was an accident, I promise. The last thing I'd want to do right now is ruin things for the team."

Izzy held her glove against her chest. "That would be a first."

The rest of the team nodded in agreement.

I sighed. "I know you all hate me, but I'm going to prove to you that I've changed and deserve to be a part of the team." I walked as calmly as I could away from the group before I said anything stupid.

All the drama was sucking the fun out of softball. Maybe I needed to look into a city team instead of playing for the school. Softball was supposed to be my release.

I slowly pulled it together for the rest of practice. I had to

take up the slack with Tamara missing. Coach had been right
—no one could play third base like Tamara. Any time I tried
to give the sub-third baseman a chance to make a play, she
messed it up, and I got chewed out by Coach for being lazy.

Then Val announced that Tamara was out for the rest
of camp.

"She can barely move her leg." Val stood with her arms
wrapped closely around herself. "It's not broken, but she'll
need to stay off it for a while." Her dramatically sad eyes
flicked over to me, anger incinerating the distress.

Coach rubbed her hand down her face. "This is going to
make tomorrow's game almost impossible to win."

I hated how negative they were all being. It was seriously
like someone had poured a pessimistic serum into their food
all week.

I licked my dry lips. "It will be hard, yes, but I think we
can manage a win. If we work together as a team . . ."

"Save your stupid speech," Ava cut in. "We aren't falling
for it. You've screwed us over."

"Again." Izzy snarled at me, and it wasn't pretty.

Everyone jogged off the field like we'd just lost the cham-
pionship.

All the hate they were throwing at me tasted worse than
the time Dylan kissed me after he'd eaten squid. Hopefully,
Liam had dug up some information. Even though I might not
make the team, I still wanted to apologize to my teammates
for whatever I'd done sophomore year. I desperately needed
to get back to being the old Camille.

CHAPTER 24

*a*t dinner, I sat by myself. I'd headed toward Mason, but there was no room around him, and a couple friends cracked some jokes about me peeing myself before he could see me. Alejandro wasn't there yet. So, I found a spot in the corner where I could see everyone. I didn't want to risk anyone pulling a prank on me.

Coming to camp had definitely drilled a hole into my kiss list. I thought it would be the perfect time to snatch some kisses, but the softball team was making it way too difficult.

Speaking of the softball players, Liam sat at their table, using his charm to woo them. He'd probably end up finding out a lot more than just what I did sophomore year.

Mason finally caught my eye, looking at me like he was debating whether to sit with me or not. I'd shut him down, which couldn't have been easy for him.

I wanted my phone. Hayley and Kaitlyn would be able to cheer me up. I missed hearing their voices.

Someone plopped down across the table, taking me from my reverie. Alejandro was in a muscle tank that left nothing to the imagination, muscles everywhere. His hair was still wet from a shower.

He smiled brightly at me. "I hear you're having a good week."

I had to resist the urge to fling my mashed potatoes at his face. "Something like that."

"Rough break about Tamara." He folded his arms on the table.

"She'll be fine," I snapped. I sighed at my rude tone and its complete lack of sexiness.

Alejandro's eyebrows shot up. "Not from what I hear."

Using my palms, I rubbed my eyes. Maybe I'd just go to bed after dinner. I could listen to music until I fell asleep. Not exactly a fun night, but it was better than putting up with all the drama.

"Do you believe everything you hear?" I stirred the potatoes with my fork. A frown came to my face, thinking of the rumor about me being a bad kisser. I hoped he hadn't listened to that one.

Alejandro leaned forward. "Not always. I like to experience things for myself before I pass judgment."

Heat flared on my face, and I couldn't stop it. Kissing Alejandro would make the entire week of hell worth it. It would definitely cheer me up.

Laughter broke out behind him. I glanced over his shoulder to see a couple tables of players in a lively conversation. Multiple heads whipped my way with amusement dancing in their eyes. Why was I letting them ruin everything for me? I had to take matters into my own hands.

Finding my smile again, I turned back to Alejandro. "Wanna get out of here?"

He didn't say anything. He just stood, waited for me to come around the table, took my hand in his, and escorted me out of the building. His skin was hot, making me shudder in excitement.

"Where should we go?" I asked. We were on a college campus and weren't allowed to leave. There was always the baseball field, but we spent all day there.

Alejandro got a scandalous look in his eyes. "Just between you and me, I snuck some Oreos into my dorm."

Aside from the last day of school, I hadn't had Oreos in the longest time. Dylan hated them. "Wow. I didn't know you were such a rebel."

He chuckled as he held the door open for me. It looked like they were setting up for another night of cards in the lobby of the boys' dorms. Another activity I hadn't been invited to. They'd probably done it every night.

A few people glanced over at us as Alejandro tugged me toward the stairs, but I did my best to ignore them and focus on the thought of his lips on mine.

He'd been there less than a week, but the dorm room he was using already rank of guy—sweat and musk floating in the air.

Alejandro shut the door and immediately went for a bag stashed under his bed. Inside were all kinds of cookies, not just Oreos.

I sat down next to him on the bed and stared inside the bag. "So, this is what heaven looks like."

His shoulders moved up and down in laughter. "Usually the girl says that to *me*, not my cookies." His laughing voice had a smoky tinge that sounded delicious.

I peeled back the cover of the Oreo box and set one in my mouth, fully intact. The second I bit down, the chocolate and cream goodness exploded, causing me to let out a slight moan.

"Again, something *I* usually make the girl do, not the cookies," he said as his shoulder brushed mine.

I held up the box of cookies. "They're just so good." I popped another in my mouth, not caring if I looked silly.

I was waiting for the moment where he looked at me in disgust like Dylan would have done, but instead, Alejandro popped an entire Oreo in his mouth just like I had.

He turned on some hip-hop music on his phone and raised the volume. We laid down on the bed and snacked away. It was nice to just hang out, listen to music, and eat junk food.

Something struck my heart. I used to do this all the time with Val and the girls on the softball team. Every Friday night, we'd get together at one of our houses and have the best time. Why had we stopped? They probably hadn't. I just stopped going because of Dylan.

Alejandro elbowed my arm. "You okay?"

"Huh?" I turned to him, his face so close to mine. I wanted to melt in his gorgeous brown eyes. When my eyes landed on his lips, mine suddenly felt dry. I'd forgotten my lip gloss in my dorm.

He lifted my chin. "My eyes are up here, Camille."

I went to playfully shove him in the chest, but he caught my hand and held it against him.

"What are you thinking about?" He turned his body on his side, so he was facing me, still keeping my hand in his.

"The team. I want back in their good graces, but I'm not sure that's going to happen."

"Can you blame them?" He intertwined our fingers. "One thing I've noticed is that girls aren't so quick to forgive. At least, not the ones I've dated."

I licked my lips, and then cursed myself. The gesture reminded me of Dylan. I didn't want to think about him when Alejandro was right next to me. "The sad part? I can't remember what I did. It's like I blocked out my life before junior year."

"Really? It was Izzy's birthday party. I think you and Dylan had just started dating, or it was right before."

I furrowed my eyebrows, trying to piece everything together. I remembered going to the party. I'd spent hours getting ready since I was going with Dylan. It was our first night as an official couple. Kaitlyn and Hayley had helped me pick out the perfect outfit, and they did my hair and makeup.

All I could remember from the party was following Dylan around wherever he went. I basically worshipped the guy, which was so embarrassing.

Alejandro let go of my hand and rested his hand on my hip. "Is this ringing any bells?" When I slowly nodded, he continued. "Val had a crush on some senior at the time. I can't remember his name."

It hit me. "Will."

Val crushed hard on him all through our freshman and sophomore years. She gushed about him. She legit had notebooks full of squiggly hearts, her name and Will's written inside them, and practiced signatures with her first name and his last name. I'd thought it so silly at the time, but really, had my actions around Dylan been any different?

Closing my eyes, I thought back to that night. Dylan loved pranks. He'd dared me to tell Val that Will wanted to talk to her outside near the pool. I never asked what he was planning on doing, I just obeyed his orders. I wanted to impress him.

So, I sought her out, whispered the news in her ear, and she giggled in excitement. I'd taken her hand, guided her out to the pool, and nudged her toward the meeting spot. She'd practically pranced over there. When she got there, Will wasn't there. Instead, Dylan and his friend took her by the arms and threw her into the pool. Pete filmed the whole thing, uploading it when he finished.

I'd thought it hilarious at the time. I mean, it was just

some water. But I never thought about the fact that Val was easily embarrassed. The whole time in the pool, she shrieked and flailed her arms like crazy.

Guests trickled out of the house, laughing when they saw what was going on. Ava and Izzy leaped in—creating a huge splash—wrapped their arms around Val, and helped her out of the pool. After they got her a towel and calmed her down, Izzy stormed over to Dylan and me, telling me that Val didn't know how to swim and had almost drowned as a kid. I rushed to Val, wanting to apologize, but she turned her back on me.

At school, I was so wrapped up in spending every single second with Dylan that I never apologized to Val.

I'd been so heartless. That wasn't me. A tear trickled out of my left eye and slid down my cheek. Alejandro's warm hand landed on my face as he wiped it away.

"You were young," he whispered. "I'm sure if you apologize, she'll forgive you."

"I hope so." I really missed having them all as friends.

Alejandro wrapped his arms around me and pulled me into him, his muscled chest comforting me.

At least I'd pieced it together. Problem was, I wasn't sure if a simple apology would be enough. It had probably been so traumatizing for Val. How would I make up for it? The best thing I could think of was to be raw and honest, letting her know the truth behind it all. Hopefully, it would be enough.

CHAPTER 25

*a*lejandro held me for a while. I could feel his heart beating wildly through his tank. His arms were solid weights around me, like I could never break and would remain safe.

I pulled back, resting my head on his pillow. "Thank you. This has been nice."

He ran a finger down my cheek. "Yes, it has." His eyes went to my lips, so I tucked a finger under his chin and lifted his head.

"My eyes are up here, Alejandro." I was trying to be funny, but it came out breathless.

"Say my name again," he whispered. So, I did.

He closed the distance between us, his arms holding me firm. His soft lips met mine, and a fire erupted inside me, heating every inch. His hand slid to the small of my back and somehow pushed me into him, even though there hadn't seemed to be even the smallest sliver of space between our bodies.

His lips moved slowly against mine. Without my lip gloss, our lips stuck together, and I could taste his salty skin. They were soft kisses, not intrusive or invading. My hands rested on his chest, squished between us to the point I couldn't move them.

His hand moved down, landing on the hem of my shirt. He slid underneath, his warm skin on mine. He kept his hand at my side for a moment before it slid up my back, inching way too close to my bra strap.

I pushed away, my chest heaving in and out as I tried to catch my breath. I couldn't look in his eyes when I spoke. "I'm not ready for anything more than kissing."

Alejandro curled a finger under my chin and forced me to look at him. His eyes were so kind and understanding. "Then we won't."

Maybe all guys weren't like Dylan.

I'd been right about one thing: Alejandro was an amazing kisser. Crossing him off the kiss list would be my greatest accomplishment to date.

The door suddenly opened, and Alejandro's roommate came in. He was the pitcher for the baseball team. "Dude, Alejandro . . ." Elijah paused when he took us in, lying in each other's arms on Alejandro's bed.

I started to move, but Alejandro held me in place, like it was perfectly normal. "What's going on?"

A sly smile crossed Elijah's face, but he quickly dropped it and replaced it with excitement. "You guys are missing all the fun downstairs."

Alejandro motioned to me. "Pretty sure this is more fun."

My cheeks burst into flames. I didn't want Elijah thinking we were doing more than kissing. In fact, I didn't want him to know we were kissing, which made no sense. The whole point of my kiss list was to stop the rumor that I was a bad kisser.

Elijah tilted his head to the side. "Since your clothes are still on, no, it's not." He came into the room and sat down on his bed. "Now that it's dark, we're going to play hide-and-seek outside."

"Are we five?" I asked.

Elijah shoved a stick of gum in his mouth, and then threw the wrapper into the trashcan across the room, easily making the basket. "I forgot you don't know how to have fun."

Alejandro had loosened his hold on me, so I sat up and glared at Elijah. "I do, too."

Elijah rubbed his hands together. "Let's go find out, shall we?"

When we got downstairs, the chatter quieted down as everyone saw us. Liam quirked an eyebrow in intrigue, but I just shook my head at him. I didn't look around for Mason. I definitely didn't want to see his reaction to me having been upstairs with Alejandro. My lips pulsed, and I wondered if it was obvious we'd been kissing.

Val and the others didn't look happy to see me, and I understood more than ever why. I wanted to go to them and apologize right then, but there were too many people watching. I didn't want them thinking I was just putting on a public show. I needed time to sit down with them and talk. In the meantime, I put on the most apologetic smile I could muster. Val's hard eyes softened into confusion.

Elijah held up his hands to get everyone's attention. "Now that everyone's here, let's play some hide-and-seek! Let's divide into teams."

Captains had already been picked—Elijah, Liam, Val, and Ava. I was hoping Liam would pick me to be on his team. Aside from Alejandro, he was the only one there who'd actually want me on their team. He picked Jordyn first, though, and I tried to hide my disappointment. On the second round, he chose a guy on the baseball team.

By the fifth round, I debated whether I should just bolt. I

could listen to some Maroon 5 and curl up in bed. Adam Levine's voice was better than hide-and-seek, anyway.

Val was the first captain up on the last round. I stood there with a few others, doing my best to conceal my disappointment. Would Liam finally pick me? Or would I end up on Ava's team, who was the last captain to pick? That option seemed the most likely, and the least tempting.

"Camille." My name coming from Val's mouth took me by surprise.

I pointed a finger into my chest. "Me?"

"Is there another Camille we should know about?" Val asked. I couldn't read her face. It was as passive as ever.

Ava scoffed. Her double Dutch braids were freshly done. "I really hope not." A few chuckled at her comment, but I chose to ignore it like I had everything else that week.

I cautiously joined Val's team, which included mostly baseball players, one being Owen. He'd been Dylan's friend before we'd started dating. I wasn't sure why they'd stopped hanging out with each other. Maybe it was a similar reason as my friends and me.

The thing that worried me, though, was Owen had been the other guy who helped push Val into the pool. Was she up to something, or was I reading too much into it?

I glanced over at Liam, hoping to get his attention, but he was fully engaged with his team. We hadn't talked since he started his secret mission. Maybe he'd found out the truth of that night and no longer wanted to be my friend. It could explain why he didn't pick me for his hide-and-seek team. I hated that I was all huffy-puffy about not being picked. We weren't in elementary school.

The temptation to take off and break into Coach Wilke's room and steal back my phone was looking awfully tempting. All I needed was advice from my mom. My heart sank at the thought. She wouldn't help me. She'd be too busy. And it would be way too much drama for Dad to handle.

But I always had Kaitlyn and Hayley. They'd stuck by me through my relationship with Dylan, which I now saw was the real meaning of friendship.

"Camille?"

I turned to find Val and the others in my group staring at me.

"Nice of you to join us," Val said, annoyance in her tone. "Don't make me regret picking you."

I smiled at her. "Thanks for picking me. It means a lot." I rubbed my hands together. "What's the plan, chief?"

She flinched at the word. It had been my nickname for her when I was on the team. Even though she was the trainer, the whole team had seen her as a leader. Val was brilliant and always had the best ideas.

I'd forgotten about the nickname until it slipped from my mouth.

Val swallowed. "Liam's team is seeking first. The rules are we can't split into groups smaller than two. I say we scatter around the campus as much as we can."

Everyone nodded as she spoke. A fiery confidence rippled across her body with every passing word. She was born to be a leader.

Val grouped us off, telling each team which direction to head so we'd know where everyone was. She left Owen and me for last. She motioned between us. "I guess that just leaves the two of you."

She'd either planned that perfectly, or she was just saving the two people she hated most for last.

"Why don't you guys head toward the workout room?" Val tucked her baggy T-shirt into her leggings, turning all business. "Hide behind some weights or something. Just don't get caught." With a tense smile, she left the two of us standing there, completely uncomfortable.

Owen and I hadn't really talked since I started dating Dylan and they'd stopped being friends.

Owen had his hands stuffed into his sweatpants pockets. "So. I guess it's you and me."

I patted his arm. "Guess so." I motioned for him to follow, and we headed out the doors.

All the other teams were scattering about, hurrying to find a good hiding spot. Liam's team was giving us two minutes before they'd come looking.

"How have you been?" I asked Owen as we jogged toward the workout room.

"Good." He stared straight ahead. "How about you?"

I beamed. "Oh, just wonderful. My boyfriend dumped me for another girl, spread a total lie about me, and the entire softball team hates me."

His eyes widened in shock as they turned to settle on me. We stopped outside the weight room. Owen put his hands on his hips, catching his breath. "Yeah, I heard about you and Dylan. Sorry."

I shook my head. "I'm not."

He pulled back in surprise. "You're not?"

"I was at first." I hooked my thumbs in the loops on my jeans. "But then I realized how much I'd changed being with Dylan. I kind of lost myself."

Owen broke out in a laugh. It took him a few seconds to compose himself. "Is it weird that I feel the same way about him? I mean, we weren't dating, obviously, but he was a really good friend."

"Is that why you stopped hanging out?"

He nodded. "Dylan has a way of bringing out the worst in people. I didn't like who I was." His face reddened. "I'm still mad I let him talk me into pushing Val into the pool. I had no idea about her past."

"Me, either," I said. "I found out after the fact." My stomach rolled. "It makes me so sick just thinking about it."

"Same." Owen motioned to the door. "We should probably hide or something."

"Right," I said.

Coach Wilkes walked up, stopping when she saw us. "What are you two doing?" She eyed the two of us suspiciously, like she'd caught us doing something completely illegal.

"Hide-and-seek." I gave her a thumbs-up. "Apparently, we're five years old again."

Owen snickered.

Coach just narrowed her eyes like she didn't believe us. "Stay out of the weight room. The school can't afford to fix anything you break from reliving your childhood days." With that, she opened the door and stepped into the weight room.

Water rained down on her, soaking her completely. My hands flew to my mouth in shock. She rounded on us, water dripping everywhere, creating a giant puddle underneath her.

"What is the meaning of this?" she snarled.

Owen's head shook vigorously. "I don't know. Honest."

Coach's glare snapped to me. I'd had nothing to do with it, but it didn't take long for me to piece it together. Val had picked Owen and me to be on her team. She'd paired us together on purpose. Then she specifically sent us to the weight room, so we'd get soaked in water like she had at Izzy's party.

We'd been set up.

CHAPTER 26

I took too long to respond.

"Was this your doing, Collins?" Coach asked. She was so mad, I was expecting all the water to sizzle off her skin from the heat.

Members of the baseball and softball teams slowly trickled into the area, like they'd been waiting for this to happen.

Except when Val saw Coach drenched, she froze in horror, her hands flying to her mouth like mine had. She obviously hadn't expected to see Coach standing there in the doorway. She was thinking it was Owen and me.

"Well?" Coach snarled. She hadn't taken her eyes off me.

I looked over at Val. She hadn't lowered her hands, but her focus turned to me. I could easily turn her in. The water had been meant for me. Most people would probably side with Val, though. They were all her friends, not mine. Earlier, I'd thought at least Liam would stand up for me, but now I wasn't so sure.

Val's eyes pleaded with mine. She didn't want to get on

Coach Wilkes' bad side. No one did. I think it was a relief for all of them that I took most of the heat off the team.

If I took the fall, I'd be done. It would be strike three, and I wouldn't have a chance of being on the team. But what good was being on a team if you didn't get along? Maybe if I was kicked off the team, I could focus on my kiss list and spend the rest of my time here flirting with Mason.

I licked my lips. "I did it, Coach. I thought it would be funny."

Murmurs sounded to the side of me, but I ignored them.

Coach shook off her arms. "Why did you even bother coming to the camp? Just so you could humiliate me?"

"No, ma'am, I just . . ." What could I say? That the opportunity presented itself, so I took it? Nothing would make sense.

She waggled her index finger at me. "This is strike three, Camille."

I nodded. "I know." I was out. Out of the softball team, out of the chance of having Coach and my teammates like me again. "I guess I haven't changed as much as I'd hoped." My voice quavered, so I cleared it and fought back the tears. The whole thing was stupid.

But I deserved it after what I'd done to Val. Not being able to play softball my senior year paled in comparison to the nightmare Val had gone through on my behalf. Yes, it had been Dylan's idea, but I hadn't stood up for Val back then.

"Do you want me to call my dad to come pick me up?" I asked. "Or should I just wait in my room until Saturday morning when we leave?" I was hoping she'd at least let me stay so I could work my magic on Mason. And maybe steal another kiss from Alejandro, because that had been amazing.

Coach took some deep breaths, like she was trying to calm herself. "Let me get dried off and talk with Coach Barnes. I'm not sure if I'm in the right state of mind to make a rational decision. Right now, I want to make you walk home."

"I'm truly sorry, Coach." I was able to choke that out. "You don't deserve this." I clasped my hands together to keep them from shaking. "I'll be in my room until you make your decision." I turned and walked away, pushing through the crowd of onlookers.

When I got to Val, I paused at her side. "I finally remembered what I did to you. I'm horrified, Val, of my choices. I was a stupid, love-sick fool, but that doesn't excuse my behavior." I took a shaky breath. "I hadn't realized how much I've missed you all until Dylan dumped me. I only wish he would have done it months ago, so I could have found myself again so much earlier."

I put a hand on her arm and gently squeezed. "You have the talent to beat the boys tomorrow. Don't let this throw you off. Crush them." With a weak smile, I walked away, heading back to the dorm.

Each step was shaky, like I could fall at any moment. Tears burned in the back of my eyes, but I would not release them. Not until I was alone in my room with Maroon 5 to give me some solace.

Pounding steps from someone running came from behind me, pushing me to move faster. Unless it was Alejandro or Mason, I just wanted to be alone.

"Camille!"

I flinched at Liam's voice. He was the last person I wanted to talk to.

He jogged up to my side. "I can't believe you did that for Val."

I wiped at a rogue tear that escaped. "It was the least I could do after what I did to her."

"You remembered?" He worked hard to keep up with my strides, which had increased.

"Something like that," I mumbled. I wasn't about to tell him about my make-out session with Alejandro.

We got to the girls' dorm, and he moved to open the door, but I got there first, swinging it wide open and stepping into the lobby.

Liam put his hands on my shoulder to stop me. "I know you're trying to do the nice thing here, but this is your future we're talking about. You really want to throw away your opportunity to play softball?"

I shook out of his grip. "I wasn't going to make it back on the team, anyway. I can join a city league or something."

"Our softball team needs you. No one else can play short stop like you."

"It doesn't matter how well I play if I can't get along with my teammates. I've already ruined too much for them. I'm not going to make it worse."

Liam scratched the side of his arm. "But that's the thing, they *need* you. You can't run out on them again. Their biggest fear was you abandoning them again. Don't make that come true."

I threw up my hands. "It's not like I have a choice here. You heard Coach Wilkes. I got strike three."

He shook his head. "Not if you tell her the truth."

"Well, that's not going to happen." I pushed past him, heading for the stairs.

He ran over and hopped onto the second step to stop me. "I thought you said you wanted to be the old Camille again."

"I do."

He set his hands on my shoulders again. "Then fight for what you want. The one thing you lost with Dylan was the ability to speak up for yourself. You were loyal to your team and your friends before him. Bring that Camille back. Fight your way back, and prove to them you want to be a part of the team." When I opened my mouth, he pressed a finger to my lips, making me roll my eyes. "Don't give up on yourself. That's what Dylan would want you to do."

His words struck me right in the heart. He left me standing there, stunned. I'd wanted to ask why he hadn't chosen me to be on his team, but his words kept replaying through my mind. Dylan wouldn't actually want me to give up. He'd just want me to spend time doing things he liked. It was never about stopping me from doing the things I loved. It was about always having his way. And I was a fool to follow.

I headed up the stairs, two at a time, to the safety of my room. I'd hoped being in there would calm me down, but it only gave me an unlimited amount of time to replay everything that had happened. Everything that had been said.

Was I giving up on my team once again? Had I thrown in the towel too early? The more I thought about it, the more I realized I never fought to be back on the team. I just stayed out of everyone's way. That proved nothing.

I could tell Coach the truth, but there was a chance she wouldn't believe me. I thought I'd been ready to go home, but Liam helped me see the truth.

I'd been so mad at Dylan for robbing me of my life, but in reality, I only had myself to blame. I'd fallen under his spell. And I wasn't doing myself any favors by giving up so easily. The old Camille wouldn't have raised her white flag. I needed to talk to Val and the others, but I wasn't sure if they'd listen.

If Coach sent me home, it wouldn't matter anyway. Maybe I could beg her to let me stay. I paced all around the tiny dorm room, my mind reeling. It wouldn't stop, or even slow down.

An hour later, a knock sounded on the door. Coach Wilkes and Barnes stood on the other side of the door, neither of them the least bit happy. I motioned for them to come into the room, but they stayed in the hall.

Coach Wilkes folded her arms. "Barnes here talked me

into letting you stay until Saturday. But I think making you stay here won't do you any favors. You need some discipline, Camille."

I nodded. "I agree."

Their eyes went wide, but neither of them commented on my response. My mom was never around to hold me accountable for my actions. Dad was too soft because he felt bad about Mom being busy all the time.

Coach Wilkes cleared her throat. "I want you down on the field at six tomorrow morning for an intense workout. Then you'll be helping me all day with the game." She pointed a finger at me. "I better not catch you slacking off for even a second."

"Of course, ma'am," I said. "I'll be there at six, ready to work and help." I shut the door and pushed my back against it.

The hard workout would give me time to think and work off my anger. Maybe spending the day with Coach would help show her my serious side.

Liam had been right. I couldn't just give up. If I wanted back on the team, then I had to take action.

I hurried to get ready for bed, so I could get a good night's rest before the busy day.

CHAPTER 27

The next morning, I was out on the field before Coach Wilkes got there. I was doing warm-ups, stretching everything out. I knew she'd push me hard, and I wanted to be ready. I just wished I had Mason with me to help loosen me up. I mean, loosen up my muscles, so they weren't too stiff.

Coach looked a little surprised to find me already there. I was doing push-ups on the grass but hopped to my feet when she approached.

"Morning, Coach," I said with a smile as I brushed off my hands.

"Good morning, Camille." She took a bite from the granola bar in her hand. "You ready to work?"

"Yes, ma'am." I adjusted the hat on my head, so it was snuggled in place.

She wasn't kidding about disciplining me. I sprinted from home plate all the way to the fence countless times. Then I sprinted around the bases, starting and ending at different locations. I did high-knee drills, crunches, plants, bridges, v-ups, and lateral oblique raises. Then she took me to the weight room and worked my arms, shoulders, and legs.

By the end, I really did need to find Mason and ask him to work a miracle again. I was dripping in sweat head to toe, and the softball team would soon be on the field doing their warm-ups. I wiped myself down with a towel and hustled out to join the team.

Coach had watched me the entire time, her face unreadable. She wasn't upset or angry, but she wasn't exactly happy or impressed with my work. At least I'd done my best.

The girls were surprised to see me when I ran out to the field. They were doing warm-ups, but not as intense as I'd been forced to do. I kept off to the side by Coach so she could yell orders at me.

"Collins!" Coach snapped.

"Yes, Coach?"

"Help Izzy get her leg straight. She's flopping like a fish."

When I jogged over to her, Izzy tried to push me away.

"I don't need your help," she said through gritted teeth. Her hair was back in a high, messy bun on her head. She was laying on her back in the grass with her leg bent toward her head. She was trying to hold her leg with her hands to help push it farther but wasn't having an easy time of it.

"I know." Putting my hands on her leg, I pushed it closer to her chest. "This is my punishment, not yours."

She snarled before she sucked in a sharp breath, so I loosened my hold. She stared at the blue sky. "Then why does it feel like I'm being punished, too?"

I held in an eye roll. "How is me helping you stretch your leg properly a punishment?"

She looked at me. "Because I have to be near you."

I pushed her leg in, ignoring her cry. "This is seriously getting old, the hate you're all throwing at me."

Ava rolled onto her side to face us, doing leg raises. Her

double Dutch braids were messy, like she'd slept on them. "You deserve it."

I lowered Izzy's leg and moved on to the other one. "Yeah, from something stupid I did over a year ago. I've apologized. Are you all going to hold a grudge forever?"

Izzy pushed me away from her and sat up. "Excuse us for not being quick to forgive."

I held out my hand to help her up, but she swatted at my arm. "Will you stop acting like a toddler?"

Izzy scrambled to her feet and shoved me in the chest, so I stumbled back. "You can't just waltz back in our lives, Camille! Not after what you did!"

Others paused their work-outs to watch us. Tamara watched from the bleachers with her leg resting on a bench with an icepack on it. I wondered how long she was going to play up the injured player routine. Val came out of the dugout, rushing over to us like something terrible was about to happen. I wasn't going to fight them if that's what she thought.

"I messed up," I said, drawing out my words. "Over a year ago. You've never made a mistake in your life?"

"Of course, I have," Izzy spat. "But I've never tormented anyone." She put her arm around Val, who had conveniently started to sulk.

I took a deep breath to calm myself. "Not that it will make a difference, but I didn't know Dylan was planning on pushing Val in the pool, and I certainly didn't know about what happened to her as a kid."

"What did you think was going to happen?" Val asked. "You knew Will didn't want to talk to me."

I tugged on the bottom of my tank top. "I actually didn't know that. Dylan just told me to get you and tell you that, so I did."

Ava stood on the other side of Val. She glared at me.

"That's the other problem. You turned on us in a blink of an eye over a *boy*."

I threw up my hands. "I know what I did! It was stupid! Hormones suck, and all I wanted to do was impress Dylan."

"Why did you need his approval so bad?" Izzy asked.

"I have issues, is that what you want to hear?" I rocked where I stood. "So I turned to the first boy who paid attention to me." I rubbed my forehead. "It's embarrassing how much I let Dylan control my life. But it's over now, and I'm trying my hardest to get my life back."

Ava scoffed. "If he hadn't dumped you, you'd still be his little puppy. It wasn't like you came to this revelation on your own."

"Does that make a difference?" Anger fumed inside. What more did they want from me? I'd confessed everything. "I'm trying now, which should count for something."

Ava turned to our teammates. "Can someone please get her a medal for her *huge* accomplishment?"

Most of the girls snickered, but Jordyn stepped forward, standing evenly between Ava and me. Her catcher's helmet rested back on her head. "Maybe you're being too harsh on Camille. She's obviously trying."

A little bit of hope sprang up inside my heart. Maybe not everyone hated me. If I had to crack at them one at a time, I would.

"Whatever she promised you, Jordyn," Val said, "she'll take it back the second another boy comes along."

Jordyn rested her gloved hand on her hip. "She hasn't asked me anything. She's just been nice and given me my space. She's actually the best roommate I've ever had."

"Thanks," I said, hope blooming inside me. "Listen, I know I left the team after sophomore year, but . . ."

Ava extended her hands like they were claws and pounced on me like a cat, shoving me to the ground. She landed on top of me and held me in place. "After? You abandoned us during the playoffs!"

I pushed her face away, trying to get her off me, but she wouldn't budge. "No, I didn't."

"Yes, you did!" Val and Izzy screamed at the same time.

I wrestled with Ava on the grass, the two of us rolling everywhere. All the other girls crowded around to watch. Coach was probably nearby, but she was the type who'd let us sort it out on our own.

"We lost because of you!" Ava yanked off my hat and tossed it. "We could have gone to state if you hadn't left."

Wrapping my arms around her, I turned her to the side until she was on the bottom. I struggled to stand up. Izzy shoved me back down before I could.

"You're the same lovesick girl now as you were back then," Izzy said. "If we take you back, you'll leave."

I scrambled to my feet. "I won't! I'm not going anywhere this time, no matter what."

Val growled. "You say that now, but the second you get the chance, you'll run."

I wanted to shout at the top of my lungs that I'd changed, but my words weren't getting through to them. Fighting them wasn't an option, either. I picked up my hat and put it back on, adjusting it into place. "I'm not leaving. I miss the team. I miss all of you."

Tears welled up in Val's eyes. "We miss you, too, but that doesn't change what you did to us, Camille. We were a team, and you left us to lose."

"We hadn't won state in years, and we had a chance that season," Izzy said.

I folded my arms. "If you want me to leave, you're going to have to make me. Otherwise, I'm staying put."

Ava, Izzy, and Val all pushed at me, sending me stumbling backward.

"We don't want you here," Ava said. Her tone bordered on frustration, but there was also a hint of sorrow.

"Please." I hoped my eyes showed the begging and longing in my heart. "Give me another chance. I won't let you down, I promise."

They continued to push at me, moving me farther away from the team and the one thing I loved most: softball.

I thought about what Liam had said, and it gave me a boost of energy. I wouldn't back down. I'd fight. So, I dug my heels into the grass, slowing their progress. It was three against one, but as they always liked to point out, I was muscular. Using my leg muscles, I buried my feet into the grass and pushed forward.

Adrenaline ignited the passion inside. I wanted to play softball. I wanted back on the team. I wanted my friends and my life back.

The three of them loosened their hold on me, their faces softening. I was making progress. Val dropped her hands first. She opened her mouth to say something when someone barreled into me, sending me flying into the grass with a hard thud.

Tamara laid on top of me, pushing my face into the ground. "Leave them alone. You've done enough damage here."

"Tamara!" Coach Wilkes' voice boomed, like she was using a microphone.

Tamara's eyes went wide as she slowly turned to see Coach storming toward us.

"The thing with lying about an injury," I said, shoving her off me, "is that it always comes back to bite you in the butt."

I expected the team to be surprised that Tamara wasn't actually injured, but most of them looked guilty. I couldn't help but laugh as I stood up. I brushed the grass off my body. "Wow, I knew you were all mad at me, but faking an injury . .

." I rested my weight on my my right leg. "Let me guess, Tamara. When we got back home, you were going to be suddenly healed?"

Red engulfed Tamara's cheeks and neck. "No. I was feeling better this morning and . . ."

Coach held up a hand. "Enough. I'm not sure what kind of game you girls are playing, but it needs to stop."

The anger inside me boiled over, and I couldn't control it. "Let me sum it up for you, Coach. I made a mistake sophomore year and did something mean to Val that I regret. And apparently, I walked out during playoffs. I honestly don't remember that, but I believe them. I obviously wasn't in the right state of mind back then." I let out a long breath. "I know you don't want to believe I've changed, but I have. I'm not under Dylan or any other boy's spell."

I turned to Coach. "That water yesterday was supposed to be for me. Payback for what I did to Val. You were just in the wrong place at the wrong time. I thought taking the fall would put me back in the team's good graces, but I was *way* wrong. They may say I'm a bad person, but not one of them has an ounce of forgiveness inside of them. Apparently, they expect everyone to be perfect all the time, just like they are."

I backed away from the group. "I've been wanting so badly to get back in, but now I'm not so sure. I've been trying to fix my life and hang out with good people who will make me a better person." I motioned to the team. "These girls aren't the girls I remember. They have turned out just as bad as me."

Turning around, I ran off the field and back to the dorm, not bothering to turn around to see their faces.

CHAPTER 28

I took a long, hot shower, trying to scrub off all the grass and dirt thanks to the other girls. I wasn't sure if Coach would let them play the game against the boys, and I didn't care.

When I was done with my shower, I threw on a tank top and shorts and hobbled back to my room. My muscles were still sore from the morning's workout. I wished I could reach out to Mason for his help, but he'd be busy practicing with the baseball team.

I settled onto my bed with Maroon 5 blasting through my earbuds, but my playlist didn't have its normal calming effect. I wanted my phone so I could look up city softball leagues. Or call Kaitlyn and Hayley to pass the time.

I'd barely fallen asleep when my bed bounced. I shot up, almost screaming, until I saw Liam sitting on the edge of my bed. I popped out my earbuds and turned off the music.

"Whatcha listening to?" Liam asked. He scooted his butt back on the bed until his back was against the wall.

I set my MP3 player next to me on the bed. "What are you doing in my room?"

"I knocked, but you didn't answer." He scanned the room, taking it all in. Not that there was much to take in.

I scooted on the bed so I was sitting next to him with my back against the wall as well. I tucked my legs close to my chest. "Isn't that the universal sign that someone doesn't want to talk?"

He pointed to my MP3 player. "Or the sign that someone is listening to Harry Styles incredibly loud."

I shook my head.

"Ed Sheeran?"

I opened my mouth to answer, but he held a finger to my lips. It was becoming a bad habit of his.

"Niall Horan."

With a sigh, I folded my arms across my knees and leaned my head against the wall. "Maybe you should stop guessing young guys."

Liam arched an eyebrow. "Selena Gomez?"

"Maroon 5." I said it as quickly as I could, so he couldn't stop me.

"I love them," he said. "Did you know they're coming to a concert this fall?"

I'd planned to go with Dylan, but obviously, that wasn't happening anymore. Then I remembered that meant I had an extra ticket. How would I pick between Hayley and Kaitlyn? "I have tickets."

His eyes lit up. "Lucky. They sold out before I could buy some. Who you going with?"

"Why are you here, Liam?"

"I wanted to see how you were. I heard what happened."

I drummed my fingers against my arm. "How does gossip travel so freaking fast?" I turned to him. "Are they playing the game?"

Liam shook his head. "The coaches cancelled it when they found out some of the baseball players helped Val plan the water prank. Everyone was running laps when I left." He grinned. "So glad I'm not on the team."

"I'm just happy I get to go home tomorrow. I can get back to a place where a few people actually like me."

He bumped my arm. "I like you." He twisted his hand back and forth. "Most of the time."

I bumped him back. "You didn't pick me to be on your team."

"Aww, is someone feeling left out?" He draped his arm over my shoulders and side-hugged me. "I had to maintain my cover. I spent the whole morning getting information out of the girls, which I didn't end up needing, and I couldn't be seen fraternizing with the enemy."

I motioned between us. "What do you call this?"

Liam looked around the room. "Are there cameras or something? Because I don't see anyone else in here."

I rolled my eyes, but a smile pulled at my lips. "I hate that it's impossible to get my old life back. If I would've known Dylan was going to screw me over so badly, I wouldn't have fallen in lust with him."

Liam lifted his arm off me and scooted away. "Fallen in lust? Who says that?"

I laughed until I snorted. "My dad." When confusion stayed on his face, I laughed harder and waved my hand. "Never mind."

An awkward silence hung in the air. Liam finally scooted back toward me. "You can have your old life back. Secret missions and all."

"Not to how it was. Val and the others didn't accept my apology, and I'm not back on the softball team, so I basically have Kaitlyn and Hayley, and that's it."

"And me," he said. "For what that's worth."

"You're my secret mission buddy." My lips were dry, so I

pulled my lips gloss out of my pocket and applied it. The instant moisture was a relief.

Liam reached into his pocket, and then held his hand out to me, revealing a wrapped mint. "You could use this, too, if we're going to kiss."

My laughter came back until I snorted again. Liam opened the package and popped the mint in his mouth.

"So, you weren't putting on your lip gloss for me?" He sighed. "I just can't win today."

I arched an eyebrow. "Did you try to kiss someone else today?"

He held up his palm. "I did *not* try to kiss you. You were preparing to attack *me*. But I did ask Val if she'd save a dance for me tonight at the after-camp dance."

"Aww." I patted his arm. "That's so sweet. You're a true gentleman." I pulled back at his frown. "Wait, she said no?"

He lowered his head in fake disappointment. "She thought I was joking, I think."

I bit back my laugh and rubbed his back. "Sorry. I'd dance with you, but I can't go, and I'm no Val."

"No, you're not." His voice was so low that it was hard to make out his tone, but he frowned in disappointment.

I removed my hand from his back and rested it on my knee. "You really like her, don't you?"

His eyes snapped up to mine. "What? No, not really. I was just trying to be nice." Something flitted across his eyes that I couldn't read. His eyes went to my mouth for the briefest of seconds that I might have imagined it.

I'd been thinking about kissing way too much. Not every guy wanted to kiss me. I wasn't that shallow, was I? I checked my watch, looking for a distraction. "Dinner is soon. You should probably get down there so no one knows you were fraternizing with the enemy."

"Aren't you going to eat?" He kept his eyes on his checkered Vans.

"I'm not really hungry. I probably shouldn't show my face down there, either."

Liam hopped up from the bed, adjusting his T-shirt. "Want me to sneak something up here for you?"

"Nah." I snapped my fingers. "Actually, yes. Mason."

His eyes bulged. "Wow. So, you and Mason?"

I shook my head. "I just need his miracle hands."

Liam rubbed the back of his neck. "Was that supposed to make it better? Because that sounded a whole lot worse."

I shimmied off the bed and went to the door, opening it for him. "He's a physical trainer, and I'm in an extreme amount of pain."

He winked at me. "Riiight. I'll pass the message along."

I pushed him out the door, and he laughed. "See you tomorrow, Liam."

He paused in the hallway, his hands in his pockets. "You're coming to the after party tonight, right? They can't stop you, especially if you sneak in."

"I'm not sure if I'm in the mood."

"Mason can get you there." He ducked when I tried to hit him. He backed away down the hall. "It's supposed to be awesome. DJ Ice came all the way up."

Isaac was here? That made things a whole lot more interesting. There was a sliver of a chance that I could have the list checked off by the end of the night.

CHAPTER 29

*M*ason never came to my room. I wasn't sure if it was because Liam never told him, or if Mason didn't want to see me.

Around eight, I slipped into my blue paisley maxi dress and slowly made my way toward the gym, where they were holding the dance. I could only go as fast as my sore muscles would allow, which was basically at my grandma's pace, who had a bad hip and knee.

I went through the back entrance, hoping no one would see me. Really, I didn't know why I was going. I didn't want to see any of the softball players, and being in the same room as Alejandro, Mason, and Isaac could be dangerous. But this weird rebellion crept in, wanting some excitement. If Kaitlyn had been with me, she would have tried to talk me out of it. Hayley would have been all for it.

Opening the door, I snuck in and headed for the corner next to the bleachers. I could get a good look at the crowd from there.

DJ Ice was on a platform on the south side, opposite

where I came in. All the baseball and softball players were in the middle of the court, dancing. Isaac had one of his famous pop remixes playing that I loved. I so wanted to be out on the dance floor.

I wished they would have picked a smaller venue to have the dance. It wasn't like there were a ton of players to fill up an entire gym. If I walked out from behind the bleachers, I'd be spotted.

So, I ducked underneath them and went to the front. Since the music was loud, there was no need for me to stay quiet. I peered out through an opening between the bleachers, watching everyone having fun without me.

Tamara was dancing like she'd never been hurt, which she probably hadn't. All the girls surrounded her, cheering her on. Izzy had her back to the guys. I suddenly remembered how timid she was around them. With her friends, she was strong and powerful. The second a guy talked to her in any way that suggested he was hitting on her, she'd crumple.

It was then I noticed the boys and girls were separated. There was a clear rift between the teams.

Out of all the guys, Mason was the only one not dancing. His gaze kept wandering over to the bleachers, like he wanted to sit down. A part of me hoped he would, because then maybe I'd have a chance to talk to him.

Alejandro glanced at the door like he was waiting for someone. From where I hunkered, it looked like everyone was there except me. All the coaches were sitting on the bleachers on the other side of the gym, completely ignoring those on the court.

A shout among the guys turned my attention to them. Liam was break dancing on the gym floor. He spun on the ground, and I couldn't help but smile. I really wished I was out there, cheering him on.

Being by myself under the bleachers was as boring as it sounded. There was no point in me being there. I turned to go back the way I came in, but a baseball and softball player had snuck over to that corner and were making out. They'd definitely see me if I suddenly popped out from under the bleachers. Though the thought of scaring them was tempting.

Peeking my head out from behind the bleachers, I scanned the distance between me and the door nearest me. It looked like most of the players were focused on what they were doing, so they might not notice me sneaking out. My eyes wandered up to Isaac on the stage. He wore a dark blue fedora with a little feather on the side. It went well with his dark blue suit and white shirt. He held a headphone against one ear, the other hand working his system. He probably wouldn't see me, but even if he did, it wouldn't matter.

"Camille?" Mason's sudden voice startled me.

My hand flew to my mouth to cover up a yell. He was leaning against the side of the bleachers. Taking his hand, I pulled him underneath the benches with me. We were toward the back, so we could both stand with no problem.

"What are you doing?" he asked.

"I got restless in my room."

Mason had on a plaid button-down shirt that fit his form well. I almost blushed at the thought of him catching me checking him out, but when my eyes wandered up to his, I saw he was checking me out as well. It was another dress Dylan never liked me wearing because it highlighted my curves, but not in a good way for him. Mason's expression said he thought otherwise. Stupid Dylan.

He cleared his throat and rubbed the back of his neck. "Why are you hiding?"

"I'm not supposed to be here." I rubbed my stiff shoulder. "Did Liam pass along my message?"

Mason stared down at his tennis shoes. "Uh, yeah. Sorry I didn't come. I . . ." His face flushed, and it was adorable.

I gently set my hand on his arm. "Don't worry about it."

He motioned to my shoulder. "Need some help?"

I turned so he could get a better angle. "Yes, please. I'm dying. Coach Wilkes was vicious this morning."

His hands were warm on my shoulder. He worked through the muscles. It hurt at first, but they slowly loosened to the point that I could relax. Mason switched to my other shoulder.

"I heard you aren't going to make it on the softball team." His voice was soft. "That's too bad. You're really good."

If his hand hadn't been on my shoulder, I would've shrugged. "Thanks. But I got what I deserved. Karma and all that."

A frown rested on his thin lips. It wouldn't take much for me to close the distance. I had no idea how Mason would react to me kissing him. But the thought of us kissing left an uneasy feeling in my stomach. I didn't think I'd feel bad about kissing a few guys, but the fact that I'd kissed Alejandro the day before took away the desire to kiss Mason. He was such a good guy. He deserved a girl who would treat him with the respect he deserved. Unfortunately, I wasn't that girl. At least not yet. I needed time to myself before I jumped into another relationship.

When I'd put Mason on my list, it was just for a fun kiss. But the more time I spent around him, the more I realized Mason was relationship material, not hookup material.

Mason took a step away from me. "Any other spots?"

I rubbed the back of my neck. "No. The shoulders were the worst. Thanks, Mason."

"Any time." He moved to duck out from under the bleachers, but then turned back around. "Hey, is Hayley seeing anyone?"

I drew back in surprise. "No. Why?"

His face turned crimson. "I wanted to ask her out." He stuffed his hands in his pockets. "I'm just not sure how. I'm not really good with that kind of stuff."

Mason liked Hayley? Hadn't he tried to kiss me the other day? I licked my lips. "Hayley likes confidence and honesty. Just call her and ask her if she wants to go out."

"Right." He looked down at his shoes. "Can I get her number?"

I'd flirted with him so much, and he liked Hayley the whole time. The more I thought about it, the more I realized he never returned any of the flirting. He never called me after Hawaii. He didn't come up to my room. "You tried to kiss me."

His eyes went wide. "What? When?"

"The other day when you were helping with my sore muscles."

His head shook vigorously. "I never tried to kiss you. I'm sorry if it looked like that. I'm just kind of awkward around girls. I'm never sure how to act."

I put my hand on my forehead. I felt like an idiot. Why did I think every guy wanted to kiss me? I folded my arms close against me. "I don't have her number memorized, and Coach has my phone. But I'll get you the number as soon as I can." I'd never been so uncomfortable in my life, so I kept talking. "When you call her, have a specific date and activity planned. She likes people who get things done."

"Is there anything she likes to do?"

"She loves going to The Shack. She has a thing for punk rock bands."

His eyes lit up. "So do I. I love The Shack. I just don't go there very often because I don't have anyone to go with."

I forced a smile. "Well, hopefully, now you'll have Hayley. I'll put in a good word for you."

Mason was beaming. "Thanks, Camille!" He ducked out from under the bleachers, leaving me completely stunned. What had just happened?

CHAPTER 30

I'd stayed frozen under the bleachers with my mind reeling. I felt so stupid for thinking Mason wanted to kiss me. I was also slightly sad that I'd never cross him off my kiss list. He'd remain a 'what if' for the rest of my life. Maybe Hayley would be able to tell me all about his kissing abilities. I had no idea if she'd say yes to him, but I couldn't think of a reason why she wouldn't. At least I knew he'd treat her much better than her last boyfriend.

That left me with only one guy left on my list: Isaac. I'd originally thought he wouldn't be too hard to get a kiss from, but now I wasn't so sure. Not everyone viewed kissing as I did: a fun activity for all to enjoy.

Kaitlyn always went on and on about how special kisses were and that they should be saved for the right person. I used to think that was silly talk, but now I wasn't so sure. I wasn't sure about anything anymore.

I was so lost in concentration, I didn't notice Liam had joined me under the bleachers. "What are you doing here?" I practically growled it at him.

He backed up and held up his palms. "Whoa. Just

checking on you. Mason said you were hiding out under here."

A scowl landed on my face, and it wouldn't go away. Had Mason told anyone else? Did he think I needed help? I was really starting to hate boys.

Liam held out his arms. "Does someone need a hug?"

The anger exuding from me made him lower his arms. I didn't need a hug. I didn't *need* anything.

"I'm fine, thanks," I snapped.

"Is this because Mason turned you down?" He tried to pat my shoulder in solace, but I squirmed away.

I had to keep my jaw from dropping. "What did Mason tell you?"

Liam set his hands on his hips and shrugged. "Just that you wanted to kiss him, but he's interested in Hayley."

That was everything. Mason had told him that? Okay, I was *really* starting to hate boys. They weren't supposed to gossip like girls.

"I didn't want to kiss him!" I totally did, but that moment had now past and would never be coming back. "I thought *he* wanted to kiss *me*," I huffed. "It doesn't even matter. I'm just tired of all the games. I want to go home."

Liam's face softened. "Go to bed right now, and the next thing you know, it'll be morning, and we'll be on our way home."

Leaning against the wall, I folded my arms. "But then I'll have to sit on a bus full of softball players who hate me. And it's not a short ride."

"Maybe I could sneak you on our bus."

"And be with Mason and Alejandro? No, thank you."

Confusion ran across his face. "What does Alejandro have to do with this?"

I did it again. I talked to Liam like he was Hayley or Kaitlyn. He wasn't a girlfriend that I could confide everything in. Why did I keep doing that?

"Nothing." I rubbed my forehead. "I'm going to bed."

Liam surprised me by taking me into his arms. "It's going to be okay, Camille. Things will work out the way they're supposed to."

I wanted to shove him away, but the warmth from his body was real nice. I relaxed into him, letting him hold me. I clasped my hands behind his back and rested my cheek on his shoulder. How come I never fit into Dylan's arms like this? It was always slightly awkward with him. I needed to find a guy with Liam's frame.

No. I didn't need to find anyone. I was fine solo.

With a deep breath, I released Liam and stepped back. "Thanks. You're the only real friend I've had this week." I twisted my lips to the side. "I never thought I'd say that about you."

He brushed off his arms, bringing my attention to how firm they were. "What can I say? I'm awesome. Now, be a good little girl and get to bed. Just don't try to kiss any guys on the way there."

"Ha. Ha. Ha." Every word was spaced out, sarcasm dripping from each one.

He patted the top of my head. "My cute Cam-I-am. You're adorable when you're annoyed."

I pushed him away as he laughed. I didn't even bother to check if anyone was looking. I just ducked out from under the bleachers and hustled toward the door leading out of the gym. The door slammed behind me, jolting me into reality.

A weird energy buzzed under my fingertips. When I'd been in Liam's arms, I had the slight urge to kiss him. Liam. What was wrong with me? I wanted to kiss everyone. But was there anything wrong with that? It was fun if the other person knew what they were doing. A part of me wanted to find Alejandro and kiss him again, just to get the thought of kissing Liam out of my head.

Ugh. Liam. Hayley and Kaitlyn were going to freak when they found out. But I couldn't deny my attraction to him. It left me all sorts of confused and slightly worried about my mental state.

The gym door opened, and I turned to find Isaac. He wasn't Alejandro, but at least he wasn't Liam.

"Any requests?" he asked. "I know you like my remixes." He glanced me over with a smile. "Where were you? I hadn't seen you all night until you just ran out."

"Shouldn't you be, you know, DJing?"

Isaac waved his hands. "I have the next song already lined up, so I'm good for a couple minutes."

A couple minutes? That was plenty of time. I may not have been able to cross Mason off the list, but I could still cross off Isaac. That would be three of my four. The buzz inside me expanded, and I craved a kiss. Craved physical contact.

In a flash, I was in front of Isaac, my hand cupped on his neck and pulling his lips down to mine. He didn't even hesitate. His arms wrapped around my back and pressed me close. He had a tropical flavor in his mouth, like he'd been sucking on a candy. His kiss was slightly wet, but not too bad.

The longer we kissed, the more I realized I really didn't like it. But I just wanted that connection. The validation that maybe I meant something to someone.

Isaac pushed me into the wall and kissed me hard, like he couldn't get enough. I felt the same way. Like we weren't as close as we could get. There was a need deep inside, smothering all sense of reason, that needed to devour him.

The thing was, it wasn't that I needed Isaac. It wouldn't have mattered if it was him or Mason or Brady or Alejandro. There was just that desire to be wanted. The desire to connect with someone on a different level. It consumed me like it was the only thing that mattered in the world.

It wasn't until Isaac broke the kiss that I realized we had an audience. The gym doors were open, all the baseball and softball players huddled in the doorway, watching us.

Isaac waved at them all. "Came to watch the show?"

Val rested her weight on her left leg. "We came to wonder where our DJ went. The music cut off."

Isaac checked his watch. "Ope. Guess I lost track of time." He winked at me, and then headed back toward the gym, pausing briefly to run his eyes over Jordyn, not even worried that I'd be able to see him check out another girl. I really didn't know the guy at all, which made everything worse.

My mouth still pulsed with the feel of his lips on mine. I pressed my fingers to my lips and wished I were anywhere else but there.

Most of the softball players were looking at me with disgust. They turned around and headed back into the gym, along with most of the baseball players, who had looked amused. Mason caught my eye. He looked disappointed. Like in my decision, not that it wasn't him.

Then my gaze swept to Alejandro. He looked . . . hurt. He shook his head at me, a frown on his lips, and disappeared into the gym.

For some reason, though, the worst was seeing Liam. His face was a mix of shock, betrayal, and sadness. His eyes kept rotating through the emotions, like they were trying to find the correct one. They finally settled on sadness, and he followed the others back inside. The gym doors closed, leaving me alone in the hall.

I'd been beyond stupid, and I wasn't sure how to fix it.

CHAPTER 31

The next morning, I was the first one on the bus. I immediately went to the back and claimed the last bench. I laid down, covered my face with my jacket, and popped in my earbuds.

I completely tuned everyone out for the whole ride. Jordyn was kind enough to get my attention when we stopped so I could use the bathroom. Other than that, everyone left me alone. That didn't mean I didn't notice the whispers and snickers. They weren't doing anything to be discreet about it.

I'd never been so excited to get to the school in my life. It meant I was that much closer to being home and in my room.

Coach Wilkes gave me my phone when I got off the bus. The problem with being in the back meant I was the last one off the bus. The second I stepped off the bus, I could feel all eyes on me.

I made the mistake of turning on my phone. It exploded with notifications. I wanted to open all the texts from Hayley and Kaitlyn, but the social media ones caught my attention. When I opened the browser, my heart sank.

There were pictures of me posted, and they weren't good ones. Someone snapped a picture of Mason and me standing incredibly close when he was working on my shoulder. From the angle, it didn't look like we were doing anything appropriate.

Then there was a picture of Liam and me hugging. I didn't realize how much I had sunk into him until I saw the picture. It was way intimate and made me blush.

Of course, someone got a picture of Isaac and me making out. I knew we'd gotten a little heated, but the picture made it look a lot worse.

The picture that really made my heart sink was one of Alejandro and me. I had no idea his roommate had snapped a picture of us in the bed when he came into the room. There was a picture of a guy and me in a bed online. All cuddled up. My only saving grace was that no clothes had come off.

I thought that would be the end. But it wasn't. Pictures from my make-out session with Brady in the cafeteria had surfaced. Along with pictures of Dylan and me kissing during our relationship.

I was officially the school skank. Six guys. Granted I hadn't kissed all of them, but to the world, it looked like I had. Even without those two, there were still four guys I *had* kissed. In my head, that didn't seem like such a big number. But seeing them back to back like that changed my entire view.

"Camille!" Hayley's voice rang out, catching my attention. I looked up to see her and Kaitlyn sprinting toward me, pushing softball players out of the way in the process.

When they reached me, both their faces fell. At the sight, everything inside me broke, and the tears came.

Both Hayley and Kaitlyn wrapped their arms around me, squeezing me tight. I wanted to disappear in their arms forever and never resurface, because that meant facing reality.

"Girl, what happened at camp?" Kaitlyn asked into my hair.

I pulled back enough to look at them but kept them positioned so they could block out the world. "I swear it wasn't what it looks like." I swallowed. "Not completely."

"I thought Liam wasn't on the list," Hayley said.

"He's not, and I didn't kiss him. It was just a hug." I rushed to add the next part. "And nothing happened with Mason, either! He was just working out some stiff muscles in my shoulder."

Hayley's red eyebrows shot up. "Wow. Okay. No need to get all defensive."

I bit my lip. "I kinda have to talk to you about him." She looked confused, so I changed the subject. Kind of. "Isaac, well, it's obvious what happened."

Hayley smirked. "It looked good. Was it?"

Man, I'd missed them so much. I twisted my hand back and forth. "It was okay."

Hayley fingered a daith earring. "Well, that's disappointing."

Kaitlyn rubbed my arm. "And Alejandro? You were in bed with him!" She grimaced when she realized how loud she'd been.

I shook my head. "Nothing happened besides a kiss, I swear. Everything looked way worse than what it was." I rubbed my forehead. "This trip was the worst mistake of my life. I have so much to tell you."

"Obviously," Hayley scoffed.

The light pounding of feet made my heart soar just a little. My brother.

Seth appeared around Kaitlyn and threw his arms around me. "You're back!"

I held him tight. "I missed you, bro."

"Same, sis." He bounced while he hugged me. "I want to

hear all about your trip! I bet you were the best softball player there." He finally released me, but turned to my side and kept his arm around me so he could face my friends. "I have the best sister ever."

The lightness in my heart disappeared. Seth was going to be so disappointed in me. I couldn't believe I'd let him down like that. I had no idea how I'd tell him that I didn't make it back on the team. He'd want to know why, and I'd have no way to explain it to him.

The second I saw my dad, I released my brother and ran into his arms like I was a little girl again. Dad let out an "umph" when I rammed into him, but he immediately wrapped his arms around me.

"Is everything okay?" he asked.

I shook my head against his chest. "I messed up, Dad. Big time."

He patted my back and let out a sigh, his other hand stroking my hair. "It's going to be okay, Camille. Let's get you home so we can talk about it."

"Is Mom home?" I couldn't look at him when I asked because I was worried about the answer.

His body stiffened. "She's working on a case. I'm not sure when she'll be home."

Even though I expected that answer, everything inside me deflated. "Yeah, okay."

Dad got my bags from the bus while my friends and brother walked me to the car. I tried my best not to look at anyone, but it was hard when I could feel all the eyes on me. A part of me wanted to find Alejandro, Liam, and Mason to apologize, but I wasn't ready to face them yet. Besides, I had no idea what I'd say to them. But all the pictures weren't good for them, either. I sighed. I'd have to apologize to Brady and Isaac as well. None of them signed up to get involved with my drama. I'd just handpicked them, and they had no say.

I hated that I'd let so many people down. I'd take some time to myself, but then I'd somehow have to fix my mess, and I hadn't the slightest clue where to start.

CHAPTER 32

I really needed to work on my public image. I didn't want to go into my senior year with everyone thinking I'd hook up with every guy. That wasn't who I was, or who I wanted to be.

I'd already had so many messages from guys wanting to get together. Some I didn't even know, and they didn't go to my school. Social media was the worst. Nothing remained a secret and people only saw what they wanted to see. Or in my case, what was thrown into their faces. I hadn't done myself any favors by putting myself in those situations.

Even though nothing had happened with Alejandro, I'd gone with him to his room and chosen to lay down on his bed. None of it had seemed that big a deal when it was happening, but seeing the picture, it was way worse than I thought.

Kaitlyn and Hayley tried their best to shut down the rumors online and stick up for me, but it didn't help. A picture was worth a thousand words. They'd never catch up with all the pictures posted of me. That was a lot of words.

I really wanted to talk to my mom about everything, but

work kept her busy. Seth and Dad tried to keep me occupied with playing catch in the backyard. It wasn't the emotional release I needed, but it was the only way my dad knew how to handle these situations.

For the moment, being out there with them, throwing the ball around, enjoying the beautiful weather and lazy Sunday, was amazing. I was able to forget everything and focus on spending time with my family. At least, the family that was there. It would have been perfect if Mom were there with us, but I could never see that happening.

"I can't wait to watch you at your games." Seth tossed me the ball, and it landed perfectly in my mitt. He'd make a great baseball player one day. I just needed to get him to try out for a team. I'd tried a couple times, but he chickened out once we got to tryouts. His anxiety would eat him alive.

I hadn't told him I hadn't made it on the team. I didn't know how. I threw the ball to Dad. "I was thinking maybe I'd try out for a city league."

Dad had the ball cupped in his glove. "In addition to school?"

I shook my head. "In place of school."

Seth frowned as he caught the ball from our dad. "Why? I think school is much better." He threw me the ball.

Dad nodded in agreement. "Better opportunities. You're already behind on college applications. We need to get you on some university's radar."

I chucked the ball a little too hard at Dad, and he had to jump up to get it. "I just think our school team isn't very good this year. I was disappointed at camp." More in myself than of the team's abilities, but Dad didn't need to know that.

Dad shook out his gloved hand. I hadn't meant to throw the ball so hard. I was still all worked up, and I needed an outlet. One that wasn't kissing. Maybe I needed to head to the batting cage.

"That was camp," Dad said. "There's still a lot of time before the season actually starts. I'm sure you'll be able to help the girls with a thing or two to get them ready."

I wanted to laugh at the irony. They didn't need my help. They were good at what they did. I just ruined the camaraderie they'd had.

I rolled out my shoulder, trying to loosen it up. "I think I'm going to go to the batting cages and work on my swing. It felt off this week." Along with other things.

Seth jumped where he stood. "Can I come with you?"

Dad pointed a finger at him. "You're supposed to help me today, remember?"

"Help you with what?" I asked.

Dad puffed out his chest. "A super secret thing we can't tell you about."

Seth grinned. "That's right." His smile turned into a frown. "Sorry, Camille, but you're going to have to manage without me."

"It'll be tough," I said, "but I think I'll be okay."

Even though I'd been behind the wheel since Dylan had dumped me, I still got excited every time I slid into the driver's seat. There was an exciting freedom about being by myself and regaining my independence.

There were a few people at the batting cages, but not many. I was able to snag one with no one on either side of me. Sometimes having a buffer was nice when I needed to clear my mind.

Mason had done wonders for my shoulders. They hadn't felt that loose in the longest time. Val was good at what she did as well, but she'd never help me out. I doubted Mason would help me anymore, either, even if he did start dating Hayley.

When I told her about his crush, she got this weird smile on her face that surprised me. Neither Kaitlyn nor Hayley had paid much attention to him before, but once I put him on my list, I think they opened their eyes.

Hayley said she'd even reach out to him on social media. I hoped I hadn't ruined everything for her, but she told me not to worry.

Each swing of the bat let a part of my anxiety go. It felt so good to release some of the steam brewing inside me. I tried to think of different ways I could reach out to the team, but nothing came to mind. They'd made it very clear they wanted nothing to do with me.

I thought about what Liam had said. Did I really want to let the team control my future? I wanted to play softball and being on the school's team was the best way for me to showcase my talent. But then again, it would be nice to have them want me there.

My chest was heaving in and out by the time the last ball flew from the machine. I hit the ball with everything I had, sending it flying to the other side of the cage and into the net.

"It's too bad you aren't on the team."

I spun around to find Alejandro with his fingers linked through the fence. I lowered my bat. "I'm actually trying to think of a way to get back on. Have any brilliant ideas?"

"Stop making out with guys?" He smirked, letting me know he was joking.

I came out of the cage and took off my helmet. "Funny. But that wouldn't interfere with my softball playing abilities."

He leaned against the fence and folded his arms. "Could interfere with your focus, though."

"I'm done letting boys control my feelings." I leaned on the fence next to him and ran my fingers through my helmet hair. "I owe you an apology."

"For what?"

I licked my lips. "For kissing you like that."

Alejandro pouted. "Why? It was fun."

I shoved his arm, making him smile. "It's not about that. I'm in such a bad place emotionally right now. I shouldn't be kissing any guys."

He rubbed the back of the neck. "Can I ask why you've been kissing around?"

I sighed. I didn't really want to tell him the truth. It was kind of embarrassing. But lying got me nowhere. "I had to prove that Dylan was wrong."

Understanding passed over his eyes. "Well, he was, in case you're worried about that. I can say something if you'd like."

I twirled the bat in my hand. "I need to draw attention off all that stuff, not highlight it. But thanks." I looked at him. "And I never kissed Liam or Mason. Those pictures were just taken at the perfectly wrong times."

"Should I feel honored I made the list?"

A pang struck my heart. He really didn't know about my list, but his words hit so close to home. "Of course." I rubbed my forehead. "Do you think the rumors will ever stop?"

He shrugged. "Eventually, people will find something else to talk about. If I could make a suggestion, though, stop putting yourself in questionable situations."

I snapped my fingers. "You know, you're right. I hadn't even thought about that!"

He rolled his eyes at me, and I couldn't help but laugh. It was nice to know that one of the guys wasn't mad at me. I highly doubted Isaac was mad, either. The funny thing was, the two people I probably hurt the most are the two I didn't actually kiss. Those rumors wouldn't have been good for them. Isaac, Brady, and Alejandro would have no problem shutting down anything bad that was said about them, or they would use it to their advantage. Mason and Liam weren't like that.

Alejandro tapped my arm. "You should come to the bonfire next Friday night. A lot of the juniors will be there."

"Isn't that the last place I should go?"

"If you want people to stop talking, you have to make them. Show them the real you." He pursed his lips. "I'm not sure if I actually even know who that is."

His words surprised me, but then they made sense. No one at school probably knew who I was anymore. I'd shut myself off when Dylan and I started dating. Then I went kiss crazy when we broke up. I needed a new and improved Camille—independent, loyal to her friends, hardworking, and fun to be around.

"Thanks, Alejandro."

He grinned. "Any time." He nodded to the cages. "Are you done, or do you want to go another round?"

I returned his smile. "Definitely another round."

At least one little piece had been put back in place.

CHAPTER 33

*M*om didn't get home until almost nine that night. I found her in the office, talking on the phone with a client. She held up a finger when I came in, telling me to hold on.

As she jabbered away, I checked out all the plaques and awards she'd received for being a lawyer. My mom really had done a lot for the community. But she'd slacked on her family in the process.

I plopped down on the leather couch and kicked my feet up on the cushions. I almost checked my phone but remembered I'd left it upstairs. On purpose. The notifications hadn't slowed down in the least, and I was sick of all the messages guys were sending me.

After ten minutes, I thought about getting up, but Mom finally ended her call. She turned toward me.

"What can I do for you, honey?" she asked, for once giving me her full attention.

"I need some advice." I laid the back of my head against the armrest of the couch and stared at the textured ceiling. "This week didn't go as planned."

"Why not?" Her tone was invested, giving me the strength to really open up.

"I really screwed things up with the softball team." I sighed. "There are so many things I'd forgotten about since Dylan became my boyfriend."

"Okay."

"I've lost myself and a lot of my friends." I folded my arms and rested my cupped hands on my elbows. "I'm just not sure what to do."

There was a long pause before she spoke, and it was then that I noticed she was typing away on her computer. "That's nice."

I sat up. "Are you actually listening to me?"

Click, click, click. "Uh huh." But she was distant.

I couldn't take it anymore. All I wanted was a conversation with my mother. It didn't even need to be that long. I just need guidance from her, which was what mothers were supposed to do. I hopped up from the couch and sprang toward her desk, shutting off her computer screen.

Mom whipped around. "What are you doing? I was in the middle of an email!"

"And I was in the middle of trying to talk to my mom!"

She sat back. "What's gotten into you? You're never like this."

I threw up my hands. "How would you know that, Mom? You'd have to actually pay attention to me to know."

Her face looked liked I'd slapped her, which I had, with my words. "Honey, that's not . . ." She trailed off, staring at her computer screen.

"That's not what, Mom?" I waved my hand in front of her face until she looked at me. "Seriously, you're the worst mom ever."

Shock and betrayal washed over her. "How could you say that?"

I threw my hands around as I spoke. "I don't know, Mom. Maybe because you're never around? Maybe because I can't talk to you about anything? Maybe because your clients are more important than your own family!"

She stood. "That's not true."

"Oh, it's not?" I tapped my finger against my lip. "Interesting. So, where was I this past week?"

She blinked, opened her mouth, and then closed it with a frown.

"Softball camp, Mom. I was at softball camp."

"But you stopped playing softball." Her words were slow and spaced apart, like she was trying to think.

I balled my hands into fists. "Yeah, over a year ago. But then I told you I wanted to go to this camp, and I wanted you to take me to get new cleats."

"You did?" She looked like she was trying so hard to remember even a fraction of the conversation we'd had. "Was that during dinner?"

I backed away from her. "It doesn't matter." I wiped a tear that had escaped down my cheek. "Why did you stop being my mom?"

"Honey, I never stopped . . ."

"Stop lying! Stop trying to work your way out of this. I'm not your client. I'm your daughter, in case you've forgotten. Any time I need to talk to you, any time I just want to tell you about my day, you're busy with work."

Heat climbed up her neck to her cheeks. "It's been super busy . . ."

"For two years! It's been super busy for two whole years, Mom." I wiped away another stray tear. "Why did you stop caring about *me*? About Seth? We need you, and you're never around. Even when you're physically here, you're not mentally." I took a few deep breaths to steady myself. "If it has hurt

Seth and me this badly, I don't even want to think about what it's done to Dad."

A flicker of life came to her eyes. "I got this job when your dad got injured! I'm trying to make money and provide for our family! You never said anything like this to your father when he was out on deployment."

I shrieked out my annoyance. "Mom, deployment doesn't even compare to this! Plus, Dad got a new job over a year ago. Unless you two have some secret gambling addiction, we're fine. You don't have to work so hard!" I pointed a finger at her. "It's your choice. You're choosing to stay busy." I backed toward the door. "I've been quiet for way too long, hoping my mom would come back to me. But you're too blind to even see the truth." I opened the door. "You know what? Forget it. I've gone this long without you, I guess I can survive the rest of my life that way, too." I spun around and left a stunned Mom in her office.

I bolted upstairs, passing Dad, who was standing in the hallway with tears in his eyes, and ran straight for my room, slamming the door behind him.

I picked up my phone, wanting to talk to someone. Instead of calling Kaitlyn or Hayley, I found myself searching for Liam's number in my phone and pressing call.

Excited nerves settled into my stomach at the thought of hearing his voice. It was then that I realized how much I liked him, more than just as a friend.

I wasn't sure if he'd answer my call. It wasn't like I'd given him a lot of time to digest everything.

But he picked up on the third ring. "What?"

I drew in a shaky breath. "Can we meet somewhere?" My words were slurred and mumbled together.

His tone softened. "Calm down, Camille. I can't understand you. Take some deep breaths."

I took a few, and then took a few more, before I could really speak. "Can I come over? I need to talk to someone."

His tone hardened again. "Call Alejandro. Or Isaac. Or Mason. Or Brady." His words rammed into my chest, and I choked on a sob.

He was so right. I was an idiot to be calling, but it was his voice I wanted to hear. He was always able to calm me down.

I covered my mouth with my hand, holding in the cries. I had to be strong. I *was* strong. I swallowed down my pain. "You're right. Sorry, Liam." I hung up and fell backward onto my bed. What was wrong with me? After everything that had happened, why was I falling for another guy? I was an idiot.

I powered off my phone, set it on my nightstand, popped in my earbuds, found Maroon 5, and curled up on my bed. I could figure things out on my own. I didn't need anyone else. Not Liam, not my mom, not anyone.

I was strong.

CHAPTER 34

$\mathcal{I}$'d fallen asleep sprawled out on my bed, still dressed in my day clothes. My music had shut off at some point. I ran out of battery.

A clink sounded at my window, waking me from my restless sleep. Rubbing my eyes, I pushed myself from the bed and shuffled to the window. Another tiny rock hit my window right before I opened it.

I wasn't sure exactly who I was expecting on the other side. I'd shut off my phone so no one could contact me. Hayley and Kaitlyn would have gone through the front door if it was open. They'd call my dad if they had to.

A small part of me hoped to see Liam. Maybe he realized how harsh he'd been on me and wanted to apologize.

What I wasn't expecting, though, was Dylan. I leaned my arms on the window sill. "What are you doing?" I checked my watch. It was just after midnight.

Dylan craned his neck to look up at me. He was shadowed by our large oak tree. "I tried calling you, but it went straight to voicemail. Can I come up?"

I shook my head. "I'm not letting you in my room after

midnight, Dylan." Somehow, another picture would pop up on social media, #makeuphookup. Lame.

"Then will you come down? We need to talk."

I pressed my palm to my mouth, stifling a yawn. I really wasn't in the mood to talk to Dylan. What did he even want? If he thought we'd get back together now, he was out of his mind. I hoped he didn't see all the pictures and think I'd loosened up and was ready to go past kissing. That was the last thing I needed. My hormones needed time to chill, not get all criss-crossed.

"Dylan, go home. Whatever it is can wait until the morning. Or until school starts in the fall." I really didn't want to talk to him before that. But I couldn't avoid him at school forever. I put my hands on my window, about to lower it, when he spoke and made me pause.

"I'm worried about you."

My arms stayed raised in shock. "Worried about me? Why?"

He shifted uncomfortably and stuffed his hands in his pockets. He glanced around before he turned his attention back to me. "Can you come down here? I don't want to shout."

I finally lowered my arms, and then folded them. "You're not shouting, and I'm not coming down." After everything that had happened to me, meeting a guy in the middle of the night outside of my house was just as bad as letting him in my room. And more likely for someone to snap a picture. "Why would you be worried about me?"

He sighed. "I saw all the pictures online. That's not you, Camille."

"Thanks for your opinion, but it doesn't matter."

His tone was soft. "You're acting out. Listen, I know it must have been hard to lose me, and then see me with someone else, but . . ."

I bit back a bitter laugh. "Are you serious? You think all of this is about *you*?" A part of it was, yes, but not in the way he thought. It wasn't about losing *him*, and honestly, it wasn't completely about him saying I was a bad kisser. It was about proving that I was worth something. That someone out there valued me. I'd just gone about it the completely wrong way.

"Of course it is," he said. "You don't need to try to save face here. Breakups are hard."

Wow. Dylan really was acting like he was Marius and I was Éponine from *Les Misérables*. I didn't care that he ended up with Cosette. All I knew was that I was so not going to end up dead at the end.

I rested my palms on the window sill and leaned my head out of the window. "Dylan, you're an idiot. I knew you loved yourself, but I didn't know you were *in love* with yourself. When did you get such a big head?" Maybe he'd always had it, and I was too much *in lust* to notice.

He frowned. "Stop trying to turn the focus, Camille. This is about you and the fact that you're lashing out. I'm worried that something will happen to you. There are a lot of creeps out there, and you're giving them golden opportunities to take advantage of you."

"Wow, look at you, so caring. You actually sound worried about my wellbeing."

"Of course I am!" He took a few breaths to calm himself. "Don't act like our relationship meant nothing. We had something good, it just didn't last, like all relationships."

The rational part of my brain knew there was truth in what he was saying, but there was a small part that needed to defend myself. "Not *all* relationships end, stupid. There are plenty of people who stay together until they die." That was actually what I wanted. A meaningful relationship with someone I wanted to spend the rest of my life with. Obviously, it would take a few failed relationships before I found the one that stuck.

"We're talking high school here," he said, annoyed.

"Dylan, I'm not having this debate, or any debate, with you. Please don't stop by again, especially in the middle of the night."

"If you kept your phone on, I wouldn't be out here!"

I growled on the inside. We were sounding like an old married couple on the verge of destruction. "I don't want to talk to you, either. Or text. We're over. Instead of throwing rocks at my window like in a freaking Taylor Swift song, maybe you should focus on your new girlfriend."

"This has nothing to do with her." He ran his fingers through his hair in frustration. "This has to do with you acting like someone you're not. I just want you to be careful."

"Noted." I went to shut the window again, but he held up his arms.

"Camille, don't shut me out. Talk to me. Tell me what's going on. I know I'm not your boyfriend anymore, but I'm your friend."

Did he really think we could just go to being friends that divulge their secrets after being in a romantic relationship for over a year? He was insane.

"Dylan, I appreciate your concern, but I'm fine. If I need to talk to someone, I'll talk to Kaitlyn or Hayley. They're my actual best friends, remember?"

"Just don't turn to Isaac, Brady, Mason, Liam, Alejandro, or any other random guy."

"Okay, did you really need to drop all their names?"

He huffed. "You're the queen of changing subjects. If you don't want to talk to me now, just know you can call me whenever. I'll always be there for you as a friend." He said it like he was being the most chivalrous guy in the world.

"You're a good person, Camille. You just need to remember that. Don't lose yourself in all this."

Now he was starting to sound like a motivational speaker. I gave him a thumbs-up. "Thanks. You've inspired me. I'll be a better person now because of you." I shut the window before he could speak again and make me listen to more of his crap.

A little spark of an idea struck me, though. I needed to remind my friends why we had been friends to begin with.

I went to my computer and typed the names of all the softball players. Then I typed everything I knew about them, like their personalities, their family situation, their likes and dislikes, and the main reason why I had liked them, and why our friendship had worked.

They'd all worried that I'd abandoned them again. I had to find a way to let them know that I wasn't going anywhere, and that they could talk to me at any time, even in the middle of the night.

After that list, I made a list of all the materials I needed. I'd once promised the team I'd make them matching name bracelets, and I was going to finally come through on that promise.

CHAPTER 35

The nice thing about getting ready and not having a guy to impress was I could just be myself. I'd worn little make-up before I started dating Dylan. I usually wore my hair down and left the natural wave. Dylan always said it made me look like I didn't take care of my hair, but I always thought it made me appear carefree. Plus, with the blue, it made it that much better.

I found my flowy satin and linen shirts in a box in my closet. They were loose-fitting and felt soft against my skin. They used to be my favorite things to wear. Then I found my capris, another thing Dylan said I couldn't pull off because my legs were too short and thick. Each thing I found that I'd discarded because of Dylan released the independent part of me that had been caged way too long.

Camille was back. The carefree, get along with everyone, extremely loyal girl had found her way back home.

I think the happiest thing I had again was my flip flops. Dylan preferred the cutesy sandals, but they were always uncomfortable. My cushy flip flops were the things dreams were made of.

Grabbing the bag of bracelets, I set off to pick up my friends. The bracelets were made from a thick leather and held three different charms in front—their first initial, a baseball, and another charm of something they liked. I made ones for Hayley and Kaitlyn, too, only I used drum and star charms for Hayley, and a basketball and hairdresser charms for Kaitlyn.

When I picked up Kaitlyn and Hayley from their homes, I handed them their bracelets.

"Love it," Kaitlyn said. She slipped it on with a toothy grin.

Hayley beamed when she saw hers. "I remember when you used to make and sell these, trying to save up money for softball." She slid it on her slender wrist. "I miss the good ol' days."

Kaitlyn smiled sweetly at us. "Let's go create some new good ol' days."

I blared Maroon 5 as we drove. I caught Hayley singing along in the backseat, even though she always claimed they weren't her style.

The bonfire was set up so much like the night Dylan had got into the fight with Brady. It was a night I didn't want to relive.

I took major deep breaths before I got out of the car. I was strong. I could handle whatever was thrown at me. I wasn't what people thought of me. I was a good person.

I sounded like an affirmation advertisement. Although, that wouldn't be such a bad thing.

Pop music welcomed me the second I stepped out of the car. I immediately wanted to dance but knew I needed to find my softball crew before I chickened out.

They were huddled in a corner near a fire, chatting away.

Kaitlyn squeezed my arm. "You got this."

"And we'll be right over here," Hayley said, cracking her knuckles. "We got your back if things go south."

Kaitlyn slapped her arm. "She needs positive thinking."

Hayley rubbed her arm where she'd hit her. "That is positive: she's not alone. We're willing to throw down for her."

I wrapped my arms around them and squeezed. "Thank you." Reciting my affirmations, I forced myself to move toward the softball team.

There were a few catcalls along the way, but I ignored them, keeping my focus on my hopefully-soon-to-be-friends-again.

Val was the first one to notice me. I expected an uproar from her, yelling at me to go away. But she surprised me by giving me a soft smile. All the others followed Val's gaze until they saw me.

I cleared my throat when I got to them. "I need to apologize."

"We've heard it already," Jordyn said, sounding bored. But I'd definitely piqued the interest of the others. They stared at me expectantly.

"I messed up sophomore year. Big time. It was wrong of me to abandon you, and I wish I'd figured this out sooner, but I have now. I'm not expecting all of you to forgive me so easily, but I want you to know I'm not going anywhere. I'll be at softball tryouts and will do my best. Softball is my passion, and I lost that along the way." I moved my purse, so it was in front of me. "I lost a lot of myself over a guy, which is incredibly embarrassing. It won't happen again, no matter how cute the guy is."

Val and others let out small laughs. It was a good sign.

I unzipped my purse and pulled out the bracelets. "These are way late, but I have them now." I went up to Val and placed hers in her hand. In addition to the softball charm, I'd gotten her a microphone.

She fingered it. "You remembered."

"Of course I did."

She'd confided in me once that she secretly wanted to be a singer. She knew how to play the guitar and piano, but never played or sang in front of anyone. One time when we were alone, I got her to play me a song, and it was the most beautiful thing I'd ever heard. She had a fun rasp to her voice that sucked you in.

Then I gave a bracelet to Ava. Hers had a chef's hat charm linked to it. The girl was an amazing cook and wanted to have her own restaurant one day. After wrapping her fist around the bracelet, Ava threw her arms around me. "It's about time. I've been waiting for this for years."

Next was Izzy. She was a little trickier, but I'd finally found a calculator charm. The girl was a whiz with numbers. She wanted to have her own accounting firm when she got older, and I had no doubt she would.

I handed out the rest. There were ones with a book, a NASA helmet, a pair of scissors, and a gavel (Jordyn would be a killer judge). One by one the girls hugged me. We weren't all of a sudden friends again, but it was a step in the right direction. I still had to prove myself. Words only got you so far.

Val twisted the bracelet on her wrist. "So, how many guys did you end up kissing after Dylan broke up with you?"

I rolled my eyes. "Way less than it looks like. I was going through a phase, okay?"

Izzy folded her arms. "This phase is over, right? We miss the old Camille."

Ava smiled at my outfit. "At least you look the part again."

"I'm working my way back," I said. "It's a slow process." I looked over at my shoulder and smiled at Kaitlyn and Hayley. I knew they'd be wondering if everything was going okay. I figured the hugs would say something, but I wanted them to be sure. They both let out breaths of relief. I turned my attention back to my softball pals. "I've been hitting the batting cages a few times a week, if anyone wants to join me."

Izzy grinned. "I'd love that. My batting needs some serious work, and you were always the best teacher."

"I'm in, too," Ava said. A few others murmured agreements.

I backed away with a wave. "I guess I'll see you guys later."

As I walked toward Hayley and Kaitlyn, I felt lighter than I had in the longest time. There wasn't much weighing me down, aside from my absentee mother. But I wasn't going to let her ruin my night. I'd just made headway with the softball team. I still needed to apologize to Mason and Liam, but I wasn't sure if Liam would talk to me.

I was almost to my friends when Isaac slid in front of me, his lips pulling up in a smirk. "How do I get the Alejandro special?"

My eyebrows shot up. "You want to hook up with Alejandro?"

His smirk turned into a frown. "What? No. I want to do with you what you did with him."

I patted his shoulder. "Sorry, Isaac, but nothing happened with Alejandro besides kissing."

"That's not what his friends are saying." Isaac took a step closer to me, and it was then I noticed the smell of alcohol on him—he was plastered.

I took a step back. "I don't care what his friends are saying, or what Alejandro is saying. Nothing happened, and nothing is going to happen between you and me."

"You can't tell me you didn't enjoy our little make-out session." He wobbled a little where he stood.

"I did," I said. Mostly for getting out all my pent-up emotions. It was an eye-opening experience for me. "But it was a one-time kiss. It won't happen again." I started to walk away, but Isaac put his hand on my waist to stop me.

He pressed his lips to my ear. "Come on, you know you want to. Don't turn back into the old Camille just yet. Let's have a little fun."

I wrapped my hand around his and ripped it easily from my waist. "No, Isaac. Try your luck somewhere else."

His gaze wandered past me. "Fine. I already have someone else in mind." With a wink, he brushed past me and sauntered away, stumbling a couple steps before he found his groove.

I would have kept on going toward my friends, but he was headed straight for Izzy—the easiest target. Her cheeks flared when she saw him coming for her. No way I was letting him dig his claws in her.

Before he could reach her, I sprinted in front of him and pushed my hand into his chest. "Not here, either. Go somewhere else." I shook my head. "Actually, don't go to anyone. I'm sure if someone wants you, they'll come to you."

Isaac grinned, looking over my shoulder. "Izzy is a big girl. I'm sure she's capable of making her own decisions."

When it came to guys, Izzy closed down. She didn't know how to speak to them. I wasn't so sure if she'd be capable of pushing Isaac away if she didn't want anything. Not because she wasn't strong, but because she'd freeze in terror.

I snapped my fingers, trying to get Isaac to look at me, but he kept his drunken focus on Izzy. I blew out a loud breath. "Seriously, Isaac, leave. You're drunk and not thinking clearly. I'm not letting you near my friends."

Isaac finally looked at me. "I just want to see if she's as easy as you."

My hands balled into fists. I had to refrain from punching him, even though I desperately wanted to.

Jordyn stepped up to my side. Then Ava came to my other.

"I think she told you to leave," Jordyn said. She had her head held high, her confidence radiating off her.

"And I think Izzy needs a chance to speak for herself." Isaac looked at her expectantly.

I nodded my head at Izzy. "Go ahead, Izzy. Tell Isaac to get lost."

"Hey, now," Isaac said. "She also has the option of saying she would love to go somewhere quiet with me."

"That's not happening," Ava said through clenched teeth.

Izzy swallowed. "I don't want to go anywhere with you." Her voice was barely audible.

Isaac took a step closer and cupped his hand over his ear. "What did you say?"

Izzy lifted her head, her voice firm. "No."

I couldn't help but smile at her. I shooed Isaac back with my hands. "Go away. There's nothing here for you."

He finally left, but not without flashing a chilling smile. I hurried over to Izzy. "I'm so sorry. I never thought my stupid actions would reflect on my friends."

Izzy lifted her shoulder in a shrug. "It was his choice to act like a creep. Besides, you stopped him before he could try anything." She threw her arms around my neck. "Thank you."

I hugged her back. "Of course. There's no way I'm letting those I love make the same mistake I did."

It still didn't change the fact that it probably wouldn't have happened if I hadn't made out with Isaac so easily.

We'd created a small crowd, which I didn't notice until I released Izzy from our embrace. Maybe people would get the idea that I'm not as easy as I appeared to be.

CHAPTER 45

*W*hen I left Izzy and the others, I went to find Mason. I needed to apologize for what happened on social media. Even though I'd made sure to say online that nothing happened, people still didn't believe me. They went off what the picture looked like.

Mason was with some of his buddies near a fire. When we made eye contact, a little bit of worry settled in his eyes. I was probably the last person he wanted to talk to.

I slowly approached him. "Hey, Mason, can we talk?"

He nodded at his friends, and then steered me away from the group. "What's up?"

"I need to apologize." Instinct made me want to reach out and touch his arm, just a friendly gesture, but I was starting to think there wasn't such a thing. "I'm so sorry that picture got put online. I didn't know we were being watched."

"I figured," he said. "It's actually kind of creepy to think that someone was watching us like that. Looks like they waited for the perfect moment to snap a picture."

I sighed. "I never expected all this blow-out." I twiddled my fingers. "I hope I didn't totally ruin your social game."

Mason laughed. "I've never had one, so we're good."

I couldn't help but laugh along with him. I glanced over to see Hayley watching us. I gave her a soft smile before I turned back to Mason. "And I hope my actions don't reflect upon Hayley. She's so much smarter than me and would never do anything this stupid."

"You didn't do anything stupid." He blushed. "There's nothing wrong with kissing a few people."

"Yeah, sure, when they're spread out. Not when they're back to back." I twisted my lips to the side. "So, are we cool?"

He nodded. "We're cool." He looked over at Hayley. "Can you, uh, help ease me into a conversation with her?"

"Of course." I motioned for him to follow me. I ignored all the stares as we maneuvered through the crowd.

Hayley had her serious eyes on me when we approached her. She stretched out her neck. "Do I need to beat anyone up?" She nodded her head toward Isaac, who had moved on to flirting with some other junior—who also didn't seem to be feeling it.

"I took care of it." I motioned to Mason. "Thank goodness Mason is the most forgiving person ever." I stopped myself before I said the rest of what I'd thought: I hated that I wasted a kiss on a guy like Isaac when it should have been a guy like Mason.

Mason waved awkwardly at Hayley. "Hey."

She barely bit her lip on the side. "Hey yourself."

His eyes slipped down to her lips, which was probably her intention.

"So, I hear to you love The Shack," Hayley said.

I caught Kaitlyn's eye, and we left Hayley and Mason alone. Mason had said he was bad at starting conversations, but Hayley wasn't. She'd put him at ease in no time.

Kaitlyn linked her arm with mine. "How's everything with your mom?"

I leaned my head on her shoulder and sighed. "Terrible. I'm starting to feel bad about blowing up at her. But she just makes me so mad. How hard is it to spend a few minutes talking to your daughter every day? It's not like I'm demanding her attention twenty-four seven."

She rubbed my arm, the breeze sending her thick, curly hair swirling around. "I wish I knew what to say. You deserve to have a mom who's in your life."

We stopped near a fire pit and sat down on the sand beside it. The light from the flames lit up Kaitlyn's beautiful eyes. She grinned at me. "I forgot to tell you this when we were still with Hayley, but she'll have to find out later. My family and I are going to the lake for a week next month, and my parents said you and Hayley can come!"

I fingered the leather bracelet on my wrist. "I'd love that. It's so what I need right now."

"Dad rented jet skis, tubes, water skis, and wake boards. It's going to be a blast."

I thought back to the last time I'd been on a tube at the lake. I'd been there with Kaitlyn's family that time as well. Her dad had sped up so fast that the waves were out of control. I ended up being thrown from the tube and smacked hard into the water. I couldn't wait to do it again.

I opened my mouth, but then noticed Kaitlyn was staring at someone. I followed her gaze to Garrett, his cheesy grin endearing. It clashed with his chiseled jaw and model appearance. They were officially a couple, and it was going so well. I'd never seen Kaitlyn this happy.

If things went well with Mason, maybe Hayley would be back in the relationship game, too. That would just leave me, and for once, I was okay with that. I didn't need a guy to define me.

I bumped Kaitlyn's arm. "Go to him. He's making lovey-dovey eyes at you, and it's grossing me out."

Kaitlyn rolled her eyes. "You love that kind of stuff."

"I do." I pushed her. "Now, go to your man."

She frowned, but there was excitement in her eyes. "What about you?"

I searched through the crowd until I spotted Liam hanging out near another fire. "I have another apology I need to take care of."

"You sure?" Kaitlyn asked, but she was already getting to her feet.

"Yep." I smiled at her as she skipped toward Garrett and threw her arms around him. He gave her the sweetest peck on the cheek, making her giggle. So freaking adorable.

CHAPTER 37

*S*tanding, I brushed off my capris and headed toward Liam. His voice got louder as I closed in. He was talking about the latest horror movie he saw. I'd wanted to see it, but had no one to go with. Plus, I hadn't had the time.

He was wearing a T-shirt that said *Director* on top, and his hair was the perfect amount of mess that I'd love to run my fingers through. I quickly pushed the thought from my head. No guys. Not yet.

The smile I had on my face faded when I saw Sadie next to him, her hands on his arm. Another party she'd sneaked into, but she hadn't been the only sophomore I'd seen.

The stupid grin on his face didn't falter when he saw me. In fact, it only got wider. He patted his knee. "We were just talking about you. Come have a seat."

Sadie frowned at Liam's hand, still beckoning to me. Before I could move—not that I would have—Sadie sat down in Liam's lap, smiling seductively the whole time. Liam just patted his other knee.

"I've got two," he said to me. When Sadie pouted, he poked her nose, and she giggled.

I had to keep myself from throwing up in the fire pit. Or all over Sadie. What did he see in her?

Sadie glared at me. "We weren't saying good things, in case you're wondering."

"I wasn't." I turned my attention to Liam. "Can we talk?"

He patted his leg again. "Sure."

I held in an eye roll. "In private."

A few people around the fire pit let out some whistles. Probably not the best approach I could have made.

Liam tilted his head to the side and shook his index finger at me. "I'm not that kind of guy, Camille. I'm sure you'll find someone else willing to go somewhere *private* with you."

A guy, who I was pretty certain was a sophomore, held up his hand. "I'm willing."

Liam chuckled, and the anger boiled inside of me, steamy and wild. He'd always given me a hard time, but he'd never let someone talk to me like that. At least, not before. Had his opinion of me fallen that hard?

I folded my arms. "Wow, Liam. I always thought you were better than the rest of them, but it turns out you're just like them."

His smile tightened. "Like you should be talking."

"Really?" I bit off the swear words that wanted to fly. "All those things posted about me weren't true, which you know."

"Do I?" He rubbed his chin. "Because it all seemed real to me."

Pete chose the wrong moment to walk up and join the group. He smirked at me. "Really gone off the deep end, haven't you, Camille? You know whoring yourself around won't make Dylan take you back."

It was like everything buried inside me broke free. I flung myself at Pete, sending us both to the ground. I punched him in the stomach a couple times before he grabbed my hand to stop me. He flipped me onto my back, holding me down by the shoulders.

The nice thing about being "thick," as Pete called it, was that I was way stronger than the guy. Pushing my hand into his face, I dug my fingernails into his skin until he jerked away, and then I kicked him hard in the stomach, sending him flying onto his back. Hearing him gasp for air was the best thing I'd heard all night.

"I said go somewhere private," Liam yelled, loud enough for everyone to hear over the commotion. "Unless you're just wanting an audience."

Pete growled at me and scrambled to his feet, sand coating his clothes. "Like I'd do anything with *her*." His disheveled hair added a feral aura to him that made me flinch.

I stumbled further back into the sand, bumping into someone. Two sturdy hands helped me up.

"Need some help?" Brady asked. His salty glare landed on Liam, and for the first time that night, the arrogance on Liam's face faltered.

I brushed off the sand. "Just keep that loser away from me, and I'll be fine." I pointed at Pete, who was holding his hand against his stomach.

Pete grimaced in pain. "What do you get in return?" He was looking at Brady.

"What?" Brady asked. He stood tall, his arms resting casually at his sides.

Pete swung a hand toward me. "What do you get for sticking up for her? I'm sure she'll reward you."

My hands balled into fists, and I went toward Pete again, but Brady got there first and punched Pete in the jaw.

Pete doubled over, holding his hand against his chin and swearing.

"Don't talk about her like that," Brady said. He glanced around at all the juniors who had stopped to watch. "What's wrong with all of you? You're acting like you've never met Camille. So what if she kissed a few guys? If it had been me kissing a bunch of girls, would any of you have said something?"

A lot of pairs of eyes went to the ground.

"Of course you wouldn't," he said. "You'd be clapping me on the back and congratulating me." He placed his hand on my shoulder before his eyes went to Liam. "A few consensual kisses is nothing. Anyone who actually knew the real Camille would know she wouldn't sleep around. She's not like that. She's better than a majority of you. I'm happy to consider her a friend."

Kaitlyn and Hayley appeared at my side, along with Mason and Garrett. They formed a pack around me, blocking people from getting to me. Soon, the softball players squeezed their way around us.

Jordyn lifted her chin. "If any of you have a problem with Camille, you'll have to go through all of us first."

An overwhelming pride swelled up in my heart. I had real friends. They were standing up for me, even when I had done something completely stupid. They knew my heart, and that was what mattered.

Alejandro joined us and looked out at the other juniors. "Being one of the guys that Camille supposedly hooked up with, I'll have you know we only kissed. Not that it's any of your business. It was a mutual kiss and a one-time thing."

Brady nodded. "Same here."

I didn't think Mason would actually say something, but he did. "Camille and I never hooked up. No kiss or anything. She's not like that."

A throat cleared, and I turned to see Dylan walking toward the group surrounding me. His eyes searched mine, like he was looking for approval. So I nodded at him.

"Camille's a good person," Dylan said. All eyes turned to

him. "I lied about her being a bad kisser." He glanced over his shoulder at Raelynn. "I was just trying to impress a girl, so I said something stupid." His gaze wandered back over to me. "I think we've all done and said stupid things to impress someone. It's in our nature." He addressed the crowd. "Just leave her alone. She doesn't deserve all the lies and rumors."

I wanted to hug the guy to thank him, but I didn't want him or anyone else to take it the wrong way. So I just smiled instead.

Alejandro turned to the group surrounding me, shutting out all the haters. "Who's up for a night wiffle ball game? I've got some glow-in-the-dark wiffle balls and bats I've been dying to use."

I rubbed my hands together. "That sounds awesome."

"And so much better than this stupid party," Hayley said.

I raised my eyebrows. "Are you going to actually play this time?"

She bumped Mason, who blushed. "Only if I'm on this guy's team."

Kaitlyn took my hand. "Let's go play some wiffle ball!"

CHAPTER 38

The next morning, I slept in. I didn't get home until well after one in the morning, and I didn't care. It wasn't like I could get in trouble. I'd have to have a mom who paid attention for that to happen. And Dad always felt too guilty about Mom to punish me.

I rolled out of bed close to noon and took a long, hot shower. While I was getting dressed, my tummy rumbled. I needed some food pronto.

As I descended the stairs, I smelled bacon, and I practically drooled. The world was a better place because of bacon.

I hopped down the last couple steps and danced toward the kitchen. "What a glorious day!" I paused, my arms raised in the air, when I saw my mom standing over the bacon on the stove.

Dad was beside her, slicing some fresh tomatoes. Seth sat at the stool in front of the counter, beaming like I hadn't seen in the longest time.

I lowered my arms and joined Seth at the counter, sliding onto a stool. "Um, what's going on?"

Seth scoffed. "They're making lunch, dummy."

Dad pointed his knife at Seth. "Don't call your sister that."

Seth raised his arms in the air, his wide eyes on the knife. "Yes, sir."

Mom chuckled as she flipped the bacon. Seeing her cook left me surprised, but also warm with happiness. It had been so long, I'd forgotten she did actually know how to cook. She smiled over her shoulder me. "You still like it crispy, right?"

All I could do was nod. My gaze wandered between my mom humming while she cooked, to Dad dancing along to Mom's music as he cut, to Seth drumming his hands on the counter. They'd created their own melody, just like the old days. A pang struck my heart, and I wasn't sure if it was good or not. The sight made me so happy, but there was the fear that it wouldn't last. Mom would go back to her regular routine the second lunch was over.

"Camille," Seth shouted to snap me out of my reverie. "You're on guitar!"

Years ago, I would have eaten that up and joined in on the fun. But the skeptical side of me couldn't do it. I didn't want to set myself up for a letdown. My heart couldn't take it. I needed to busy myself to keep from crying. When had I become such a crybaby?

I hopped down from the stool and joined Dad. "Anything I can do to help?"

Dad nodded at the bread on the counter. "It's time to toast the bread for those who want it that way."

Seth held up his hand. "I do! But not too dark. A golden brown would be perfect." He pressed his fingers to his lips, and then kissed them away.

"Yes, your majesty." I curtsied, making him laugh. "Anyone else have special orders for their *toast*?"

"The golden brown does sound nice," Dad said.

"Yes, it does," Mom said.

I popped four pieces of toast into our large toaster. I set the dial to medium and pressed down, the electricity buzzing. "I'm so glad they installed a golden-brown setting on here. Makes my life easier."

Seth jumped down from his seat and ran around to my side. "They did not!"

I ran my palm over the top of his Mohawk. "Of course they didn't. But I got you off your butt."

"Dad! Camille said 'butt!'" He stuck his tongue out at me, which was difficult with the wide grin on his face.

"She was referring to your buttocks, or your gluteus maximus. Therefore, it's okay." Dad grabbed the lettuce out of the fridge and took it to the sink to wash it off.

Seth cracked up and couldn't stop. It wasn't long until I was laughing as well, because it was so contagious.

When Seth had finally calmed down, Dad had him help set the table. That left me alone with Mom in the kitchen. She'd just finished with the bacon. I was on my last set of toast. I stared at the toaster, willing it to go faster.

"Camille." Mom's soft voice came from my right side.

I kept my focus on the toaster so I wouldn't have to look her in the eyes.

She draped her arm around my shoulders. "Sweetie, I'm sorry I've been absent lately. I've been thinking about everything you've said, and you're right. I'm going to do my best to dial back on my work." She smiled at Dad in the dining room, who was deep in a place setting competition with Seth.

The toast popped up, so I grabbed a piece.

"Dad's going to take my phone from me every weekday from six to nine," Mom said.

The warm toast in my hand fell onto the counter. I quickly scooped it up and set it on the plate with the others. "Do you think you can handle that?"

She bumped my hip with hers. "Very funny." Then she

sighed. "But I'm not sure. It will definitely take some getting used to."

Mom wrapped her arms around me, pulling me into a hug. "I hope you can forgive me, Camille. I'm going to try to be better, I promise."

I'd stiffened at first, not wanting to fall into a trap. But then my body relaxed into hers. It had been so long since my mom had hugged me. I missed it. I breathed her in. Past the smell of bacon that now clung to her hair, I could smell her warm vanilla perfume.

"The food is getting cold!" Seth did his unfortunately amazing whine, making Mom and me end our embrace and laugh.

Dad beamed at the two of us, probably happy to see us getting along. But it was still a small step. Mom was there for lunch on a weekend, but that didn't mean I'd be able to talk to her whenever I wanted. I'd gotten to the point where I wasn't sure I wanted her advice. It didn't hold the same value that it used to. It would have to be something we worked toward.

We sat down at the table and enjoyed our BLTs as a family. No cell phones allowed. It was perfect.

Things were slowly falling back into place. I'd mended my relationship with my mom. The softball team didn't hate me anymore, and I had the possibility of getting back on the team for my senior year. Coach Wilkes would be hard to crack, but with the girls on my side, we might wear her down.

My anger toward Dylan had melted. There was no way we'd be friends like he'd been hoping, but I could say hi to him at a party or passing in the hall at school without wanting to vomit.

I was in a good place with Hayley and Kaitlyn, but I always had been. They'd stayed by my side through my entire idiot Dylan phase.

My kiss list hadn't all be checked off, but I was okay with that. In fact, it made me happy. There was a small victory in knowing I came to my senses before I was done. Granted, there was only one guy left, but it was still something.

Brady, Alejandro, and Mason were all in a good place with me, and that alone made me happy. My eyes had been opened to the fact that Isaac was such a jerk, but I didn't regret kissing him. I think I learned the most from that kiss. Kissing wouldn't solve all my worries. It was something to be saved for a meaningful relationship with someone I cared about, and they cared about me in return.

Something still felt off, though. And I knew exactly what it was.

PART 3: BACK TO SCHOOL

CHAPTER 39

*T*he rest of the summer passed in a blur. I spent a lot of my time with Hayley and Kaitlyn. Whenever they were with their boyfriends—they'd both reached that phase with Mason and Garrett—I was either with my softball friends or my family.

It was really hard for Mom at first, dialing back her work. But she finally found a groove that worked for everyone. The ironic thing was that she started winning more cases as her hours went down, giving her more clients. Spending time away from work and being with her family had reduced her stress considerably, so she was happier and more pleasant to be around.

By the time my senior year started, we were all in a good place.

But I still hadn't been able to crack Liam. Anytime I saw him at a party or get-together, he'd ignore me. There were a few times when we'd gone to the movies with him and Brady, and he still wouldn't talk to me.

So, I kept my interactions with him short and polite. I smiled whenever he looked at me. I complimented him on things he said and did. But the wall he had built wouldn't crack. Not even the tiniest bit.

I missed having him as a friend. I'd forgotten how much we had in common. I wanted him to be my movie buddy. I wanted to go to him when I was having a bad day because he always knew how to cheer me up in such a natural way.

Mostly, I wanted to be with him. He was the kind of guy I could picture settling down with. Years in the future, of course. But he'd keep me grounded. He liked me for who I was. I just needed to remind him of that.

Anytime I saw him in the hall at school, I'd try to stop him for a short chat, but he'd get away as soon as he could. If the anger boiled to the surface, I turned off the heat. I didn't want to get mad at him to get my way.

It was a month before Homecoming, and I wanted to ask Liam to go with me. I didn't want to wait long because I knew he'd be snatched up fast. He'd hurry to ask someone just to make sure I couldn't. But I wouldn't let that happen.

I had to think of something creative to get his attention. Something to tell him that I liked him and wanted to be with him.

Hayley, Mason, Kaitlyn, Garrett, and I were sitting in the cafeteria during lunch one day. I'd gotten used to being the fifth wheel, and I was okay with it. There were times when Brady or Val would join us, but that day it was just the five of us. They were all lined up on the other side of the table from me, like some panel at a comic convention, and I was the captivated audience with a million questions.

I popped a grape into my mouth. "How can I ask Liam to Homecoming?"

Mason flushed. "Are we supposed to be asking people already?" He swallowed, staring at his food. I loved that no matter how long he and Hayley had been together, he still got nervous about things. She still made his heart flutter. By the wicked grin on her lips, he did the same to Hayley. They just showed it in two completely different ways.

I shook my head, pointing a grape at him. "I gotta make a move before someone else does."

"Why do you think so many girls want him?" Hayley asked, massaging the back of Mason's neck. "He's not *that* great."

I threw the grape at her nose. "He is *that* great, and it's not so much that other girls will be asking him, it's that I know he'd ask anyone just to avoid me asking him."

Garrett lowered the massive sandwich that had almost made it to his mouth. The guy could eat a surprising amount of food, but he needed the calories. He was always in motion, playing sports or working out. "If he doesn't like you, why do you want to go with him?"

Kaitlyn rolled her eyes and pushed him on the arm. She had her curly hair down, falling around her shoulders like an exotic waterfall. "He does like her. He's just being stupid."

"They'd go perfect together," Hayley said. "Like pickles and peanut butter."

Kaitlyn gagged, ruining her exotic charm. "That's a terrible combination."

Mason grinned and wrapped his arm around Hayley. "To most people, yeah, but it's her favorite." He kissed her on the cheek. She acted nonchalant about it, but excitement danced in her eyes. The knowing smile from Kaitlyn told me she noticed it as well. I loved seeing them both so happy.

I tapped the table. "We're getting off topic here. I need a clever way to ask him to Homecoming. A way he can't say no to."

Kaitlyn placed her hand over her heart, the charms on her bracelet clinking together. "Or a way for him to realize his undying love for Cam-I-Am."

Her use of his nickname for me made me more determined than ever. I wanted to hear him say it again. I'd once hated it, but now I kind of liked it.

"Why can't you just go up to him and say, 'Hey, you wanna go to Homecoming with me?'" Garrett leaned his folded arms on the table. We all turned to him, and he pulled back his long neck in surprise. "What?"

Kaitlyn held up her index finger, her charm bracelet sliding down her arm. "First off, you better be thinking of an amazingly creative way to ask me." She held up another finger. "If Camille asks him flat-out like that, he'll say no."

I pulled out a piece of paper and a pen from my backpack. "I need to make a list of all the things he loves." Caramel popcorn, horror movies, and Dr Pepper were on top of the list.

The bench shifted next to me as someone sat down. I looked up to see Brady straddling the bench. He stared down at my list. "This looks like a Liam list." He raised his eyebrows at me. "Is this a Liam list?"

I nodded, pushing my bag of grapes closer to him. "I'm trying to think of a way to ask him to Homecoming. I thought it would be best to start with the things he loves."

Brady pointed to the paper before he grabbed a handful of grapes. "Add *Stranger Things*. He's been binge-watching the series. Again."

"Me, too!" I added it to the list. We could have been binge-watching the show together, but Liam had to go and be stubborn.

"Bocce ball," Brady said.

"Bocce ball?" Hayley had her red eyebrows scrunched together in confusion. She wasn't one to play outdoor sports or sports in general. She stuck to the music scene.

"It's a yard game." I wrote it down on the paper. I smiled, remembering the shirt he'd worn to summer camp.

Brady juggled his last three grapes, his gaze on super

focus. "The guy is obsessed lately. He wants to start a bocce ball league and do competitions and everything. I told him the school probably wouldn't get on board with that."

"Why not?" Garrett asked, scratching Kaitlyn's back. "They have clubs for everything. Why not a bocce ball club?"

I snapped my fingers. "I could start a bocce ball club. In his name, of course. I'll just get the ball rolling." I laughed at my pun but stopped short when I noticed I was the only one. Liam would have laughed.

"*We could have a bocce ball together at Homecoming,*" Kaitlyn said in a haughty tone. When everyone snickered, I put my hand on my hip.

"Really? That got a laugh?" I asked.

Hayley shrugged. "Hers was just real cheesy."

Kaitlyn slapped her on the arm. "It was brilliant."

I stared at the paper. There were so many things to work with. I could get Liam a basket of things he likes and say I'd be a basket case if he didn't go to Homecoming with me. Or I could somehow work *Stranger Things* into the question. I could make a creative poster for it.

A sly grin spread across my face. I would find a way to make Liam say yes, whether he liked it or not.

CHAPTER 40

$\mathcal{M}$om helped me put together a basket full of goodies for Liam when she got home from work. We made caramel popcorn—and consumed as much as we gave away—using our family recipe that was a hit every holiday season.

I stuffed the basket full of Twix, Rolos, and Caramellos. Then I lined the outer area with Dr Pepper. I made my mom write out the letter since she had way better penmanship than me. She wrote exactly what I'd thought of: I'll be a basket case if you don't go to Homecoming with me. I signed my name in the scribbly way he always made fun of in elementary school.

Together, my mom and I drove over to his house, and I set the basket on the front porch. I rang the doorbell, and then sprinted toward the car. I'd left the passenger door open so I could just slip on in.

"Hurry!" Mom hissed as I ran toward her.

I hopped in the car and slammed the door. "Go! Go! Go!"

She took off down the street, and then rounded back so we could sneak a peak of Liam's reaction from far away.

Only, his dad answered the door. He picked up the basket, stuffed a Rolo bar into his pocket, and shut the door.

I slumped in my seat. "Now I'll have to wait to see what he says."

Mom reached over and patted my arm. "I'm sure he'll be calling any second now. He would be crazy to turn you down. I mean, that's homemade caramel popcorn in there."

I grinned at her. "He'd be stupid to say no after that."

We left Liam's street, and I smiled the whole way home. As the night dragged on, the smile slowly fell off my face. I checked my phone dozens of times. I scoped out social media to see if he'd uploaded a picture or tagged me in anything.

Nothing.

It took forever to fall asleep that night. My eyes were like lead weights the next morning, but I forced myself up and to school. Liam was nowhere to be found. I know because I searched. Everywhere. By the time I got to the class we had together, I slumped in exhaustion.

Liam was casually sitting in his seat, leaning so his elbow was resting on the back of his chair. And he didn't look in my direction or give any indication that he'd received the best basket of his life. Maybe his dad hadn't given it to him. I mean, he did pocket one of the candy bars. Maybe he stole the rest of it because it was so tasty.

As soon as the bell rang to signal the end of class, I hopped from my seat and jogged over to Liam. "Hey, Liam!"

"Hi." He pushed out the door and down the hall.

I hurried to catch up to him. "Get anything exciting yesterday?"

"No." He kept his eyes trained forward.

Had his dad really kept the basket for himself? I did write Liam's name on the card. It wasn't like a first come, first serve basis with the gift.

"Nothing was delivered to your house?"

He finally looked at me, his blue eyes lacking emotion of any kind. "I have no idea what you're talking about." He took a Caramello bar out of his pocket, pulled back the wrapper, and took a huge bite. With a grin, he left me standing there, stunned.

So, he had received the basket. And he was flat out refusing me.

My cheeks burned hot as I glanced around the hall. Obviously, no one would know what had just happened, but I was still so embarrassed. How could he be *that* mad at me? Everyone else had forgiven me. The rumor mill had moved on to other people.

Kaitlyn rounded the corner and spotted me. Her constant smile turned into a frown as she rushed to me, her long legs having her in front of me in no time. "What happened?"

"It didn't work."

She threw her arms around me. "I can't believe he didn't say yes. What's wrong with him? He's never been this stubborn before."

A little rational part of my brain said I was being stupid by trying so hard, but I didn't want to give up quite yet.

"I guess it's time for round two," I said.

CHAPTER 41

After school, Hayley and Kaitlyn came home with me so we could work on a poster. I drew the *Stranger Things* logo on top, taking my time so it looked halfway decent. Then I wrote: "In the newest season, Liam accepts Cam-I-Am's Homecoming proposal. Stranger things have happened." Underneath that I wrote: "Starring Liam Elliott and Camille Collins." I also gave it a four-star review, saying it was "Breathtaking and unbelievably captivating. Critics are going wild."

I held the finished product up for my friends to see.

Hayley snapped a picture with her phone. "He'd have to be an idiot to turn this one down. It screams *Liam*."

"You have to stay this time," Kaitlyn said.

My hands shook. I thought I'd just drop it off like the day before. "Why?"

She stood, straightening out her jean shorts. "So you don't have to wait for an answer."

"So he can't say no to your face," Hayley said, fiddling with a daith earring.

My heart thudded in my chest. "What if he does say no?"

"He won't," Kaitlyn said.

At the same time, Hayley said, "Then we'll go get a Dr Pepper slushy from the Fill-N-Go. The biggest size they have." She smirked. "And maybe we can buy an extra one and chuck it at Liam's car."

I made Kaitlyn drive so I wouldn't have to. My stomach was clenched tight, my heartbeat so loud in my ears, it drowned out the blaring music. If Liam said no, there was no way I could drive after that. I wasn't sure if I could handle another rejection from him.

Kaitlyn left the engine running when she pulled along the curb in front of Liam's house. I had the poster rolled up in my lap, my legs bouncing like crazy.

Hayley leaned forward from the back seat. "You can do this, Camille. Just go ring the doorbell."

"You don't even have to say anything," Kaitlyn said. "Just hold up the sign."

Closing my eyes, I took lots of deep breaths, hoping to get my heart to settle down. When I was convinced that it wouldn't, I forced myself out of the car and up the walk. My legs were like two thick sticks of putty on the verge of a complete meltdown.

I was a warrior. I could do this.

I applied some lip gloss real quick, and then put it back in my pocket. My trembling finger pushed the doorbell, and then I held the poster in my shaking hands. After thirty seconds—I counted—I knocked on the door. After another thirty seconds, I rang the doorbell again. Liam's car was in the driveway. I knew he was there.

Unless he'd gone somewhere with his family. I was about to walk away when the door swung open. Liam leaned against the doorway and munched on one of the Twix bars I'd given him.

He lazily read my sign as I held it up for him to see. He

threw his head back and swallowed the candy in his mouth. His attention went back to me. "I already have a date. Sorry." He moved to close the door, but I finally found my voice.

"What? Who?"

Liam grinned. "I believe you met her. Sadie."

I placed a hand on my queasy stomach. Sadie? He asked *her*? "When did you ask her?"

"Today." He took another bite of his candy and put his hand on the door. "Can I shut this now, or are you just going to stand there all night?"

I lowered the sign to my side. "Why are you being like this?"

"Being like what?"

I threw out my arm. "This arrogant jerk. What happened to the Liam I adore? The one who'd run secret missions with me, watch horror movies, and eat all the caramel popcorn we could find?"

He shrugged. "He grew up and realized he lives in reality land, not fairytale land." He huffed. "Listen, I'm just not into you like that. You need to learn to take a hint."

Licking my lips, I took a step back. "It's funny that you got on my case for changing and losing the real me, yet you've gone and done the same thing." He opened his mouth, but I cut him off. "I miss the old Liam. The one who would banter with me and make me feel better when I was having a bad day. I miss the guy I fell in love with." I slapped my hand over my mouth, realizing what I had said.

Liam finally dropped his bored look and replaced it with utter shock, the same emotion I was feeling.

But I wouldn't take it back. I *had* fallen in love with him. It had been a slow process, but in the end, he was the one I wanted to be with.

I held out the poster. "Here. Keep it, so maybe one day you'll remember us and think about what we could have had."

He took it from my hands, looking it over like he was finally reading it for the first time. Then his stunned blue eyes found mine.

"I was stupid, I know that," I said. "I messed up big time. Making a kiss list was the biggest mistake of my life. I guess I was just so desperate for approval." I folded my arms, wishing he was holding me. "But I got my mom back, so things are looking up." Though, that was only one piece of my broken heart replaced.

I stepped closer to him, hoping he could hear my pounding heart and know how much I meant every word. "Just know, Liam, that you're the only guy I ever want to kiss." Standing on my tiptoes, I choked down the tears and lightly pecked his cheek. I couldn't meet his eyes when I turned and walked away.

Hayley and Kaitlyn were watching me the entire walk back to the car, Kaitlyn having to really lower her head so she could see out the window. It wasn't like it was a long walkway, but it sure stretched on, getting longer with each step. It was my walk of shame. I'd finally found *the guy* I wanted to have a serious relationship with and kiss only him, and I'd completely blown it with my stupid hormones.

I got into the car and buckled up. "Let's go."

"What happened?" Kaitlyn asked, tapping her long fingers on the gear shift. "We couldn't tell if it was good or bad."

"Bad." I folded my arms. "Now drive."

Kaitlyn glanced at Hayley before she put the car in drive and pulled away from the curb. I filled them in on the entire interaction on the drive back to my house.

"You admitted you're in love with him?" Hayley whistled. "Camille, that's huge."

"It's stupid." I wiped at a stray tear that had escaped my left eye.

Kaitlyn shook her head, her curly hair bouncing. "It's

huge. You never told Dylan you loved him, and you were with him for over a year."

I pinched my skin, trying to keep myself from crying. If I started, I worried I might not stop. I'd never felt this strongly about a guy before. "That's because I never loved him."

"Which is why this is *huge*," Hayley said. "You've finally found someone to love."

"And you're so not going to pout and throw it all away." Kaitlyn's hands were wrapped tightly around the steering wheel, the chair far back to accommodate her long legs. "We can fix this. We can fix anything. It's what we do."

I leaned my head against the headrest. "He's already said no twice. He's going with Sadie to Homecoming. What else can I do without being desperate? No guy wants *that*."

Hayley swore under her breath, then sent a quick apology skyward. "I bet you anything he's not going with Sadie. He probably just said that to upset you."

"He can't even stand her," Kaitlyn said. When I turned to her in surprise, she continued. "Brady told me. We've been talking about you guys, wondering how we can get the two of you together. It's like everyone can see you're meant to be except for Liam."

I stared out the window. "Maybe that's a sign we aren't meant to be."

"He's being stubborn," Hayley said with a growl. "He likes you, he just can't lower his pretentious manly guard."

"Brady said Liam has been wary of relationships since his first girlfriend broke his heart," Kaitlyn said.

I thought back, trying to think of who Liam had dated. The only girl I could think of was in middle school. "Jill?"

"Yep," Kaitlyn said. "She cheated on him and wasn't even sorry for doing it. She just toyed with Liam, playing him like a puppet to get him to do whatever she wanted. She knew what a nice guy he is, so she used him. He was like her picture-perfect boyfriend, and she was getting the action on the side with someone else."

Hayley scoffed. "Why do girls like the bad guys so much? They're bad. I mean, it's in their title." She tapped the center console. "Mason? He's a good guy, and the best guy I've ever dated. There's nothing wrong with a guy who respects you."

Hearing those words out of her mouth made a smile find its way to my face. She would have never said that with her old boyfriend. He'd been one of the bad boys and lived fully up to his name. I'd worried she'd never see the truth, but she finally did.

"What about the bocce ball club?" Kaitlyn said, stopping at a light.

"I don't think that would actually work," I said. "It's not exactly like asking him to Homecoming."

Kaitlyn's eyes lit up in excitement. "He just wants a grand gesture. He wants you to prove that you really do like him. Actions speak louder than words." She glanced in my direction. "You of all people should understand that."

"He probably wants to be the one to ask *you* to Homecoming," Hayley said, plopping back in the middle seat. "Because of his overrated man-card."

Kaitlyn looked in the rearview mirror at her. "I could so see that. He's the type who would have planned the whole thing out years ago, and she went and did it first."

I turned to them. "He wouldn't have asked me."

Hayley rolled her eyes. "Well, not now. Not after everything that's happened. But he probably planned the perfect way to ask a girl to Homecoming back in middle school in a color-coordinated planner, and when you show up with some killer invites, he was reminded of it."

"You're just making up stories to make me feel better," I said, twirling my bracelet around my wrist.

"Is it working?" Kaitlyn asked.

I smiled. "A little." I tapped my finger against my lips. "Maybe I could challenge him to a game of bocce ball. If I win, he has to go to Homecoming with me."

"And if you don't?" Kaitlyn asked, intrigue in her tone.

"I'll drop it all and leave him alone." I hated the thought of not having Liam in my life, but I couldn't force someone to love me.

Hayley clucked her tongue. "Do you even know how to play bocce ball?"

I shrugged. "I've played it before. How hard could it be?"

Hayley whistled. "Famous last words."

Question was, would Liam accept the challenge?

CHAPTER 42

$\mathcal{W}$hen I talked to the front office about starting a bocce ball club, they said I had to go through Coach Wilkes. She usually passed on any new athletic clubs. I tried not to take it as a bad sign. But I also brought Val and Izzy with me for backup.

We caught Coach Wilkes at the end of her last math class of the day. She was walking out of the building with a scowl on her face, setting her visor into place on her head. Not the best start, but she looked over and saw us, so I couldn't turn back now.

I smiled at her. "Hey, Coach! Do you have a minute?"

She folded her arms, glancing between Val and Izzy like she was wondering what they were doing with me. "A few. What can I help you with?"

"I want to start a new club." I used my excited voice that usually got people's attention. Mom always called it my 'over-eager' voice, but whatever.

Coach arched an eyebrow. "What kind of club?"

"A bocce ball club," I said. "Have you played before? It's so much fun, and a great way to get people socializing. It's not that complicated to learn or play."

Coach tapped her shoe on the ground, a steady, impatient beat. I was about to add something when she finally spoke. "No." She turned to leave, so I hurried in front of her.

"Why not?" I asked. "It's a super easy set-up, and I'm going to donate a couple bocce ball sets to the school, so there's no money involved. And I already have a captain in mind."

"Let me guess, you?" Coach adjusted her visor, scratching her forehead in the process. "No."

I pursed my lips at Val and Izzy. They were doing nothing to help. In fact, they were both on their phone. So much for sticking by my side.

I turned my focus back to the coach. "No, not me. Liam Elliott. He's a natural leader and great at bocce ball. I think he'll be the perfect person to get people to join and make them feel a part of the group. The guy can make friends with anybody."

Coach Wilkes looked over her shoulder at Val and Izzy. "What do you girls think?"

Val tucked her phone into her back pocket and came to my side. "I think it's a brilliant idea."

Izzy skipped to my other side, her phone put away. "Great way for us to work our arm muscles during the off-season. It helps with aim and accuracy."

I hadn't thought of it like that, but I liked where she was going. I nodded. "The balls are the size of softballs, just slightly heavier. Perfect for members of the softball team. And anyone else who wants to join. This won't be an exclusive club or anything." I was rambling. Coach's expression hadn't changed a bit the entire time we talked.

She stared at the three of us, so we all gave her our best

smiles. She sighed. "I'll think about it. Have Liam come to me with his vision for the club. I want statistics and research that shows he knows what he's talking about." With a nod, she left us.

Izzy tucked her hair behind her ear. "I think that went well."

"Do you think Liam would be able to put that all together?" Val asked.

I chuckled. "I'm sure he already has."

The trick would be getting Liam to go talk to Coach. He couldn't hear about her conditions from me—he'd turn it down in a heartbeat. There was one person he'd listen to, though.

I stopped by Brady's house on the way home from school. I'd never get used to the weird feeling of pulling up in front of his exquisite home. I was awed by it every time. I hadn't thought to text him, so I hoped he was home.

After a few taps on the door, plus a doorbell ring, Brady finally answered the door. Shirtless. Sweat slid down his perfect abs.

"Hey, Camille!" He sounded out of breath. "You caught me during a workout. Come on in!"

He held the door open for me. I scanned the foyer and kitchen but didn't see anyone else there. Both his parents worked full time, so it was typical for him to be alone. He motioned for me to follow him.

Brady led me down the hall and into the fitness room. His family had treadmills, ellipticals, bikes, and a huge weight area. They could basically start a fitness club inside their home.

He laid down on a bench and set his hand on the bar holding huge weights. "Spot me."

I went around and stood behind him, my hands held out in front of me as he lifted.

"So, what's on your pretty little mind?" He blew deep breaths out of his mouth as he spoke.

"I talked to Coach Wilkes about starting a bocce ball club today." I tried counting the numbers on the weights to see what he was lifting, but I couldn't see all of them. Whatever it was, I doubted me being there would help if they happened to fall.

Brady smiled. "Liam will be excited! Have you told him?"

I shook my head. "That's why I came here. I thought he'd be on board if it came from you."

His smile faltered. "You can't avoid him forever."

"I'm not avoiding him. He's avoiding me."

"Don't you want him to know that it was your doing? I thought you were trying to get him to like you?"

It was so much more complicated than that. I'd originally planned on doing it as a grand gesture. But I didn't want to risk it not working out. Liam really wanted a bocce ball club, so I really wanted him to have it, whether I was involved or not.

Brady finished his reps, and then moved on to the leg machine. I sat down in his vacated spot—after I wiped it down with a towel.

"I want Liam to be happy," I said, staring at the tiled floor. "If that doesn't involve me, then so be it." I forced myself to look at him.

"I didn't take you as the type to give up," Brady said. I tried not to stare at his pecs as his chest heaved in and out from the strenuous work.

"I'm not. But I know when I've been defeated. If I keep throwing myself at him, it will just look pathetic. He knows my feelings for him. The ball's in his court."

Brady grinned. "I heard you're in love with him. I didn't know it was that serious."

Of course, Liam had told him. They were best friends,

after all. I put my hands over my face, wishing I could hide the embarrassment flaming on me. "I didn't know, either. Not until it came out of my mouth. I think I had been avoiding the obvious, just like most things in my life." I took a deep, shaky breath. "I hate that I screwed everything up so bad. We could be perfect together, Liam and me. But I blew it. I didn't realize I loved him until it was too late."

Weights grinded and thunked to a stop. Brady took a seat next to me and wrapped me up in his sweaty arms. I didn't even care how gross it was. He rubbed my back, trying to console me, but it wasn't working. I wanted to be in Liam's arms, not Brady's. I mean, I know Brady wasn't hitting on me or anything, he was just trying to be a good friend.

But then I thought about how it would look if anyone walked into the room. Me, in Brady's shirtless, sweaty arms, and it so wouldn't look good. It was another picture disaster waiting to happen. So, I gently separated myself from Brady, as to not appear rude.

I wiped at some sweat on my arm. "Can you just tell Liam you talked to Coach, and she wants a full report from him about the club?"

Brady nodded. "If that's what you really want, of course. But I still think you should be the one to tell him." He snatched a towel from a nearby rack and wiped himself down. "I hate seeing you like this. I've tried to talk some sense into Liam, but the guy is stubborn. I'm not even entirely sure why he's acting like this. The guy has had a crush on you since elementary school."

I pulled back in surprise. "He has?"

"Um, yeah. Super obvious. Well, that and the fact he's talked about you so much over the years."

My phone buzzed in my pocket with a message from Kaitlyn with a 9-1-1 code. I quickly stood. "I have to go. Thanks for doing this, Brady."

"No problem." He grinned. "See you tomorrow!"

With a tight smile, I hurried down the hall. I threw the front door open and stopped short. Liam stood there, confusion on his face. He looked past me before his gaze landed on my hair. I smoothed it out, realizing it was wet with Brady sweat. I was hitting the shower the second I got home.

"Hey, Liam." I stepped around him and outside of the house, trying not to breathe him in, because if I did, I'd lose control and do something stupid—like kiss him. "Brady is in the fitness room." Liam wore a baby blue shirt that brought out the blue in his eyes, and, gah, I wanted them to look at me with the longing I felt. "That's a good color on you."

"Uh, thanks." He looked down at his shirt with a frown. "I didn't know you would be here."

I waved my hand in what I hoped was a nonchalant manner that wouldn't give away my trembling nerves. "I just swung by for a few minutes. Had some questions about weight-lifting. I need to get back into shape if I plan to make it on the softball team again. I lost so much of my muscles thanks to . . ." I cut off.

There I went again, talking too much. I'd been about to crack a joke about losing my muscles from being Dylan's girlfriend, something I would have said to Kaitlyn or Hayley. Maybe I view Liam more like a best friend than relationship material. But every time I saw him, I buzzed with an energy that made it hard to breathe, and all I wanted to do was slip my hand in his and feel the warmth and every contour mold with mine.

I had the perfect opportunity to challenge him to a bocce ball game, but for some reason, I couldn't get the words out of my mouth. It was such a stupid idea. What if he said no? What if he agreed, but then I lost?

When I realized I was just standing there staring like an idiot, I backed toward my car. "See ya."

After hurrying to get in, I peeled out of the driveway way too fast, my tires screeching. I let up on the gas, my cheeks flushing with embarrassment. I stupidly looked through the rearview mirror to see Liam laughing.

I couldn't get mad at him for laughing, though. I hadn't seen him laugh like that in the longest time, and I wanted it to remain forever.

But then my focus went back to the 9-1-1 code. I wasn't sure if I wanted to find out what was going on, but I drove toward Kaitlyn's house anyway.

CHAPTER 43

*B*oth Kaitlyn and Hayley were waiting in the driveway when I pulled up to Kaitlyn's house. By their faces, whatever was going on wasn't good. Kaitlyn wore her sympathetic expression, while Hayley's was murderous. It meant someone had done something I wouldn't like. Which, really, with everything that had been going on, how could it possibly get worse?

I was to the point of saying, "Just throw it on me. I can take it." After I pulled up to the curb, I put the car in park, took a deep breath, and joined my friends on the driveway.

Hayley had her arms folded, the anger almost making me take a step back so I wouldn't get torched. Kaitlyn put her hand on Hayley's arm, as if to tell her to rein it in, but that wasn't something Hayley knew how to do.

"I'm going to kill her." Hayley ripped her arm away from Kaitlyn and shook her fist. "I'm going to literally murder the self-righteous brat. I'm going to rip her piece by piece until she's nothing. I'm going . . ."

Kaitlyn shouted to be heard over her, throwing out her hands. "Okay! We get it. You want to kill Sadie. We all do.

But we can't because we'll go to jail for murder, which would suck."

My heart sank. Sadie. What had she done? Is that why Liam had gone over to Brady's and had been so shocked to see me? He was about to tell Brady whatever brilliant thing Sadie had done and had felt sorry for me?

My whole mouth went dry. I wanted to ask, but I also didn't, because then I wouldn't have to face reality.

Kaitlyn held up her palms. "Just know that Sadie was just trying to get attention."

"Which she got," Hayley said through gritted teeth. She rounded on Kaitlyn. "I'm not sure why we're still standing here, and not finding her and beating the crap out of her!"

"When did you get so murderous?" Kaitlyn asked, placing her hands on Hayley's shoulders and gently pushing her away.

"Think she's always been that way." I'd finally found my voice. They turned to me, their faces softening. "What did Sadie do?"

They both took deep breaths, and for once, neither of them would speak. They had a fight with their eyes about who had to be the one to tell me.

I pulled my phone out of my back pocket. "I'm sure it's on social media. I'll just see for myself."

Kaitlyn moved to snatch my phone away, but Hayley stopped her and shrugged. "Maybe it's better this way. It will explain everything, and we won't have to."

Kaitlyn dropped her arm with a frown, but also with a nod of agreement.

I found the post right away. Everyone had tagged me in the story. One Sadie had created. If I thought the rumors about me before were bad, I was wrong. Way wrong.

If it hadn't been about me, I would have been impressed with her creative abilities. It was basically a showcase of my desperation and undying love for Liam. There were pictures and videos of my Homecoming proposals—and rejections—to Liam. Then there was my last attempt to win his approval by creating a bocce ball club at school.

My cheeks flushed with anger and embarrassment. All those ideas that I thought were brilliant now looked incredibly pathetic, thanks to her.

Of course, everyone was commenting about what a loser I was, and how I'd never get another guy to date me. No one was focused on the fact that Sadie had a video of me asking Liam to Homecoming. Twice. It meant she was watching from the sideline like some sort of stalker. I could have brought that up, but that wasn't me. I wasn't like her.

How could Liam like a girl like her? He was better than that. At least, I thought he was.

"So, what are we going to do?" Hayley cracked her knuckles. "My mind has already flooded with ideas. So much sabotage and destruction can be done."

I shook my head and tucked my phone away. "No."

"No?" Kaitlyn quirked an eyebrow. "What do you mean, no? This girl humiliated you. You have to do *something*."

Just like Hayley, my mind was racing, just not in the same way. I took a deep breath. "I'm going to do a post and confess everything."

Hayley scrunched her nose. "Why? How will that fix anything? We need to find some dirt on Sadie and . . ."

I cut her off. "No. Just, please, listen. That's not who I am. I've spent the past few months getting smothered in wrong perceptions of me. Revenge would just add to that. I'm not a spiteful person. Sadie can say whatever she wants." I rubbed my forehead, wishing away the headache that was forming. "I just need to put out my side of the story. I'll let everyone choose who to believe."

Hayley scoffed. "Are you insane? The kids at our school have already proved their idiots. They'll choose her!"

"I don't care!" I took a few deep breaths to calm myself. I wouldn't get worked up over this. "They're not all idiots. They're siding with her, and everyone else, because they've only seen one side of the story. No one has seen *my* side. I just need to be honest and open." I backed toward my car. "Now, if you'll excuse me, I have a blog post to write."

Kaitlyn beamed, showing off her pearly whites. "Go get it, girl."

Hayley shook her head but smiled. "You're so much better than me. But go do your thing."

With a grin, I rushed to my car.

*A*s soon as I got home, I headed for the stairs, but Mom called out.

"Camille? Where have you been?"

With a sigh, I turned toward her voice and went into the kitchen. Mom, Dad, and Seth were all setting the table for dinner. The sight softened the need to write. This was exactly what I had wanted—Mom to be home for dinner. The blog could wait.

I turned on a smile. "What's for dinner? It smells delicious." I took a quick sniff to make sure I had been right. I'd been too preoccupied to actually notice the smell when I came in. But then it hit me. "Enchiladas?"

Seth whooped. "I know! It's been too long!"

"You came home at the perfect time," Dad said. "It's all ready."

I joined my family at the dinner table. Seth rattled on about his day as we ate. He'd loved having Mom around as much as I did. Mom and Dad's eyes kept flickering over to me. I was doing my best to stay focused on the conversation, but my mind wandered. I was trying to piece exactly what I would say to hopefully clear my name. I didn't have much going in my favor. I'd put myself in terrible situations.

I hated that these moments I thought had been innocent were perceived as bad. It made me realize how much my actions reflected on my character. I had no one to blame but myself. If I wanted the world to see me in a different light, then I needed to show myself in a different light.

Leaning forward, I pulled out my phone and held it up to Seth, who had just stuffed a huge bite of enchilada in his mouth, and snapped a picture.

"No phones at the dinner table," Dad said with a warning tone.

I smiled sheepishly. I'd given my mom such a hard time about it. "Sorry, but I'm working on a social experiment."

"What kind?" Genuine curiosity danced in Mom's eyes, and I had to wrestle back the smile that tried to take over my face.

"I've made some stupid mistakes lately," I said. Mom and Dad both raised their eyebrows, so I continued on before they could ask any embarrassing questions. "Nothing major, but it's changed people's perceptions of me. I wanna see what happens when I start posting the things I love and my day-to-day doings, as opposed to the things that focus on being popular." I shook my phone. "Can I take a family selfie at dinner?"

Mom and Dad exchanged a look. When Mom nodded, Dad nodded as well. I held the phone out, and my whole family squeezed into the photo, goofy grins and all. I waited until after dinner to post the pictures. It was about time the world saw the real Camille Collins.

CHAPTER 44

*A*fter I finished helping clean up after dinner, I went up to my room to get all the thoughts out of my head. I'd already had some positive feedback from my posts. Mostly saying how delicious dinner looked, and laughing at Seth's silly face with his cheeks full of food.

I'd had a blog years before with softball tips. It died down the same time I started dating Dylan. But blogs were becoming outdated, anyway.

I stared at my laptop screen after I opened it. Maybe writing down my feelings wouldn't be the best idea. A video would be better. It was exactly what Emma Stone had done in *Easy A*. They'd hear my tone, see my face, and know if what I was saying was real or not. It was hard to portray emotion through text. They might not believe me.

I got up to fix my hair and make-up, but then forced myself back in my seat. If I wanted to portray the real Camille, I needed to look like the real me. Not the fake, dolled-up version that I'd created to make Dylan happy.

It was probably crazy of me not to check the mirror.

Hopefully, there weren't any leftovers from dinner on my face.

Closing my eyes, I took some long, deep breaths to calm myself. I just needed to be honest and raw.

I pressed record, and my natural smile spread across my face.

"Hey, everyone, I'm Camille Collins. There have been lots of rumors going around about me, and it's time I set the record straight. I think the easiest way to start is at the beginning. Softball and my friends used to be my world. I lived and breathed for them. Then I met a boy."

I held up my palm for a second. "Let me be clear that this is not the boy's fault. It's completely my own. I was having trouble at home, personal issues I don't want to get into, and I hope you understand. But it left me craving, no, *starving* for attention. I needed it so badly that I would do anything for it, including losing myself. Which is exactly what I did. Because I had to be around this boy, I turned my back on my friends, family, softball, and most importantly, me. I lost the true me to the point that no one knew who I was anymore."

I paused to wet my lips, but also compose myself. I didn't want to break down crying. No one would be able to understand me through my blubbering cry. "I got so wrapped up in what this boy thought of me, and how I thought he needed to see me, that I made a fool of myself.

"To all my friends, I'm truly sorry. I was an idiot and let my hormones control my life. None of you deserved the way I treated you. I hope to work past this, but I know it will be a long road of proving myself. I think we can all agree that actions speak a lot louder than words.

"This leads me to my next mistake. I let that same boy get to me. He told a few people that I was a bad kisser, and it spread like wildfire. Honestly, it doesn't even matter if I am or not, but I thought it did. I thought I had to prove myself."

I took a few deep breaths before I pursed my lips. "So, I created a kiss list. In my stupid brain, I thought if I kissed a few guys, I could prove that boy wrong. I chose guys that I wanted to kiss, and hoped wouldn't turn me down." I chuckled. "Unfortunately, one did turn me down in a really embarrassing display on my part, but it all worked out in the end. He got the girl he really wanted, and they are happy together. Mason, I'm sorry for everything I put you through. You're a good guy and didn't deserve any of this. Thank you for forgiving me. It means a lot.

"Alejandro was my second kiss." I tilted my head to the side. "And before any of you think I'm going to rate the guys on their kissing, I'm so not. That's a private matter not to be shared with the world. But Alejandro and I did kiss. It was a mutual choice. But it didn't go beyond that, no matter what the pictures looked like. Again, it was me putting myself in a stupid situation that felt innocent at the time, but looking at pictures, it tells a whole other story. Well, multiple stories, because people just filled in the blanks how they wanted to. Alejandro, I'm sorry I got you messed up in this. You're also a great guy and deserve someone who treats you well. I think you're brilliant and are going to make it to the major leagues."

I paused to collect my thoughts. "Isaac, I got carried away with you. The kiss looked heated in the picture because it was. All those pent-up emotions came flying out at you. I'd say I'm sorry, but you enjoyed it and aren't mad at me for it, so I'm really only mad at myself. Just do me a favor and be respectful of girls. I know you're a good person. Don't lose yourself like I did."

I rubbed my hands together. "The last guy on the list was Brady. Well, he was the first, but you get my point. Thanks, Brady, for playing along with my madness. We were both coming off a bitter breakup and in bad places. You're a good friend, and I'm glad we've stayed as such. You honestly make this world a better place with your smile and laughter. Just between you and me, and however many people actually watch this, she was an idiot for leaving you. But, I guess if we're all happy in the end, that's all that matters."

I glanced down at my keyboard, my eyes unfocused on the buttons. "This leads to me making the biggest mistake of my life." I forced myself to look at the screen. "There was this guy that was beyond amazing. Any time I was sad or in a bad mood, that guy could snap me out of it in seconds. We were good friends back in elementary school, and I let the years fade between us into nothing. I lost my focus over another boy, and in return, lost the guy I really wanted.

"Liam, you're the most amazing guy I've ever met. You're honest, kind, smart, devoted, loyal, and unrepentantly hot. It's almost not right. You were right in front of me all these years, and I was too blind to see. You've made me realize the kind of person I want to be and how I want people to perceive me, which is definitely *not* how I've been representing myself lately.

"I know a certain girl has called me desperate for throwing myself at you, but all I wanted to do was let you know how I feel. You've always struck me as a forgiving guy, so I guess I was hoping for you to forgive me, even though I didn't deserve it.

"Liam, I *know* you. You're not petty, and normally not this stubborn. I'm almost wondering if you got that from me, because we all know how stubborn I am. You have big dreams that I know you'll turn into realities. I'd really love to go on the journey with you, but only if you want me to.

"The girl may say this is another desperate plea, but all I want to do is say this: I love you, Liam Elliott. I know we could be good together if you'd give me another chance. I'm not the stupid girl I was before. I've learned and grown a lot, and I'd treat you with the respect you deserve.

"Even if you don't return my feelings, I hope one day you can find your way back to me. I've missed having you as a friend." I sniffed. "It's funny that it took me this long to realize that you need to be friends with the person you're dating. It shouldn't be a competition, or a cry for attention. It should be two people who have stuff in common, love each other at their worst moments, and see each other's hearts. I didn't have that with the boy I lost myself over. But I know I could have it with you."

I checked the clock. I'd been going on for so long. I had no idea if anyone would watch the entire video. I needed to end it. "So, to wrap this all up, I need to make a few things clear: My name is Camille Collins. I'm a virgin. I have kissed a total of five guys, none of which I'd take back, because I found myself in them. I'm not kissing another guy until I'm in a committed relationship. I love softball. It's the one thing that clears my mind. I have the best Mom and Dad, the perfect little brother, and the best two friends a girl could ask for. Thanks, Kaitlyn and Hayley, for never giving up on me during this whole ordeal. You both mean the world to me, and I couldn't imagine my life without you.

"Thanks, everyone, for listening. If you have any questions, hit me up. I'll be as honest as I can. I just hope you'll all keep in mind that we all make mistakes. Mine were, unfortunately, aired for the world, but there's nothing I can do about that except speak my peace." I waved at the camera. "Bye."

With a smile, I pressed the button to stop the video. I thought about going through it and listening to what I said, but that wouldn't make it the raw, honest truth. So, I uploaded the video to social media and let the world take it into their greedy hands.

CHAPTER 45

*W*ithin twenty minutes, I had to turn off my notifications. My phone and laptop were exploding with them. There were still a few haters out there, but for the most part, people were starting to understand my side of the story. All my softball mates were sticking up for me if anyone said anything negative. So were the guys I kissed.

Of course, Kaitlyn and Hayley were rapidly firing away. I'd called to tell them about the broadcast, and after they watched, they put on their fighting gloves and went to work on the responses, so I didn't have to. They really were the best friends.

I thought about replying to the comments, but I needed to take a step back from social media for a while. Aside from posting pictures of me doing happy things with my friends and family. But that was all the world was going to get.

I'd have to be careful of my actions during the following weeks. A lot of people would be watching me and waiting for me to mess up. I liked the challenge it provided.

The next morning, I dressed with care. Conservative was

basically my theme when it came to clothing, make-up, and hair.

Kaitlyn and Hayley had the biggest hugs for me when I picked them up for school. Kaitlyn even had a can of Dr Pepper for me, and I would have kissed her on the cheek if I'd known no one would be watching. But Sadie was probably hiding in the bushes in her typical stalker fashion, and I didn't want to give her anything to work with.

I wasn't sure what I was expecting when I got to school, but overall it was a warm welcome. For those who even paid attention to me. We had a big school, which sometimes helped you sink into the background in a beautiful way.

The moment Izzy, Ava, and Val saw me, they hugged me and let me know all was forgiven. Jordyn even gave me a hug.

What really surprised me was Coach Wilkes. She stopped me in the hall. Kaitlyn and Hayley stepped away to give us some privacy.

"Hey, Coach," I said.

She smacked her lips. "I owe you an apology. I was a little hard on you at camp. I realize now that you really were trying."

I smiled. "Thanks, Coach, that means a lot."

"I better see you at tryouts in a couple months," she said. "Our team could really use you."

I wanted to hug her, but again, that wouldn't help my public image. Instead, I just grinned like a little girl. "Thanks, Coach! I'm really excited to play this year."

She patted my shoulder. "We're excited to have you." She glanced around the hall at the passing students. "Don't worry too much about what others say about you. You're a good person, Camille." She quirked an eyebrow. "Just do us all a favor and don't lose yourself again. Especially over a boy."

A laugh bubbled up inside me, and I let it loose. "Trust

me, Coach, that's the last thing I want to do. It didn't turn out so well last time."

With a nod, she left me alone in the hall. It felt good to be back. I mean, I still had to try out for the team, but I'd work out daily and practice until then, so I wasn't too worried about making it back on the team.

I swiveled back to Hayley and Kaitlyn, and they were staring down the hall, their eyes wide. I turned back around and saw Liam standing in the middle of the hallway, staring at me. He shifted uncomfortably where he stood. He had his hands stuffed in his jeans pockets, his uncertain eyes blinking rapidly.

We stood there, staring at each other, neither one of us moving. By his reaction, he'd seen my video. I couldn't quite read his face, except for the nerves radiating off him.

All the sounds around us drowned out. It suddenly felt like Liam and I were the only two people in the hall. He was probably twenty paces away. I could close it quickly, but I had no idea how he'd respond. Besides, I was done making the moves. I'd thrown myself out there multiple times. If he wanted me, he'd have to come to me.

It felt like our whole relationship boiled down to this moment. If he came to me, talked to me, then everything would be okay. We could get back to a good place and be friends, maybe even more.

But if he turned around and walked away, it would be over. No Liam and Camille. Ever. The thought sent my stomach rolling. I couldn't handle a life without Liam in it. Not in a dramatic "I could never survive without a guy" kind of way. Just that there would be a hole without him there. He was my balancing force, and there was nothing wrong with that. It was the perfect relationship if you could get two people who made each other whole, filling the void they never knew was there.

I was motionless, so afraid to move, or even breathe. He licked his lips and took a tentative step, coming toward me. But then he stopped. Just one step. Was that good or bad? Should I run away and save myself the embarrassment?

No. No running away. I needed to face my life head-on. I needed to show Liam that I was a safe place. That he could relax and be himself around me.

So, I finally made myself move and pulled out a bag of caramel corn from my backpack and munched on it, keeping my eyes on Liam. I rested my weight on my left leg, standing casually. His eyebrow slowly lifted as he watched me eat the popcorn.

Then that perfect smile of his, the one that made my heart flip, spread across his face, almost splitting it in two.

The next movements were so fast, I could barely keep up with them. He was walking toward me, no, running toward me. He came to a stop right in front of me, his eyes an ocean of excitement.

I held the bag of popcorn in front of my chest, blocking out how much it was heaving in and out from the lack of air around me.

He moved, slowly, his hand coming up, barely brushing my cheek before it landed in the bag. He grabbed a couple pieces of caramel corn and popped them in his mouth, smiling the whole time.

I didn't want to be the one to speak first. I was afraid that anything I said would scare him away, and that would be it.

He finished off the popcorn in his mouth, leaned toward me, and my world exploded. His soft lips landed on mine, perfectly caramel-coated. They were sweet, slow kisses, nothing too hungry or sloppy, just the perfect amount of lip to make it the most amazing kiss I'd ever had. Heat ignited inside me, but I pushed it down before I lost control. I wanted to savor every moment I had with Liam. I would *not* let my hormones ruin it.

His lips left mine, leaving mine pulsing. He stayed close and intertwined his fingers with mine. He popped another piece of popcorn in his mouth before he broke the silence. "I love you."

A grin burst across my face. "I love you, too."

He smirked. "I know. You broadcasted it all over the world. It was a little over the top, and the lighting was wrong, but the sentiment was nice."

I snatched the bag away from him and put it back in my backpack. "No more popcorn for you, mister."

He took me in his arms. "I think I left out that it was actually perfect, and you looked beautiful, and I've been in love with you since elementary school." He kissed my cheek. "Took you long enough to return the feelings. I should get an award for my patience."

I would have slapped his chest if he wasn't so close. "What patience?"

"Camille. Ten years. I've waited for this moment for ten years. If that's not the definition of patience, I don't know what is."

I clasped my hands behind his neck. "How come you never told me before? I didn't start dating Dylan until like the eight-year mark, so that was plenty of time."

He leaned his forehead against mine. "I knew I had to wait until you were ready. If I would have made a move before, you would have rejected me."

I opened my mouth, but then snapped it shut. He was right. I probably would have. I wasn't ready for a Liam-caliber relationship back then. His was the lasting kind that I hoped never ended. I'd needed to find myself before I dove into something that deep.

He smiled and pulled back. "Your video reminded me of

Easy A. If you're not busy tonight, we should watch it." He glanced over my shoulder. "Kaitlyn and Hayley should come, too. And their guys. I should probably get to know them now that we're together."

"So, we're officially together?"

"Duh. You said you wouldn't kiss someone unless you were in a committed relationship with him."

I tilted my head to the side. "We weren't in a relationship when you kissed me. just now"

Liam sighed. "Camille. When I was standing back there, you pulled out a bag of caramel popcorn and took a bite. That's total girl code for 'let's officially start our relationship.' Then, I closed the distance and took a bite of popcorn, which is guy code for 'sure, I think that sounds like a swell idea.'"

I bit back a laugh. "Did you just use the word *swell*?"

"I'm a gentleman. That's how gentlemen speak."

"I wasn't aware of that fact." I snuggled into his chest, happy that I could do that openly, and it felt so perfect. It was where I belonged.

The bell rang overhead, so Liam wrapped his arm around my shoulders and steered me toward my class.

"Did you hear?" he asked. "There's going to be a bocce ball club. You should join."

I put my arm around his waist. "That sounds fun. Is the captain of the club hot?"

"Smoking. You should get his number."

I wiggled my eyebrows. "I already have it."

Liam found my ticklish spot on my side, and I broke out into a fit of laughter. It wasn't until that moment that I realized we had a lot of people watching us, some holding up phones. But I didn't care. It was the kind of attention I wanted. Liam and I were in a committed relationship, and there was nothing embarrassing about it.

Besides, I wanted the world to know how much I loved the guy. And how comfortable I was with myself.

THE END

*If you enjoyed *The Kiss List*, would you do us a solid and leave Sara an honest review? You can leave one on any book retailer or review site online. The more reviews Sara gets, the more visibility she has. Then, she can connect with even more fantastic readers like you!

ACKNOWLEDGMENTS

Once again, all the thanks in the world to Cammie Larsen and Mary Gray at Monster Ivy Publishing. You two are rock stars, and the best editors and publisher a girl could ask for. Thanks for taking a chance on me, and making my stories all glossy and make-out worthy.

Chad, thank you for standing by my side through all of this and making sure I never give up. I couldn't have come this far without you. Also, I tell you this all the time, but now let it be publicly known, you seriously have the most kissable lips in the world, and they're in my top five favorite things about you.

As always, thank you to my family for being so supportive. Not all authors have that, so it means the world to me.

A big thanks to Ellie Tate, Hannah Hales, Kira Gagnon, Brinley Babcock, and Hailey Sullivan for being my most passionate fans. You young ladies are the reason I keep on writing, and you mean the world to me. *squishy hugs*

A huge thank you to all my readers. You make all this worth it.

And to the few guys on my kiss list in high school, thanks for giving me something to daydream about.

ABOUT THE AUTHOR

Sara Jo Cluff grew up in Yorba Linda, California, right next to the Happiest Place on Earth (aka her second home). Now, she resides in Utah with her husband, Chad, and their definite mama's-girl cat, Princess Buttercup.

She loves creating stories from scratch and seeing where the characters take her. When she's not writing, she's hanging out with her husband, watching Netflix, reading, or doing jigsaw puzzles.

She's a proud #PepperPack #Ambassador for the Most Delicious Beverage on Earth: Dr Pepper.

Visit her author website, www.sarajocluff.com, and for merchandise, visit shop.spreadshirt.com/awkwardpepper.

After a catastrophic friendship, Elinora decides that having any relationship isn't worth the heartbreak. Her parents still want her to socialize, so she starts her Filler Friend operation, unbeknownst to them. She'll fill-in as a friend for anyone at school, whether it's getting a gamer out of the house, or being a plus one at their parent's boring work party.

When a client becomes a regular, the lines of fiction and reality begin to blur, making Elinora unsure of what she really wants. Adding to the confusion, she's slowly falling for the cute guy she met at the library. Before the operation blows up in her face, Elinora will have to decide if friendship and love are worth the risk, or if she's better off shutting out the world forever.

FILLER FRIEND

Chapter 1

*S*peaking of serial killers, I was currently watching Tomahawk Tully draw her latest battle scene with way too much gory detail. Tully sat next to me in eleventh-grade English and made the last class of my day go by faster—grosser, but faster.

We both loved to write. We were critique partners because we were basically the only people we knew who wrote novels and could be trusted to read each other's work with honest and open minds. Although sometimes Tully was *too* honest. She was a fan of epic fantasy/horror (yeah, she mashed them together), and I stuck mostly to paranormal and psychological thrillers. I loved anything that messed with the mind.

I also had a secret stash of romance novellas I'd written buried in the bottom of my desk so my parents wouldn't find them. Some of the scenes would have been a little too heated for them, especially when it was their daughter writing them.

Tully handed me the finished drawing. It was complete with dead bodies littering the grassy field. She only drew in black and white, but it was done so well that I could see red blood dripping everywhere.

"Hey, Elinora," she said, trying to get my attention. "That goes with the last chapter I gave you."

I stared at the paper, swallowing to keep the bile down. "Yeah, the chapter was more than enough. You explained everything so well, the picture isn't needed."

She gripped the top of her short blue hair in her usual irritated fashion, giving it a little yank. "But now you can visualize it."

I didn't *want* to visualize it.

"Got any other chapters?" she asked.

I rifled through my bag until I found the latest chapter of my YA thriller about a girl who contacts her mother on the other side and accidentally lets a ghost into our realm during the séance. "Here you go."

She took it from me, her eyes hesitantly glancing over the first page. "This one isn't all sappy, is it? That last chapter was a gag fest."

"They shared a tiny peck on the lips," I said.

Her thick eyebrows pinched together. "Yeah, gag fest."

The bell rang, and I stood. "Get over it, Tully. Sometimes people like each other, and they kiss. Just read it."

"Whatever." She stuffed the pages in her backpack and sulked out of the room, pushing some guy out of the way in the process. Once you got past the angry scowl and her I-hate-everyone attitude, she was actually a decent person.

The sun warmed my skin the second I walked outside to head home. I watched all the other juniors get in their cars and drive off. I had a license, but no car. Plus, I only lived two blocks away from the school. Driving there and back would be overkill.

My earbuds were safely in place, my Kelly Clarkson playlist ready to go, when I heard someone shout my name.

If my parents had done their duty and named me something generic, I could have ignored the person and claimed I'd thought they were shouting for someone else.

But my parents sucked and named me Elinora.

Don't get me wrong. I loved my name. And my parents. But it made me stick out on days I wanted to blend in.

Luckily, everything else about me was average—average height, average weight, average boobs. I kept my straight brown hair shoulder length year-round. For either good or bad, no one did a double-take when I walked by. It was perfect.

"Elinora!"

With a sigh, I pulled out one earbud and spun around.

Jacqueline Mercer, aka Jackie Meaner, was jogging toward me. Her nickname was stupid, but I hadn't given it to her. She'd gotten it back in elementary school before I'd known her, and it had stuck all these years.

"Tomahawk Tully" was all my doing, though, and I was proud of it. Even Tully said she'd liked it once I'd been brave enough to tell her. I had to make sure she wasn't actually a serial killer before I'd dropped that bomb on her. Turned out her killing was strictly fictional.

I switched on my public-nice smile when Jacqueline finally reached me. "Hey, Jacqueline." All her friends called her Jackie, but she'd once told me she preferred Jacqueline, so I went with it. I hated when people shortened my name.

She ran her fingers through her long brown hair, swishing it to the side. Two guys and a girl all paused to watch, causing Jacqueline to give her hair an extra shake. She had double-take hair, and she owned it.

"Are you free this Friday night?" she asked.

I checked the calendar on my phone. I had a game night scheduled with the family, but Mom and Dad would be cool if I canceled. "I can be. Why?"

She stepped in close, keeping her voice low. "I need another favor."

"If it involves overly chatty ladies at teatime, I'm out."

Jacqueline laughed, the musical sound making people turn toward us. She cleared her throat and waited for them to pass. "I'm sorry about last time, okay? I didn't know I was taking you to hell on a crumpet."

My phone buzzed, and a message from my twelve-year-old brother popped up. He wanted to know where I was. We had a fort to build and Nerf guns to fire. I texted him as I talked to Jacqueline. "You're forgiven. What is it this time?"

"Dinner at the country club," she said, her smile and tone overly charming.

"That sounds like the same exact thing," I said, putting my phone away. "A bunch of pompous, rich people talking about mundane things no one in the world cares about."

Jacqueline pouted. "Please, Elinora? You know I can't bring any of my friends. My parents hate them."

I shrugged. "Maybe you should get new friends."

She stood on her tiptoes like my little sister did when she really wanted something. "Like you?"

I backed away, moving toward home and creating some distance between us. "Yeah, pretty sure I'm busy Friday night. Something super crazy important to do."

She rushed to me, taking my hands in hers like we were long-lost bosom buddies. "I'll pay you."

I arched an eyebrow. My clients never paid me. When it came to being a filler friend, all I asked was that they cover the cost of everything involved. "You're that desperate?"

"My brother was supposed to go, but he can't. I don't want to be alone with my parents. I don't have your charm. They adore you, and it would take all the attention off me."

Lifting my arms, I held our clasped hands between us. "Dearest Jacqueline, you have so much charm. Four guys have passed out just walking past you during this conversation. You can survive your parents."

She yanked her hands from mine. "I don't have the charm *they* want. Can we not have this debate right now?"

My phone vibrated with another text from my brother. He was losing patience. So was I.

She pulled forty dollars out of her pocket and handed it to me. "I'll give you the same amount after dinner on Friday."

I stared at the cash in my hands. "You're going to give me eighty dollars to go with you?"

She huffed. "Fine. I'll add another twenty. One hundred even."

That wasn't what I'd meant, but it was a lot of money. Dad's birthday was coming up, and I could get him something nice. I also really wanted her to shut up so I could get home. I tucked the money into my back pocket. "What time?"

Jacqueline clapped her hands, a squeal escaping her. "Thank you! I'll pick you up at six, and we can go back to my place to get you a dress, shoes, makeup—the works." She looked me over. "Make that five o'clock."

I returned her clapping, trying to hold in the sarcasm. "Can't wait!"

With a bounce, she jogged to her hot pink BMW. I couldn't believe she was that desperate to make her parents happy. She was hiding something from them, though I didn't know what. The last time I was her filler friend, I'd told her to just tell her parents the truth, but she wouldn't.

I added the dinner to my calendar and walked home. So far the filler friend operation had been easy—simple tasks that didn't require much effort on my part. When it came to the Mercer family, though, I had to turn on the charm. I was drained by the end of the night. Jacqueline was starting to become a regular client, and I wasn't sure if I liked it or not.

The money in my pocket was nice, but something felt wrong. When I was a filler friend for free, I didn't feel bad about it. There was nothing anyone could point to and say we weren't real friends. But once money was added to the situation, suddenly there was a paper trail of my deceit.

I hoped I hadn't made the biggest mistake of my life by taking Jacqueline's money. But deep inside, I knew I had.

Available at book retailers online.

CPSIA information can be obtained
at www.ICGtesting.com
Printed in the USA
LVHW041553220119
604810LV00016B/555/P